MURDERER'S TRAIL

Ben the tramp is back at sea, a stowaway bound for Spain in the company of a wanted man – the Hammersmith murderer.

Son of novelist Benjamin Farjeon, and brother to children's author Eleanor, playwright Herbert and composer Harry, Joseph Jefferson Farjeon (1883–1955) began work as an actor and freelance journalist before inevitably turning his own hand to writing fiction. Described by the *Sunday Times* as 'a master of the art of blending horrors with humour', Farjeon was a prolific author of mystery novels, with more than 60 books published between 1924 and 1955. His first play, *No. 17*, was produced at the New Theatre in 1925, when the actor Leon M. Lion 'made all London laugh' as Ben the tramp, an unorthodox amateur detective who became the most enduring of all Farjeon's creations. Rewritten as a novel in 1926 and filmed by Alfred Hitchcock six years later, with Mr Lion reprising his role, *No.17*'s success led to seven further books featuring the warm-hearted but danger-prone Ben: 'Ben is not merely a character but a parable—a mixture of Trimalchio and the Old Kent Road, a notable coward, a notable hero, above all a supreme humourist' (Seton Dearden, *Time and Tide*). Although he had become largely forgotten over the 60 years since his death, J. Jefferson Farjeon's reputation made an impressive resurgence in 2014 when his 1937 Crime Club book *Mystery in White* was reprinted by the British Library, returning him to the bestseller lists and resulting in readers wanting to know more about this enigmatic author from the Golden Age of detective fiction.

Also in this series

J. JEFFERSON FARJEON

Murderer's Trail

COLLINS
CRIME
CLUB

COLLINS CRIME CLUB

An imprint of HarperCollins*Publishers*
1 London Bridge Street
London SE1 9GF
www.harpercollins.co.uk

This paperback edition 2016

First published in Great Britain for The Crime Club Ltd
by W. Collins Sons & Co. Ltd 1931

A catalogue record for this book is
available from the British Library

ISBN 978-0-00-815591-9

Set in Sabon by Palimpsest Book Production Limited, Falkirk, Stirlingshire

Printed by Clays Ltd, St Ives plc

MIX
Paper from
responsible sources
FSC™ C007454

FSC™ is a non-profit international organisation established to promote
the responsible management of the world's forests. Products carrying the
FSC label are independently certified to assure consumers that they come
from forests that are managed to meet the social, economic and
ecological needs of present and future generations,
and other controlled sources.

Find out more about HarperCollins and the environment at
www.harpercollins.co.uk/green

CONTENTS

1

Invisible Fingers

'Now, then,' frowned the policeman, 'where have *you* come from?'

The human scarecrow, of no address and with only half a name—the half he had was Ben, and the other half had been lost years ago—removed his eyes from the poster he had been staring at. The poster said, 'Old Man Murdered at Hammersmith,' and it was a nasty sight. But the policeman wasn't much improvement. Policemen were blots on any landscape.

Where had he come from? Queer, how the world harped upon that unimportant question! As a rule it was an Embankment seat, or a coffee-stall, or a shop where they sold cheese, or an empty house where one could pass a night rent free. What did it matter? But the nosey-parker world seemed to think it mattered, and was always worrying him about it. Policemen in particular.

'Didn't you hear me?' demanded the policeman. 'Where've you come from?'

'Not 'Ammersmith,' answered Ben.

His eyes wandered back to the poster. The policeman's frown increased. Bent on being a nuisance, he persisted, with a tinge of sarcasm:

'Quite sure of that?'

Faint indignation stirred within the scarecrow's meagrely-covered breast. That was another thing about the world. Ben couldn't do anything, but the world was always accusing him of everything!

'Orl right, 'ave it yer own way,' he said, with a sarcasm that far exceeded the constable's. 'I was walkin' by 'im and I didn't like 'is 'ead, so I chopped it orf.'

'I suppose you think that's funny?' inquired the policeman.

'Yus,' retorted Ben. 'There's nothink like a nice little murder ter mike yer larf!'

Then the policeman decided that, unless the interview were concluded, the law stood a good chance of losing its superiority in the encounter without gaining anything in return; so, uttering a warning generality against the dangers of loitering and of back-chat, he leisurely adjusted his belt, turned, and trudged away.

Ben shivered. Despite the way in which he stuck up to them, policemen always made him shiver in his secret heart. If they never did anything to him, they always carried the threat! It wasn't only the policeman, however, that made Ben shiver as he stood blinking in the gloaming. He had holes in his clothes, and the gloaming got through. There was a place on his knee open to three square inches of breeze. He had torn it on a nail seven weeks ago, and it occurred to him that it was about time to try and bump into someone with a needle and cotton. After seven weeks, the spot was getting cold.

But, even more than the holes and the policeman, the

poster made Ben shiver. At first he had stared at the words vaguely. You know—as one does, when one is hard up for hobbies. Then the words impressed themselves upon his mind, with all their unpleasantness. This murderin' business—it wasn't no joke! Yet Ben had made a joke about it, as he often did about the things that scared him most. He had suggested that he had committed the murder himself, and had cut the old man's head off! There was a nasty idea! And suppose the policeman had believed him . . .

'Oi!' he gasped.

Somebody had blundered into him. He hit out wildly—the rule is to hit first and to think afterwards—but his fists went wide, and the somebody toppled in between them. For an amazing moment he held the somebody in his arms. It was an amazing moment because the somebody wasn't in the least like the somebody he had expected to find there. It was a rather small somebody who clung to him, limply, gasping; a somebody with a bit of hair that tickled his cheek, and a little ear, and a rather nice sense of soft warmth. Then the amazing moment passed, and the somebody shot away from him in a panic.

Ben saw her more distinctly now. He saw her eyes, bright with fear, and the flutter of her heaving breast, and her slender legs, slim and taut, beneath her short brown skirt. For an instant she stood there, poised before the grim background, 'Old Man Murdered at Hammersmith.' The word 'Murdered' leered between her knees, and 'Hammersmith' between her ankles. Pretty ankles, alive with grace and elasticity. Then the ankles got to work, twisted as though suddenly touched by electricity, and bore their owner round a corner.

"Ere! 'Arf a mo'!' called Ben.

But the girl had vanished.

Ben decided that it was time *he* did a bit of vanishing. The sensation was creeping over him that unpleasant things were happening, and that invisible fingers were stretching towards him to draw him in. He knew the signs. He'd been drawn in before. He'd been drawn into cupboards and coffins and corpses, into cellars and wells and dark passages, and had been tossed about by the invisible fingers like a blinkin' shuttlecock! Well, he wasn't having any more of it. All he wanted was a quiet life, same as he'd heard about, and he meant to get it, if there wasn't an old man left alive in Hammersmith!

So he departed from the corner where a poster had delayed his aimless wanderings, and shuffled along the moist streets to a coffee-stall a couple of blocks away. It wasn't raining, but the streets were moist as though with their environment. Water was in the atmosphere, and the damp aroma of London docks.

'Cup o' tea,' he said, to the stall-keeper.

The stall-keeper looked up from a coin he was holding. In the pleasant little glare of his temporary shop, and surrounded by cheering edibles, hungry folk would have described him as handsome.

'Who's going to pay for it?' he asked.

'You are,' replied Ben.

'Oh, *am* I?' exclaimed the stall-keeper, and reached the conclusion, after a close scrutiny of his impecunious customer, that perhaps he would. We've all got to try and get into heaven somehow, and the ticket would be cheap for a cup of tea. 'Well, you can share my bit o' luck, if you like. Last customer left in too much hurry to take his change.'

4

He held up the coin he had been examining. It was a two-shilling piece. A new one. Then he turned his head and glanced along the road, where the last customer was vanishing into the murk.

'One o' them—well, *jerky* chaps,' the stall-keeper went on, as he slopped tea into a thick cup. 'Up they come like a jack-in-the-box. "Sandwich!" And they've hardly got their fingers on it before they're off. I reckon when they say their prayers they jest say, "Hallo God, good-bye!"' He chuckled at his little joke while he shoved the cup across. He always served spoons with his saucers, to prove that he knew Ritz manners, but the spoons were always drowned. 'Couldn't have gone quicker, not if a bobby'd been after him.'

Ben did not offer any comment at once. The tea claimed first attention. But when he had drunk half of it and the warmth began to percolate through the chills in his soul, he observed, meditatively:

'P'r'aps one *was*!'

'Well, you never know, do you?' replied the stall-keeper, now becoming meditative himself. 'New money and old clothes always makes me suspicious if it ain't Christmas-time. And, then, there's another thing. There was a nasty mark on his face. That's right. A nasty mark. And *not* one he'd got in the war.' He paused, to visualise the nasty mark. It had been on his left cheek. 'Read about the bloke they've done in at Hammersmith?'

Ben frowned. Wasn't there any way of keeping this old man from continually popping up?

'It's in the paper,' said the stall-keeper.

'Well, I ain't read it,' answered Ben. 'I belongs to one o' them inscripshun libraries.'

The stall-keeper's head disappeared behind the expanded pages of an afternoon journal. Invisible, it announced:

'Ah, here we are. "Old Man With His Throat Cut. Hunt in Hammersmith. Rich Recloosey." Don't seem no end to 'em. But they've got the knife, I see, and it ses here that the police are on the track of an important clue.'

'Well, the dead bloke's a clue, ain't 'e?' queried Ben, making an effort.

'And we're to look out for a feller six foot one, in a dark suit.'

'And wot do we do when we finds 'im?' inquired Ben. 'Go hup ter 'im and hask, "Beg pardon, guv'nor, but do you 'appen to 'ave done a murder terday?" They tike us fer blinkin' mugs, don't they?'

But the stall-keeper wasn't listening to Ben. He was thinking. 'Six foot one. Six foot one. And a dark suit. Well, that's queer—or am I barmy?'

A couple of sailors came along. They were noisy and half-drunk. Not feeling social (and you need to feel social if you are going to get any change out of half-drunks), Ben finished his tea, thanked the good-natured stall-keeper, and slipped away. In two minutes, the pleasant coffee-stall was merely a memory, and the dark, moist streets were closing in upon him again.

From beyond the dimness on his left came the depressing sound of a tram. The sound was some way off, and painted no sylvan picture. Ahead, moist vistas. On his right, a wall. A high wall. An interminable wall. Every now and then the wall was punctuated by an opening guarded by a gate or a door. The doors, being solid, revealed no glimpse of what lay beyond the wall, but through the occasional gates one got little peeps of a queer, derelict land, of unpopulated spaces, of rails that seemed to have no purpose, of large, barren buildings and of other walls. One could not see water, but one knew it was there. It hung in the greyness, and breathed up above its level. It was both depressing and invigorating—it whispered of lapping ooze and of vivid colours, of blue seas and blackened bodies. It gave you the taste of salt and the tang of wet rope. It filled your subconscious soul with a prayer for liberty and a knowledge of captivity, even the subconscious soul of a scarecrow like Ben, who had no knowledge of his soul or of what it was passing through.

'Gawd, wot a smell!' he thought once. 'Tork abart dead fish!'

Yes, even his nose was shocked. Yet there was something about the smell . . . Ben, in almost-forgotten days, had been to sea . . .

Hallo! One of the doors was ajar! Hardly conscious that he did so, he slipped through. Perhaps he thought that, on the inner side of this wall, there would be fewer inquiries when he found his pitch for the night. Perhaps the water's breath, or that queer, dead-fish smell, had led him to follow an unreasonable impulse. Or perhaps the invisible fingers from which he was endeavouring to escape had stretched out through the open door, had closed round his frail frame, and had drawn him in. A moment of sudden terror, born of he knew not what, supported the latter theory as he stood on this threshold of dockland.

'Garn, yer idgit!' he rounded on himself the next instant; and he comforted himself by his time-worn philosophy, 'One plice is as good as another, ain't it, when there ain't nowhere helse?'

So, quelling his fear and imagining himself a hero once

7

more, he advanced over the derelict spaces of the dock to find a corner where he could lie down and dream of kings and queens.

And the invisible fingers closed the door in the wall behind him.

2

Ben versus Ghosts

'Oi! Git orf me!'

Ben sat up abruptly, with a clammy sensation that a nightmare had pattered over him. Then fear of death was succeeded by indignation against life. Why had life, as momentarily represented by a black and shadowy dockyard, nothing better to offer a weary man than the horrible spot on which he lay?

Ben did not often sleep between clean sheets, but he had his standards. A bit of a carpet, with a footstool under your head—the corner of an empty attic, particularly if the attic were triangular to improve the wedge-like snugness of the angle, and if the peeling wall-paper kept off your nose—a couple of chairs with a minimum of seven legs—even a table, either on it or under it, according to which least reminded you of granite—these were supportable and permitted you to retain the one per cent of self-respect unfeeling life had left you. But cold and slippery stone, an equally cold and slippery post that vanished from behind you every time you moved your head half an inch to scratch it, leaving you outstretched, and *rats*!—these were conditions that even a worm might turn at, destroying its faith in the god that looks so inadequately after the Lesser Things!

Yes, the rats in particular. Ben hated rats. Nasty, slimy creatures, with evil eyes and bodies four sizes too large. Mice, now—they were different. You could chum up with a mouse when you knew how, and give them little bits of cheese. But rats took the cheese without waiting to ask. They just watched you from a dark corner or a crack, then darted forward with a swift swish, clambered heavily over you like giant slugs fitted with feet, used your face as a floor, and left their foot-marks on your soul.

'Next rat I see,' thought Ben, 'I'll wring its neck!'

A large dock rodent accepted the challenge, leapt at his cheek, and bounced away again into the blackness. Ben's eyebrows only escaped contact through being raised out of the rat's route in terror. A month previously an Asiatic's eyebrows had been less fortunate in Smyrna.

'Blimy, wot a life!' muttered Ben, wiping his forehead with a red handkerchief. The handkerchief was already four weeks late for its annual laundering, but, even so, handkerchief was preferable to rat, and he wiped hard to make certain that no trace of rat remained. 'I 'opes I'm born somethink dif'rent nex' time!' He carried the thought a stage farther. 'I 'opes there ain't no nex' time!'

Indeed, it *was* a life! Why did one hang on to it? Not far away dark water oozed and sucked around big, stationary ships. All one had to do was to get up, feel one's way over the damp ground, avoiding posts and chains and ropes—there wasn't any need to hurt yourself on the way, was there?—until there wasn't any wet ground, but only the dark water. 'Couple o' gurgles, and yer've done with knocks,' he reflected. Then he chided himself. Wot, 'im a swizzicide? 'Im wot 'ad been in the Merchant Service and 'ad once asked a captain for a rise? 'Ben, yer potty!' he announced to his weaker nature. 'Come orf it!' And so, instead of seeking the dark water, he sought the post again, with the more temporary sleep it offered, discovered too late that the post wasn't there, and found himself flat.

He gave a yelp. The yelp was echoed. Now Ben was no longer flat. He was on his feet, shaking like a struck tuning-fork. For if the second yelp had really been an echo of the first, its character had changed uncannily in the tiny space of time between!

Ben's yelp had been the yelp of one in sudden pain. The other seemed to have come from one in sudden panic.

'Well, I'm in a panic, ain't I?' chattered Ben, struggling for comfort in the thought.

He stood, listening—for thirteen years. The echo was not repeated. Then, deciding that any place was better than where he was, a condition which possibly explains the source of most human energy, he groped his way through darkest dockland in search of a happier spot. He did not know in what direction he was walking saving that, if the second cry had come from the north, he was unerringly walking south.

He came upon another post. It wasn't a nice post. It was unnaturally white, and it fluttered. All at once it occurred to Ben that it wasn't a post at all, and that he had better hit it. The blow proved, painfully, that it was a post, but the fluttering white costume still needed explaining. A match explained it. Matches, at certain moments, are wonderful company. The service performed by the present match, however, might have been improved on. The

11

costume turned out to be a newspaper poster tied round
the post with a piece of string, and the poster said:

OLD MAN

MURDERED

AT

HAMMERSMITH

'Gawd! Ain't I never goin' ter git away from it?' muttered
Ben.

For a few seconds the match-light flickered on the gruesome words—words against which the holder of the match
might have laid his head. But sleep was no longer in the
immediate programme. A rat, an echo, and a placard had
combined to demonstrate that dockland—or, at any rate,
this particular corner of dockland—was unhealthy, and
that the best thing to do was to get right out of it.

The match-light touched his fingers. He dropped it spas-
modically, but suppressed the exclamation. He had an idea
that ears were listening, and in the darkness that followed
the match's descent the policy of retreat became instantly
more appealing. Even in the darkness the horrible placard
was still visible. It shivered palely as a little night breeze
slithered from the sides of ships, and suddenly Ben turned
and darted away. His foot caught in a chain, and he made
a croquet-hoop over it.

He remained, croquet-hooped, for nearly half a minute.
Only by utter staticism, he felt, did he stand any chance
that Fate would lose him and pass him by. He knew for
certain by now that Fate was hunting him, and that the
invisible fingers were groping to make their catch. It was
only when he considered that it would not be dignified to

be caught in the shape of a croquet-hoop that he cautiously rose and proceeded on his miserable way.

He trod gingerly. He raised his feet high over many chains that were not there, and failed to raise them over another that was. He didn't fall this time, however. As the ground rose up towards him, like the deck of a rolling ship, he lurched his left leg forward with a bent knee, recalling a trick of his old sea days. 'Not this time, cocky!' He glared at the chain. But a couple of seconds later he looped over some fresh obstacle, and his hands descended on something soft.

'Wot's 'appened?' he wondered. 'Is the bloomin' ground meltin'?'

Or was it grass? But what would grass be doing here? Soft. Soft and warmish. Now, what was soft and warmish?

The solution came to him in a sickening flash. Suddenly weakened, the human croquet-hoop went flat, doing a sort of splits north and south from the stomach. Then it bounded up towards the unseen stars. It is doubtful whether anything in dockland had risen so high in the time since the days of bombardments.

Obeying the laws of gravitation, Ben came down on the spot from which he had vertically ascended. In other words, he came down on a dead man. After that, he ran amok.

He ran without knowledge of time or direction. Actually, the time was five minutes, and the direction was a very large circle. He fought imaginary foes all the way, and at every fifth step he leapt high over imaginary corpses. By the time he had completed the circle, his breath was spent. But, as events were soon to prove, that needn't stop you. You can always borrow a bit of breath from the future if you're really pressed.

Back at the spot where he had started from, he paused. He knew it was the same spot for various reasons. One was the chain—the chain over which he had nearly tripped just before falling over the dead body. There it was. No mistaking it. Another reason was a shape looming on his left. A bit of a boat. He remembered that too. Another reason—the strongest reason—was instinct. He *knew* this was the same spot. Couldn't say why. Just knew it. It was as though he had stepped back into a picture he had temporarily deserted, completing it again . . . Yes, but one thing wasn't in the picture. What was it? What was missing?

He stared at the ground ahead of him. His eyes glued themselves to the spot.

'Lummy!' he murmured. 'Where's 'e got ter?'

A splash answered him.

Several nasty things had happened during the last few minutes, but this splash was among the nastiest. If it had been followed by a cry, or by further splashing, or by any sound denoting movement, it would have seemed less ominous. But it was followed by nothing. Just silence. Whatever had caused the splash had made no protest.

And then, suddenly and without warning, a dark form came vaguely into view, and stopped dead.

The form was tall and shadowy, and the reason of its abrupt halt was obvious. If it had come into Ben's view, Ben had also come into its view. Each was a dim shadow to the other. Too frozen to move, Ben stared at the spectre, while the spectre stared back. Then, when the silence at last became unbearable, the weaker broke it.

''Allo!' said Ben stupidly.

He heard himself saying it with surprise. He did not recall having instructed his tongue to say it. And, now he came to think of it, *had* he said it? The spectre made no sign of having heard it.

"Allo!" He tried again.

He was sure he had said it that time. His voice rattled like hollow thunder. But the spectre still made no sign. Slightly encouraged by the astonishing fact that he was still alive, Ben became informative.

'There was a deader 'ere jest now,' he said.

The spectre moved a little closer. Ben backed a little farther.

"Ere, none o' that!" he muttered, and then added, in nervous exasperation, "As somebody cut out yer tongue?"

He closed his eyes tightly the next instant. He was afraid the spectre would answer the question by opening its mouth and revealing that its tongue *had* been cut out. He couldn't have stood that. The darkness of closed lids was momentarily consoling, for it not only shut out the spectre, but it induced the theory that perhaps there really wasn't any spectre at all. The whole thing might be just imagination. There were not many things, come to think of it, Ben had not imagined in his time. Once he had even imagined a transparent tiger with all its victims. 'Wot you gotter do,' he told himself soberly, 'is ter stop bein' *frightened*. See?' Then he felt two arms around him, and forgot the advice.

Ben's accomplishments were few, but he could carve little statues out of cheese, and he could bite. He bit now, and fortunately what he bit proved vulnerable. The spectre emitted a savage oath—there was no doubt now that it possessed a tongue—and Ben felt a pain somewhere. He didn't know where. There wasn't time to find out. But he knew he felt it, and the knowledge was so acute that he was urged to give a second bite. The second bite produced a

15

second oath and a temporary loosening of the tentacles around him. He slid down, dodged left, slid up, dodged right, twisted, turned and ran.

He heard a heavy fall behind him. The chain that had once proved his enemy now proved his friend. His pursuer had tripped over it.

Profiting by this incident, Ben ran as he had never run before. That is to say, his legs moved as they had never moved before. For some reason, born of the nightmare atmosphere, his body seemed to be insisting on slow-motion, and as his legs raced beneath him he had a queer feeling that he was travelling in first gear.

That wasn't the only trouble. As he ran, everything about him appeared to have increased in size and in height. The posts he sped by had grown four yards. The iron rings in the posts could have encircled Carnera. A wooden partition actually became taller as he passed it. The roof of a vast shed was as distant as the stars. And while his eyes grappled with these grim illusions, his brain grappled with the grim realities that had brought him to this sorry pass. The realities formed themselves into another chain, a chain this time in his mind. It was a chain of six links. Rat—cry—poster—body—splash—spectre. Rat—cry—poster—body—splash—spectre. But wasn't there something else? Wasn't there a girl some-where? A girl who had blundered into his arms? And a man who had hurriedly left a coffee-stall without waiting for his change? Girl—man—rat—cry

Oi! What was this? *Another* link? The dark world began to swim. The spectre was behind him, twenty feet, or two, but this new apparition was before him. Short, thick-set, and stumpy. And motionless.

16

Ben, also, became motionless. When you're the middle of the sandwich, you just wait to see which way you get it from. He expected to get it from the new apparition, and couldn't understand the delay. Then, all at once, he discovered the reason. The new apparition had his back to him.

Fate was giving him a chance, and he took it. He could not advance, and he could not retreat, and on his right was a brick wall. On his left was another wall, but this was of iron, and in the iron a black hole gaped. It was a short distance from Ben's feet to the hole. Just the length of a board that spanned a few inches of water.

''Ere goes fer Calcutter!' thought Ben.

And into the hole he shot.

3

The Stomach of a Ship

The ship you know is probably a very pleasant affair. It has scrupulously scrubbed decks, luxuriously carpeted stairways, palatial dining-rooms, and snug cabins. In these surroundings you meet clean, trim officers, talk with some of them on polite subjects, stretch, yawn and play shovel-board. But the ship you probably do not know—the ship that provides the real service for which you pay—is a very different matter.

It is dark, and it is hot. It is honeycombed with narrow passages and iron ladders. You go up the ladders or down the ladders or along the ladders. Some are fixed at an angle, some are vertical, and their only object seems to be to lead to other ladders. Your Mecca may be the scorching side of a huge boiler, or a little gap in the blackness through which hell peeps, or a metal excrescence bristling with a thousand nuts, or a mountain of coal. None invite you to stop, unless economic pressure has forced them upon you, or some other strange necessity has brought you to seek their ambiguous consolation. On you go, sweating, through the bewildering labyrinth, from ladder to ladder, from passage to passage, from dimness to dimness, from heat to heat. A germ in the ship's stomach.

And so Ben went on. When he had first entered the black hole in the ship's side he had shot across a dark space in a panic, and then, striking something—whether human or not he had no notion—he had shot across another dark space in another panic. He had stopped dead on the edge of a dip. He had heard a movement near him. Human, this time, he swore. He had shot down the dip, fallen, clutched, and discovered a rail. Thus he had arrived at the first of the interminable ladders.

Now he was in a maze of ladders. A metallic city of descents. But he did not always descend. Sometimes he went up. The main thing was to keep moving, and to move in the least impossible direction. Presently one would come to a dead end, and then one would stop because one had to.

It is probable that if Ben had never been in a ship's stomach before he would have been killed or caught during the early stages of his journey. A ship's interior is not designed for the speed of those who dwell in it. In his zenith, however, Ben had stoked with the best of them, and a long-dormant instinct was now reasserting itself and leading him towards coal.

But it was the simple law of gravitation that finally brought him there. He was descending a particularly precipitous ladder, a ladder that seemed to be hanging down sheerly into space, and all at once something caught his eye between the rungs. He became conscious of a sudden flutter. A small shape, like a detached hand, loomed momentarily, and it gave him a shock that loosened his grip. 'Oi!' he gulped. The rung he had been grasping shot upwards,

19

while he shot downwards. A short, swift flight through space, and he landed on the coal

He was oblivious to the impact. As his long-suffering frame rebelled at last against the indignity of consciousness, he swam into a velvet blackness, and this time the blackness was utterly obliterating.

Thud-thud! Thud-thud! Thud-thud!

Ben opened his eyes. He came out of the greater blackness into the lesser. Cosmos was replaced by coal.

Coal was all about him. Under him, beside him, on top of him. He could understand the coal that was under him and the coal that was beside him, but he couldn't understand the coal that was on top of him. When you fall upon coal, it doesn't usually get up and lay itself over you like a counterpane.

But that wasn't the only thing that puzzled him. There was something else. Something new. Something . . .

Thud-thud! Thud-thud! Thud-thud!

'Gawd—we're movin'!' thought Ben.

Yes, undoubtedly, the boat was moving. The engines were thudding rhythmically, like great pulses, and although there was nothing visible by which to gauge movement, Ben's body felt a sense of progress. How long had he been unconscious, then? More than the minute it seemed, obviously. Was it ten minutes, or an hour, or twelve hours, since he had seen the little waving hand and had pitched down here from the ladder? Or . . . even longer?

He moved cautiously. Very cautiously. This surprising roof of coal must be treated with respect, or it would cave in. As he moved, his foot came into contact with something that, surely, was not coal. Something soft. Something warm.

Then he remembered the last warm, soft thing he had touched, and he stiffened.

The fellow he had tripped over in the dockyard! Was he here, beside him?

No, of course not! Steady, Ben! There was that splash, don't you remember? That fellow had been pitched into the water. And, anyhow, this soft thing was different, somehow. Quite different. Ah, a cat! That was it! The ship's cat, come to see him, and to give him a friendly lick!

Now Ben moved his hand, groping carefully through the cavern towards the cat's body. 'Puss, puss!' he muttered. ''Ow's yer mother?' He opened his fingers, and prepared to stroke whatever they made contact with. His fingers met other fingers. The other fingers closed over his.

'That's funny!' thought Ben. 'Why ain't I shriekin'?'

It wasn't because he wasn't trying. He was doing all he could to shriek. Well, wouldn't *you*, if you were lying in a cavern of coal, and somebody else's hand closed over yours? But the shriek would not come. It was merely his thought that bawled. P'r'aps he had a bit of coal in his throat? That might be it! How did you get a bit of coal out of your throat when one hand was under you, and the other was being held, and your nose was pressing against another bit of coal?

Then Ben realised why he wasn't screaming. The other person's hand, in some queer way, was ordering him not to. It kept on pressing his, at first in long, determined grasps, but afterwards in quick, spasmodic ones. 'Don't scream—don't scream—don't scream!' urged each pressure. 'Wait!'

What for?

A moment later, he knew. Voices were approaching.

At first they were merely an indistinguishable accompaniment to the thudding of the engines, but gradually they drew out of throb and became separate and individual. One voice was slow and rough. The other was sharp and curt. Ben had never heard either of them before, yet he had an odd sensation that he had done so, and instinctively he visualised the speakers. The first, tall; the second, short, thick-set and stumpy.

'This the spot?' drawled the first speaker.

'Yes. Charming, isn't it?' said the second.

There was a pause. When the first speaker answered he had drawn nearer, and seemed so close that Ben nearly jumped. He might have jumped but for another little pressure of the fingers still closed over his.

'Can't say I'd choose to live in it,' came the slow voice.

'Well, no one's asking you to live in it,' came the curt one. 'It'll do, anyway. That is, if we're driven to it. But there may be another way.'

'Seems to've been made for us.'

'P'r'aps it was! Old Papa Fate hands one a prize once and again, doesn't he? He handed *you* to *me*, for instance!'

'And he handed you to *me*!'

A short laugh followed. Then the curt voice said:

'Well, it's fifty-fifty. Only, don't forget, son of a gun, you don't get your fifty unless I get mine!'

'I'm not forgetting anything,' retorted the slow voice; 'and if there's any damned double-crossing, I sha'n't forget *that*, either! What's beyond there?'

'Water.'

'Don't be funny. Is all this coal?'

'Ay.'

'Just coal?'

22

'Of course, just coal! D'you suppose we feed the fires with diamonds? Have a feel!'

Ben bared his teeth to bite. God spared him the necessity.

'What's all this curiosity, anyhow?' demanded the curt voice abruptly.

'Nothing special,' responded the slow voice. 'But there's no harm in knowing, is there?'

'None at all. And you can trust *me* with the knowing! I expect I know my own ship, and—hallo! What's that?'

The curt voice broke off suddenly. Four pairs of ears listened tensely. Two pairs by the coal, two under it.

'I didn't hear anything,' growled the slow voice.

'P'r'aps I didn't either,' muttered the other.

'Getting nervy, eh?'

'Nerves your hat!'

'Then what was it?'

'A blankety rat, probably, running across the coal. Oh, shut your mug and let's get back to it! Do you think you can find your way here all right? That is, supposing you have to?'

'I suppose so. But wouldn't you be coming with me?'

A contemptuous snort followed the question.

'Bit of a darned fool, aren't you?' said the curt voice. 'How am I going to manage *that*?'

'How am I going to manage fourteen ladders and seventeen corners and ninety-six passages?' came the retort, delivered with warmth.

'You may have to!' The warmth was reciprocated. 'Anyway, Sims would manage the first half of the journey for you.'

'What! With that load?'

23

'Yes, with that load! Sims has muscles. And d'you expect I'd have taken *you* on board if I hadn't seen yours?'

'Maybe one of these fine days you'll *feel* 'em!'

'Maybe elephants grow grass on their heads! You're a useful sort of a tyke, aren't you? How the blazes could *I* get away? It'll be all hands on deck if this little business comes along, don't you worry!'

'Yes, but s'pose—'

'Do *you* suppose an officer can afford to be missing during an affair of that sort?' cried the officer under consideration. 'God, you used your brains at Hammersmith, didn't you?'

Hammersmith! Ben stopped breathing. *Hammersmith* . . .

'I used something else, as well, at Hammersmith,' snarled the other; 'and you're going the right way to get a taste of it.'

'Say—have you ever been at a murder trial, and seen the old man put on his black cap?' asked the curt voice, after a momentary pause. 'I reckon *you're* going the right way to get something too. Now, listen! We've been here long enough. Get back to your quarters, Mr Hammersmith Stoker, and lie low till you're wanted. And if you think of using that pretty little spanner I see in your hand, just remember the black cap.'

There was a silence, and the sound of moving feet. Then the slow voice observed, contemplatively:

'We've all got to die some time, you know.'

'Like hell, we have,' agreed the curt man. 'But there's ways and ways. I prefer a bed to a rope.'

The voices were farther off. Now they ceased altogether. But Ben did not move. His spirit was lying, frozen, in Hammersmith.

A whisper close to his ear brought him back to coal. 'For God's sake, let's get out of this before we suffocate!' it said. 'You and I've got to talk!'

Thud-thud! Thud-thud! Thud-thud!

4

Confidences in the Dark

''Oo are yer?' muttered Ben.

'Wait till we're out,' came the whispered response.

'Yus, but 'ow do we *git* aht?' Ben whispered back.

This time a brilliant little light answered him. It illuminated the improvised coal cavern, and revealed it as considerably smaller than he had imagined it to be. A few points and sharp edges dazzled close to his eyes; then, as the little light became more distant and the shaft changed its direction, shadows shot towards him from the points and edges, which now became blurred outlines beyond moving pools of black.

Suddenly the little light went out, and all was darkness again. Ben tried to hold his breath, and discovered that he was already holding it. When terrified, he had not the power to keep anything in reserve. That was why he frequently went beyond the reserve. Five long seconds ticked by. He thought he heard them ticking, but couldn't be sure. Then the light was switched on again, almost blinding him.

'Wotcher put the light aht for?' he demanded weakly.

The situation was complicated by the fact that he did not know whom he was talking to. He was entirely vague as to what attitude he ought to adopt.

'I thought I heard them coming back,' replied the person who held the light.

'Oi!' said Ben. 'Yer got yer foot in me marth.'

The foot moved away. So did the rest of the little warm bulk to which it belonged. Cautiously, Ben followed.

By painfully slow degrees, the journey proceeded. It seemed a mile long, but actually its length was only a yard or two. The foot that had been in his mouth proved, subsequently, of use as a sign-post. It was small and shoe-less, and Ben developed a strange affection for it. While he saw it, there was hope. When it disappeared, over-whelming loneliness descended upon him, accompanied by a kind of panic. It must be remembered that Ben had been through a lot.

Once he caught hold of the foot just as it was vanishing, and hung on to it like an anchor.

'What are you doing?' came the sharp whisper.

'Not gettin' fresh,' mumbled Ben; 'but I ain't got nothin' helse ter go by.'

The foot slipped out of his grasp. He glued his eyes on it. Then it slipped over a precipice and vanished.

'Oi!' chattered Ben.

As there was no immediate response, he repeated his observation, and then a voice whispered up from some-where below him.

'You seem to love that word,' said the voice; 'but I wish you'd say it a bit softer.'

'Where are yer?' asked Ben.

'On the ground.'

'Where's that?'

'Be quick! Want any help?'

'Yus. Me boot's got on top of me some'ow, and seems to 'ave caught on a 'ook.'

Two small hands appeared from the precipice over which his companion had vanished. He stretched one of his own hands towards them, giving the hooked boot a jerk at the same time. There was a crackle overhead, and the roof descended upon him.

Fortunately the roof caved in where it was thinnest, or Ben might not have replied to the anxious question, 'Are you hurt?' As it was, he was able to answer, 'Dunno,' and to feel about himself to find out. He couldn't feel very fast, because heavy things lay all about on top of him, but the two small hands were deftly removing them, and when his back had been cleared he was able to report, to his considerable astonishment, that he was still alive.

'On'y I think me spindle's broke,' he added.

'What's that?' asked his companion.

'Dunno,' blinked Ben. 'Ain't I got one?'

The only thing he was certain of was that he wouldn't want anything more to eat for a week.

The two hands gripped him, and assisted him down to the ground; but when you reached the ground it wasn't easy to keep your feet. You swayed, and had to catch hold of something. And then you missed the something, and it caught hold of you . . .

As Ben stared at the something that caught hold of him, he had a confused sensation that history was repeating itself, only inversely. Yes, there had been a situation similar to this only a few hours ago! A few hours? More like a few years! In that previous situation, however, it was Ben's outstretched arms that had received a tottering form. Now, the form he had received was supporting *him*!

The same hair, the same eyes—bright this time with concern, not with terror—the same slight, girlish figure, the same short brown skirt, now much blackened, the same soft warmth . . .

''Corse, miss, this beats me!' muttered Ben dizzily.

'Beats me too,' responded the girl. 'Don't move for a jiffy, if you're groggy.'

Ben overstayed the jiffy. He did feel groggy. Then he leaned back a little, tested himself without her, and found that, with great care, it could be done.

'O.K.,' he reported. 'I got me legs back. And, now—'oo bloomin' *are* yer?'

'Who are you first,' she answered.

'Oo am I?'

'I want to know.'

''Corse yer does!' nodded Ben. 'Heverybody wants ter know. That's the way, ain't it? Hothers does the haskin', and I does the tellin'.'

'Please don't get huffy.'

'Oo's 'uffy? Well, 'ave it yer own way. I'm Hadmiral Beatty. Now fer your'n!'

A faint smile flickered in the torchlight. Then the smile vanished as the light was snapped off sharply. Admiral Beatty swung round with a gulp.

'Keep steady, admiral!' said the girl's voice, through the darkness. 'It just occurred to me that we'll be fools if we show our lights.'

'Yus, that's orl right,' complained Ben; 'but don't do things so sudden—'

29

'*Or* if we raise our voices,' continued the girl. 'Sometimes you forget there's a war on!'

'It's never orf, fer me!' muttered Ben. 'But wot's the pertickler war yer torkin' abart?'

'Meaning you can't guess?'

In the darkness her hand stretched out, and took hold of his sleeve again. He was beginning to know the touch of those firm little fingers. He liked the touch of them. At least, when he got a bit of warning it was coming.

Could he guess? He tried hard not to. Then he faced it.

''Ammersmith?' he whispered sepulchrally.

The grip on his sleeve tightened. He was answered. The answer wound round them as they stood there motionless, binding them grimly and inexplicably together. It sifted through the blackness, coiled through the unseen coal, and journeyed on invisible sound-waves to the engines, wedding itself to their muffled thudding.

'Yus, but—*you* ain't done it?' muttered Ben, in a sudden sweat.

'No,' she answered. 'I do bar *that*!'

Her voice came in a sudden choked hiss. Something in the vehemence of the denial brought consolation to Ben. Wot—*she* done a murder? This bit of a gal? There's a blinkin' idea! Still, it was good to be sure.

'It was done by the bloke wot was 'ere jest nah, wasn't it?' said Ben.

'How do *you* know?' shot out the girl.

'Well—you 'eard wot they sed.'

'Yes, yes, I heard! But—is that all?'

'I don't git yer.'

'As far as *you* are concerned?'

'Oh, I see. No, it ain't. It's never all as fur as I'm

concerned! Things jest go on 'appenin' as soon as they sees me comin' and I can't stop 'em. Gawd, they've 'appened ternight orl right!' He shuddered. 'It *is* ternight, ain't it?' Then, suddenly becoming conscious again of the fingers gripping his arm, he went on, 'Yus, and you're one of 'em, miss. Ain't yer never goin' ter tell me 'oo yer are, and 'ow yer got 'ere?'

'What else has happened to you—tonight?'

'Tork abart oysters!'

'Please! What else happened? Why did you come on this boat? Were you following me?'

''Corse not!'

'Well, you might have been. After the way I blundered into you like that.'

'Yus, that did git me thinkin', miss. But yer was too quick. Like a rabbit. Any'ow, I didn't know *you* was on this ship.'

'Then why are you here? Stowaway?'

'That'll be the nime, when they finds me. And you too, eh?'

'They're not *going* to find me!'

'I 'ope yer right.'

'I'll see I'm right!' Then she added quickly, 'I don't suppose *you'll* give me away?' She paused for a moment, and ran on, 'I've done you a good turn, you know. Don't forget that! When you pitched down from the ladder I got you under the coal with me. Some job! I—looked after you.'

Ben nodded. He knew that he owed his present security to her, and he also knew why she was informing him of the fact. She was trying to enlist his gratitude.

That puzzled him. Why should she do that? Wasn't it

obvious that he would not give her away? Bit of dirty work that'd be, wouldn't it? The world had got its heel on both of them, and he'd hardly turn upon a fellow-sufferer. Perhaps there was something else, though! Yes, there might be something else. Perhaps . . .

Ben thought hard for several seconds. He was trying to straighten things out with insufficient material to work upon. He fell back upon a generality.

'Look 'ere, miss,' he said, and the simple solemnity of his voice was not lost upon his companion, 'you're in trouble, ain't yer? Well—so'm I. Ain't that enuff?'

There was a little silence. Then the girl answered, in tones equally solemn.

'Seems as if I've found a pal. You're white, aren't you?'

'Like blinkin' snow,' replied Ben uncomfortably. He never knew what to do with compliments. He hadn't had much practice. Then, partly to change the conversation, and partly to settle the point that was worrying him most at the moment, he asked, 'Wot are yer runnin' away for?'

'I'll tell you as soon as you tell me why *you* are?' Ben reflected. Why was he running away? The nightmare reverted to him in all its horror—the nightmare that was still to be played out.

'Some'un went fer me, miss,' he said.

'Where?'

'In the stummick.' No, that wasn't right. 'In the dock.'

'Why?'

'There you are!'

'Don't you know?'

'P'r'aps 'e thort I'd seed too much.'

'Oh! What had you seen?'

32

'Well—it ain't pretty, miss.'

'Life isn't pretty.'

'Ah, but this—this wasn't life. No, miss. This was—the hother thing!'

He was conscious that she shuddered. He felt her draw closer, as though for comfort.

'You mean—someone—dead?' she whispered.

'I might 'ave bin mistook,' he murmured, unconvincingly.

'Don't hide anything, please. *Nothing'll* help but the truth. The—person you saw—*was* dead?'

'As a door nail,' Ben confessed. ''E'd bin done in orl right. Funny—'ow yer can tell.'

'What did you do?'

'Oo?'

'What did you do, after you came upon him?'

'Oh. Well—I tikes a little walk rahnd, see?' There was no need to mention that it had been rather a rapid walk. 'And when I comes back agine, the deader's gorn.'

'Gone!'

'Yus.'

'But—'

'I'm tellin' yer. 'E was gorn. "'Allo!" I ses. "That's bad." And then I 'ears a splash. Like wot—well, then I 'ears a splash.'

He paused. He didn't like the story. The girl made no comment, and he decided to get the rest of it over in one sentence.

'Well, arter that, this hother feller comes along and goes fer me, and so I 'ops it—well, 'oo wouldn't, and I comes on another feller and I shoots onter the ship, see—well, 'oo wouldn't?'

He paused again. For a while the girl made no comment.

The throbbing of the engines seemed to grow louder and more ominous. Then, suddenly, she shot a question.

'Do you know how long you've been on this ship?' she asked.

'Couple of hours?' guessed Ben.

'Couple of days,' she replied.

Ben gasped.

'Wot—couple of—days?' he murmured. 'Are you tellin' me, miss, that you've bin lookin' arter me fer a couple of *days*?'

'That's right,' she nodded. 'Hospital nurse and general provider. Part of the time, you were off your nut.'

Off his nut! Wasn't he still off his nut! His mind swung backwards and forwards. Then, suddenly, it stopped swinging, and *he* shot a question.

'That fust feller—that feller wot was called Mr 'Ammersmith Stoker,' he said. 'Is 'e arter you too?'

'Like hell, he is,' answered the girl. 'He's killed two people, and if he finds me, I look like being a third!'

What Happened at Hammersmith

Ben received the bad news numbly. For one thing, although it shocked him, it hardly surprised him. For another, his brain was getting a little dizzy and stupid. Two days . . .

'Arter you too, is 'e?' he muttered. 'Wot for?'

'P'r'aps—*I've* seen too much, like you,' suggested his companion.

'Ah!' blinked Ben. 'Sight ain't always a blessin'. Wotcher seen?' As she did not reply, he made a guess. It was a nasty guess, but they'd got to get straight with each other. 'Was it—at 'Ammersmith—wot you seen?' he inquired.

She nodded. He detected the faint movement of her head against a ghost of light that dimly marked the position of the iron ladder mounting above them. His sympathy for her grew. And for himself.

'Yus, but you didn't *do* it,' he said, as though he were informing her of a fact she did not know.

Now she shook her head. She was quite aware of the fact.

'Then you ain't got no cause ter fear the police,' went on Ben.

'Haven't I?' she replied.

It was an unsatisfactory reply. It told nothing, but it implied a lot. He put himself in her position—as much of her position, at least, as he knew—reviewed himself from her angle, and then advised her.

'If I was you, miss,' he announced, 'I'd tell me.'

'It mightn't do you any good to hear,' she answered.

'There ain't much I can't stand,' he retorted, 'in the way of 'earin'. If you was ter say Windser Castle was blowed hup, I'd 'ardly notice it.'

'You know, but for our tight corner,' said the girl, 'you'd make me laugh! I hope I meet you one day at a party. Meantime—well, let's see if you can stand this! That—murdering fellow is my working partner.'

'Is 'e?'

'Well done! You're sticking it! Want some more?'

'Well, we're orf now like, ain't we, miss?'

'You've said it! We're off! And the next tit-bit is that I was *in* on the Hammersmith affair.'

'Was yer?'

'*Feel!*'

He heard a swift little rustle, and a wad of paper was thrust against his hand. He guessed correctly, with a shiver. A dead man's notes.

''Ere, you must git rid o' them!' he gasped, diving straight to the kernel.

Then his mind began to go back on him. He was advising a girl to get rid of evidence that would connect her with a murder. She hadn't done the murder, but she was implicated in it. In another minute, Ben himself would be implicated. He began to speculate on how he stood. 'I knows they can nab yer if yer knows and don't tell,' he thought; 'but can they nab yer if yer knows and don't tell abart some 'un helse as knows and don't tell?' It was much too difficult. He gave it up, and tried to concentrate on the words that were now being whispered to him through the darkness:

'Get rid of them? I'm not quite a fool! They'll have the numbers taped all right! And, anyway, I don't feel I want to touch the wretched things. Yes, but don't think I'm squeamish!' The voice rose a little, in sudden defiance. 'I'm the stuff, all right! I could pick your pocket while you winked. That's my speciality. But—no, not *murder*! That's outside the ring. I do bar *that*!'

''Corse yer does,' agreed Ben hopelessly.

'And when I joined with this fellow—Jim Faggis—the name'll be in the papers soon enough—we had it all clear first. You've got to make sure where you stand, you know, or you're soon in the soup. And on our very first job he—does this!' She paused. 'Say, I'm telling you a lot, aren't I?'

'Everythin' but,' replied Ben. ''Ow did it 'appen?'

'God knows! It was Faggis's show from the word go. He'd already marked the man and the house—sort of old miser who collects money just to keep it away from other people, and then leaves it to a cat's home—you know—and we got in easily enough, and everything was going all right till Faggis knocks over a chair. That scared me. I don't like inside work, anyway. Never did. God's good air for this child! Yes, and when I heard him coming downstairs—I did a bolt, and don't mind admitting it!'

'So'd anybody,' sympathised Ben.

His mind was in a terrible tangle. She had said she was telling him a lot, and it was the truth. He was learning things that were very awkward indeed for a law-abiding citizen like him—because, after all, lying down on seats and being moved on wasn't actually breaking the law, was it? You had to lie somewhere . . .

'But Faggis wouldn't go, even then, the fool! No, he must stay and see it through. You see, we'd only done downstairs, and he knew there was more on the first floor. That's the worst of people like Faggis. Never satisfied! Well, by God, I hope he's satisfied now!'

It had taken her a long while to start, but she was thoroughly wound up now. Hours of emotional repression and tightly-closed lips had had their effect upon her, and now, in this queer sanctuary, before this queerer audience, her tongue was loosened, and words flowed fast from where they had waited frozen.

'Yer can see she ain't one o' the *real* bad 'uns,' argued Ben to himself, as he listened. He didn't know it, but he was actually arguing her case at the gates of Heaven. 'Never 'ad a proper chance, that's wot it is. You gotter 'ave a charnce. And, as fer pickin' pockets—well, didn't I nearly pick a pocket once, on'y I didn't 'cos I couldn't, me 'and was too big. Well, then . . .'

'When I got outside, I waited for him. I'd got the wind up properly. Faggis had been getting on my nerves, you see.' She always tried to make it clear that she wasn't really soft. 'He hadn't exactly got the bedside manner. I waited goodness knows how long. *Years!*'

'I knows 'em,' murmured Ben.

'And then he came. And—and the moment I saw his face, I knew what had happened. "You've killed him!" I said. Just like that. "You've killed him!" He didn't answer. But that didn't make any difference. It was written all over him. The poor old fool I'd heard coming downstairs to look after his silly property had been bumped off!'

She spoke through her teeth. Suddenly, as Ben tried hard not to visualise the scene she was describing, and failed, he became conscious of the engines again and their ceaseless throbbing. They throbbed like Fate, with all Fate's indifference and domination. 'Go on whispering, if it amuses you,' said the engines. 'It won't alter things. You're being carried on, just the same.'

Throb-throb! Throb-throb! Throb-throb!

'I don't know how long we stood there, staring at each other. Only a second, I dare say. Then I got giddy, and turned to run. But he got hold of my arm, and asked me what I was going to do. "I don't know," I said. "You're not going to be a damned fool?" he said. "I don't know," I said. I didn't. And then I managed to get away, and he came after me. You see—he'd got the wind up too. He thought I might tell the police.'

'Why didn't yer?' asked Ben, to fill in a pause.

'D'you take me for a saint?' she retorted. 'It would have looked well for me, wouldn't it? Besides—when you take on a bargain—it's for better or worse, isn't it? Still, I thought of it. And then, there's another thing. If Faggis was caught, he'd drag *me* in. He's that sort. Oh, he'll do it, don't worry! And that's why he'd been after me all day. He knew I'd either make for a police station or a getaway, and he wanted me in either case. And he nearly got me that time I barged into your arms! . . . I've been through it!'

'There yer are,' said Ben to St Peter. 'She *thort* o' goin' fer the police! Tha's somethink, ain't it?' Meanwhile, to the girl whose case he was pleading, he held out a more immediate crumb of comfort. 'P'r'aps 'e wasn't dead, miss,' he suggested. 'The miser bloke. Arter all, yer never seed 'im.'

'Yes, I *did*!'

Ben gulped. Seen him, had she? *Seen* him! Lummy! Now Ben visualised St Peter thrusting her out—thrusting Ben out, also—and slamming the golden gates in their faces. Ben's St Peter, of course, was not known to him by name, nor was he the St Peter of your and my conception. The nearest his vision could get to heaven's gate-keeper was a picture he had once seen of Mark Twain, with wings added.

'So—yer *seed* 'im?' whispered Ben.

'Yes. Somehow—I *had* to,' she whispered back. 'You see—as you said—he mightn't have been dead. And, if he hadn't been—'

'Yer could 'ave gorn fer a doctor and p'r'aps saved 'im?'

Ben jumped in quickly with that. Again in the dimness he caught the girl's nod, and this time it rejoiced him. 'Wot abart *that*, yer blinkin' fool!' he cried to his winged version of Mark Twain. 'She went back agine, see? Might 'ave bin copped, but she goes back. Puts 'er 'ead in at a winder, eh? Ter mike sure she carn't do nothin' fer 'im. Bet *you* wouldn't 'ave! Hopen yer gate!'

Then, leaving the future and swinging back to the more vital present, he exclaimed:

'Gawd, and now this blinkin' murderin' bloke is on the boat with us!'

'Sh!' she warned him.

The exclamation had been rather on the loud side.

'Yus, but does 'e know *you're* 'ere?' he asked hoarsely.

'I don't know,' she answered, after a pause. 'P'r'aps you've got an opinion?'

Ben held a consultation with himself.

'Well, miss, this is 'ow I sizes it hup,' he said. ''E may

think yer 'ere, but 'e don't *know* it. 'E may think *I'm* 'ere, but 'e don't know it. 'Cos why? That ain't why 'e come aboard, see? No. 'E's come aboard as a blinkin' stoker—Mr 'Ammersmith Stoker, the hother feller called 'im—and 'e's got some gime on that ain't nothink ter do with you—*hor* with me!'

'I believe you're right,' nodded the girl. 'You weren't asleep under the coal, then!'

'No—seems as if I jest come aht of me two days' snooze when they comes in. Yus, and if your 'and 'adn't give me the wink, I'd 'ave 'ollered.'

'Then you *do* see you owe me something?'

'Fifty-fifty, ain't it? And them two blokes is fifty-fifty on that hother gime too. They said so, didn't they?'

'But what *is* the other game?'

'That's wot we gotter find aht,' said Ben. 'Orl we knows hup ter nah is that they've marked the spot where you and I are standin'—and that they're *comin' back*!'

His voice dropped to its most sepulchral depth. The girl did not appear to be attending.

'Comin' *back*!' he repeated. 'Comin' back right 'ere!' Then, as she still made no comment, he became worried. 'Wot's hup?' he demanded.

'Do you—smell anything?' came the question.

Ben sniffed. The thing he instinctively sniffed for was fire. No, he didn't sniff fire.

'I don't smell nuffin',' he said. 'That is, barrin' coal.'

He sniffed again. Ah, yes! There *was* something. He went on sniffing.

'Where is it?' He blinked.

He looked towards the girl and missed her. 'Oi!' he whispered. But she was merely bending down, and her

41

position answered his question. The smell was coming up from below them.

Ben got a sudden queer vision. It was of a hospital. He saw rows of small white beds, and nurses moving about and doctors. He saw a man being brought in on a stretcher. He discovered himself on a stretcher, moving towards an operating room. Things happened very swiftly in Ben's mind.

But why had this vision come to him? They were in a ship, not a hospital. Of course, he did remember coming out of gas once and hearing a throbbing something like that of the engines. Still, this wasn't gas, even though it brought gas to his mind. Something that reminded him of gas, but not gas. Something . . .

'Lummy!' he gasped. 'Clorridgeform!'

6

The Third Officer

The chloroform was in a small green bottle that lay on the ground in a little arc of light produced by the girl's torch. For several seconds they stared at it. The sight brought recent events ominously close.

"'Ow did it git there?' asked Ben.

As he put the question, the bottle disappeared. The girl had snapped off the light again.

'Wotcher doin'?' demanded Ben.

He heard a swift whisper, but it was too low to be intelligible. Then another sound caught his attention. It came from above, in the vicinity of the ladder.

The swift whisper had been a warning. Gawd—now fer it! Ben whispered back:

'Doncher move, miss! Stand steady! They'll 'ear yer!'

There was no time to climb back to their original hiding-place and, in a matter of seconds, to re-cover themselves with coal. Perhaps, by standing perfectly still under the wall of coal, they might escape notice. The originator of the noise above, whoever it was, might pass on to another ladder, giving this dead end a miss, or he might poke his head in, see nothing during a quick glance, and then poke his head out again. Sound—that was the thing to avoid. Sound!

Why does one always want to sneeze at the most inconvenient moment? In terror Ben seized his upper lip and fought against the tragedy of explosion. He thought hard of a monkey sitting on the North Pole—he had heard this was one of the best remedies—but as the monkey sneezed this only made matters more insupportable. He hastily sent the monkey packing, and substituted a snake, which hasn't a nose. At least, Ben's snake hadn't. Then a shaft of light struck him from above.

There being no object in keeping the sneeze back any longer, he let it go.

When he opened his eyes he received another shock. The light was still on him, revealing him mercilessly, but it did not reveal anybody else! The girl was no longer by his side. He appeared to have sneezed her away.

The source of the light drew nearer. He did not move. He was too stunned. A second edition of himself moved, however. His black shadow. It swelled enormously as the light approached, creating envy in the breast of its responsible substance. 'Gawd, if I was as big as that,' thought Ben, 'I'd give somebody somethink!'

Then he turned round to see who the somebody was. It was the short, thick-set, stumpy man.

The unwelcome visitor did not speak until he had reached the bottom of the ladder and had settled himself securely on *terra firma*. Then, after a curt scrutiny, he opened fire.

'Well, what's *your* game?' he demanded.

Ben became child-like.

'Stowaway,' he answered.

'I see! Riding without a ticket, eh?'

'Tha's it. Somethink fer nothink.'

'Not a hope!' retorted the other. 'You don't get anything for nothing in this world. Thought you people had learned that by now.'

'I've give hup learnin',' returned Ben. 'Well, wotcher goin' ter do abart it?'

His inquisitor did not answer. His eyes were on the ground. He stared at the bottle of chloroform.

'Where did *that* come from?' he inquired.

'Fell out of me button 'ole,' said Ben.

'Joking won't help you,' frowned the other. He stooped and picked the bottle up. Then he looked at Ben quizzically. 'Do you know what this is?'

'Yus.'

'What?'

'Ginger beer.'

'Ginger beer! A pretty strong brand! Ever heard of chloroform?'

A bit of coal shifted somewhere, and made them jump.

'What's that?' exclaimed the officer.

'Ever 'eard o' rats?' asked Ben.

The officer frowned. Not long since, in this very spot, he had himself offered the same explanation to another man. All at once he looked at Ben sharply.

'Say, you—how long have you been in this little funk hole?'

That was an awkward question. Two days, apparently. But if he admitted it, the officer would know that Ben had overheard a certain conversation. In a panic he responded:

'Jest come 'ere.'

45

'Are you sure?'

'Fack.'

'I didn't see you as I came along.'

'Tha's why I come along.'

'Damned fool!'

''Oo?'

'Look here, do you know you're speaking to an officer?'

'On'y third.'

'Only—' Indignation was succeeded by interest. 'So you can read a uniform, eh?'

'Better'n the Bible.'

'How's that? Been to sea before?'

'Yus. Ain't you never 'eard o' the Battle o' Jutland?'

'And haven't *you* heard that even third officers are called "sir?"'

About to submit, Ben suddenly changed his mind. His ear had caught the sound of coal shifting again, and his brain was working.

'Git on with it!' he retorted, deliberately rude. 'This ain't a children's party!'

'By God, it isn't!' cried the third officer angrily. 'You'll learn what sort of a party it is before you're many minutes older.' He held up the bottle of chloroform. '*This* isn't going to help you, you know!'

'Wotcher mean?' asked Ben uneasily.

'Clear enough, I should think! Stowaway! We'll see about that!'

Ben blinked at the bottle, and backed a little. The third officer was brandishing it rather close. That, however, was not the point that worried him most.

'That ain't nothing ter do with me!' he declared, with vehemence.

'Oh, isn't it?'

'No, it ain't!'

'I thought it dropped from your button hole?'

'Go on! I was bein' funny! Doncher know a joke when yer sees one?'

The third officer suddenly grinned. Apparently he was seeing some joke at that moment.

'I tell yer, w— I fahnd it on the grahnd!' He just saved himself from saying 'we.' 'I was lookin' at it when you come along.'

'Really, now?' responded the third officer, still grinning. 'Without a spot-light?'

Ben perspired. The joke had passed out of his hands. Staring at the grin in front of him, he wondered how hard he could hit, if he really tried. But he did not hit the grin. He suddenly interpreted it, instead. And perspired more freely afterwards.

'So *that's* yer gime, is it?' he thought. 'You dropped it 'ere, did yer, and now you're puttin' it on *me*! Orl right, Sunny Boy, I got a gime too, that'll send the sun in!'

Aloud he said:

''Oo wants a spot-light fer clorridgeform? I got a nose, ain't I?'

'Yes, and you'll feel something on it, if I have any more of your back chat!' exclaimed the third officer. 'Now, then— up the ladder with you. And step lively!'

Ben hesitated. 'I gotter go fust?' he asked.

'Bet your life, you have!' retorted the third officer. 'Well, what are you waiting for?'

He was waiting because he didn't want to go first. He wanted to see the third officer out of the place before he followed. Those movements among the coal were troubling him. He knew who was making them. She'd nipped into cover somehow . . . Lummy! There was another one!

'Have I got to help you?' cried the third officer angrily.

'No, you ain't!' shouted Ben suddenly. 'I don't want no 'elp, not from you—no, nor not from *hanyone*. See? Not from *hanyone*!'

The third officer thought Ben was speaking to him. As a matter of fact, Ben was addressing the coal. A piece of coal responded, by dislodging itself and toppling to the ground.

'Hey! What's that?' exclaimed the officer, and flashed his torch towards the spot.

'Gawd—now 'e's got 'er!' thought Ben, and clenched his fist, just to give the world one good bash before it crushed you.

Two bright eyes gleamed from the illuminated coal heap. Then their owner sprang at the third officer.

'Damn these blasted rats!' he cried.

Ben felt himself feeling sick.

7

The Faggis Jigsaw

More ladders. More dark passages. More climbing and squeezing through the tubes and arteries of the ship's stomach. But this time Ben did not have to select the tubes and arteries himself. They were selected for him by the third officer.

And thus he was free to grope among other dark passages—the dark passages of his mind. He tried to illuminate them. Some of them needed illumination badly. To avoid further tripping.

Where was he going now? That was one question. What was he going to do when he got there? That was another. Answer to the first question—captain. Answer to the second—Gawd knows!

Other questions: How was he going to re-establish contact with the strange little pickpocket down among the coal? If she were caught, what would happen to her? And if *he* were caught, and had prevented her from being caught, what would happen to *him*? . . .

'Now, then, look where you're going!' barked the third officer.

Then there was that murdering chap. Faggis, she'd called him, hadn't she? Where was Faggis now, and what new game was *he* up to?

In order to obtain some clarity on this particularly vital question, Ben took his mind back to Hammersmith, and tried to piece together Faggis's actions and motives. Perhaps if he could complete the first part of Faggis's story, he might make something out of the second part . . .

'Of course, if you *want* to step straight into a hole, it'll be your funeral, not mine,' said the third officer.

Faggis had been working on his own. Right. Fell in with the girl, and got her to join forces with him. Right! And this Hammersmith affair had been their first job together. The girl had said so. Right. All clear so far.

Why hadn't Faggis continued to work alone? P'r'aps he had had his eye on the old miser's crib but required a partner to help him crack it. P'r'aps he needed someone small, like this girl, to shinny up a water-pipe, and then slip in through a window. P'r'aps he was tired of his own company, and liked the girl's face. Anyway, into the house they get, and start collecting. Find plenty of new money. (The chap at the coffee-stall, who had left in a hurry, had paid in new money.) Then the old miser comes down, the girl does a bunk into the garden, Faggis attacks the old man, and kills him. Didn't mean to kill him. But kills him. And, once you've started killing, you ain't too pertickler if you have to go on . . .

'Turn to the right, man, unless you want to get your face scorched off!'

Faggis rushes out into the garden. The girl scoots. Faggis follows. She gives him the slip, runs back to the house for a quick squint—plucky, that was!—and then off she goes again, with Faggis after her.

P'r'aps Faggis never let her out of his sight at all. That might be. Anyhow, he must have stuck pretty close, and he gave her a scare when she came barging round that corner, and bumped into Ben. Then Faggis probably lost sight of her till he picked her up again near the coffee-stall. That was why he slipped away from the coffee-stall so quickly. And after that, one by one, all three of them—the girl, Faggis, and Ben went into dockland through that open gate!

The girl got into the ship. Either to escape from Faggis, or from the police, or from both. By this time, she'd probably decided *not* to tell the police, but to concentrate on her own get-away. Her mind would be in a terrible tangle.

Yes, but something happened to Faggis before *he* got into the ship!

Ben's mind grew dark, and he shuddered, for now he was dealing with the evidence of his own eyes, and not with mere theory. In spite of the unpleasantness of the business, however, he grappled with it, and tried to complete the story. He realised that his future actions, and possibly his future fate, might depend upon the extent of his knowledge.

Now, then! Get on with it! Girl in the ship. Faggis, not yet. Ben, asleep against a post. What happens?

Faggis wants to get into the ship, if he knows the girl has got in. If he doesn't know, then he's still poking around for her. Along comes a man.

'Who are you?' says the man.

'Who are *you*?' replies Faggis.

Something like that. Or perhaps Faggis doesn't wait to inquire! He'd be in a stew. Anyway, there's a tussle. P'r'aps the man is from the ship, and is trying to stop Faggis getting on it. P'r'aps the man recognises Faggis, and threatens to give him up. Or p'r'aps the man doesn't know anything, but is going to make a row, and that's the last thing Faggis wants. Slosh! The man goes down, hit with a spanner or a knuckle-duster. Probably a spanner. The third officer had referred to a spanner in the conversation in the coal bunker, and the report in the paper had said that the knife had been found by the police. Very likely Faggis had plenty of tools on him, and the spanner was one of them.

Down goes the man for the count. Death does the counting. He cries out as he goes down. Ben hears the cry, and thinks at first it is an echo of his own. The echo was this poor fellow's death cry . . .

'Now you're for it,' said the third officer. 'We're nearly there.'

What happens then? Faggis gets the wind up. He starts lugging the man he has killed towards the water, hears Ben approaching, drops the body, darts away, and leaves it for Ben to topple over.

Was Faggis watching Ben as he croquet-hooped over the dead body? Whew!

Next? That's easy. Ben rushes off on his circular tour. Faggis returns to the body, continues with his journey, and drops the man into the water. Splash!

'Stoker?' thought Ben suddenly at this point. 'The deader was a stoker!'

The thought was illuminating. Dead man, stoker. Faggis, who had killed the dead man, referred to by the third officer as 'Mr Hammersmith Stoker.' Taken on in his place, eh? By the third officer, who somehow got to know all about it! Now, why would the third officer take a murderer on to his ship, allowing him to fill the vacancy caused by the murder?

Ben turned suddenly, and stared at the third officer. The third officer stared back.

'What the hell are you stopping for?' demanded the third officer.

'I was jest thinkin',' answered Ben, ''ow much I loves yer.'

The third officer swung him round and kicked him in the back.

'Tha's orl right,' thought Ben, struggling not to cry. '*You wait!*'

8

In the Captain's Cabin

The stomach of a ship, as has been indicated, is not the pleasantest place to reside in. The brain is more appealing. There are instruments in it which may fill a novice with a certain awe. There are wheels and levers, intricate barometers, compasses with bulbs and lights, and other electrical devices, all bearing the mute message, 'Do not touch!' But sunlight plays about them, and clear air bathes them, driving away one's nightmare thoughts; and in the adjacent sanctuary where the brain rests, luxury mixes very pleasantly with necessity.

While Ben was ascending from the stomach, two men sat in the brain's sanctuary. One was dressed in immaculate dark blue. His sleeve bore four imposing gold lines, the middle two interwoven to form a diamond. (The third officer's sleeve had only one line, and his diamond was just tacked on.) His face was as immaculate as his cloth, but the immaculateness of both the face and the cloth spoke of efficiency, not of dandyism. The chief engineer can give orders with grease on his clothes and smuts on his face, but the captain's appearance, saving in emergency, must be irreproachable.

The other man possessed quite another kind of distinctiveness. His clothes too, were of the best, if money stands for quality. Brown tweed, of expensive roughness. A coloured shirt that glowed in daring contrast to the suit. 'I am right!' it shouted to the doubter. 'Notice my silk. Men who can afford me can *make* fashion!' Brown boots, solid and highly polished. A tie that cost even more than it could show—it is a tragedy that mere appearance is so limited—and a pin to bring tears to covetous eyes. The pin was secretly secured against the covetous eyes, however, by an eighteen-carat gold clip.

And presiding above all this was a large monarch of a head, full of ancient business furrows that were now comfortable creases. A grey moustache, also large and comfortable, concealed the upper lip. But today something disturbed the usual ostentatious comfort of this man, and his eyes as they gazed at the captain sitting opposite were bright with restlessness.

'Say, I've heard of your silent navy,' said the large man, breaking a pause that was getting on his nerves; 'but I didn't know it spread to the Mercantile Marine!'

The captain, quite unperturbed by the little sarcasm, allowed a few more seconds to pass. Then he replied, unnecessarily informative:

'I'm thinking, Mr Holbrooke.'

'Well,' growled Mr Holbrooke, 'I should say even thought's got a time limit.'

'In your country, perhaps,' said the captain. 'Not in ours. I'm thinking of what you've told me just now—and wondering—'

'Yep?'

'If you've told me everything?'

Mr Holbrooke frowned, looked away for a moment, and then hastily looked back.

'I don't get you!' he exclaimed.

'It ought to be easy,' observed the captain. 'What's *really* making you so scared?'

Mr Holbrooke did not like that, and his large eyebrows went up in protest.

'Say, who's scared?' he demanded.

'Well, suspicious, then,' the captain corrected himself dryly. 'Choose your own term, Mr Holbrooke.'

Mr Holbrooke regarded the cigar he was smoking thoughtfully. It was one of the captain's cigars, and, to his surprise, it was quite as good as his own.

'Ah—I see what you mean,' he murmured. 'Yes, I'm suspicious, don't worry. Suppose I say it's just a hunch?'

'A hunch,' repeated the captain, nodding slightly. 'And do you seriously expect me to search the whole of this ship for you on account of a hunch?'

'Eh?'

'And to watch every passenger? And to ring a Curfew at eight? And to send a wireless to Scotland Yard? Because that's really about what it comes to, Mr Holbrooke, isn't it?'

Mr Holbrooke's frown grew.

'Maybe that's putting it rather strongly, sir,' he protested. 'I'm not aware that I've said anything about any Curfew!'

The captain shrugged his shoulders.

'Then what *do* you want me to do?' he inquired.

Mr Holbrooke stared at the ground, and then suddenly banged his fist down on the arm of his chair.

'No, by Gosh, you're right!' he exclaimed. 'That's what I *do* want you to do! Within reasonable limits, of course— and I dare say we can spare the Curfew! The point is, as I've mentioned, that you're not dealing with—well, sir, just an ordinary person. You understand me? What I'm telling you is that I'm able and willing to pay for what I'm asking—'

He paused, as the captain raised his hand. The captain spoke a little stiffly.

'The normal protection of passengers on board the *Atalanta* is included in the price of their passage,' he said. 'And, even if it were not, the expense of the extra service you suggest would be rather high for—well, just a hunch.'

'Wouldn't that be my affair?' suggested Mr Holbrooke, unhappily.

'In the strictest sense,' responded the captain, 'everything on board the *Atalanta* is my affair.'

'Then, by golly, *make* it your affair!' cried Mr Holbrooke, exasperated. 'You call it a hunch! It's a darn sight more than that—'

'Ah!'

'Yes, sir! It's—' He broke off, and stared at the captain speculatively. 'Say, do you never have *enemies* in your country?'

'What sort of enemies?'

'Well—I don't mean wives.' He smiled rather foolishly at the cumbrous jest. 'No, you can deal with wives. Flowers—a theatre—that's easy! I'm talking of—' The smile faded. 'This kind—people who are jealous of you—jealous of your success and your position—jealous of the money you've made and the brains and industry you've made it by—people who hate you like poison, and will do any sort of God-darn trick to bring you down a bit to their level!'

His eyes narrowed. For a moment, he almost seemed to forget that he was in the captain's cabin, and the captain regarded him with increased interest. He had been on the point of ending the interview. It was not to his taste. But now he decided to continue it.

'I see,' he commented quietly. 'So you've got enemies of that kind?'

'There's not a successful man in the United States who hasn't!'

The statement was delivered in the form of a retort. The captain interpreted it as an attempt to modify the significance which, a moment earlier, had been insisted on, and he was unable to suppress an ironical smile at the awkward manœuvring of his wealthiest passenger. It was child-like in its inconsistency. When a clever millionaire became child-like, there must be some solid reason behind it. Was the reason, in this case, stark terror?

'I'm quite ready to help you if it's necessary, Mr Holbrooke,' said the captain; 'but you haven't made out your case yet. If your enemies are the sort that every successful American possesses, then every successful American would require the captain of every ship he travelled on to give him special protection. Captains would have a busy time. It seems to me that these enemies of yours must be more malicious than the average. Otherwise, you'd hardly waste my time over them.'

'Well—we'll say they are?'

'Then may we also say, perhaps, that they have more reason to be?'

'Eh?'

'I merely put the question.'

'Well, suppose you *explain* the question?' grunted Mr Holbrooke, with an exclamation of annoyance.

He did not relish the question. His face grew rather red. The captain's own face became a trifle sterner.

'Please try and be calm, Mr Holbrooke,' he said. 'I really can't assist you otherwise. What I've got to find out is how real this danger you talk of is—'

'It's real enough!' interrupted Mr Holbrooke excitedly. 'Say, do you suppose I'd be here if it weren't? You English— if you'll forgive me saying it—want shaking up. You're so darned *slow*! You can't see things that are right before your nose. Now, listen here! Something's *wrong* on this ship! Why, there's even a rumour that a stoker fell in the water before we moved out of dock. Suppose he *didn't* fall in the water. Say he was *pushed* in?'

Someone knocked on the cabin door. 'Come in,' said the captain. A small man entered, in spotless whites. It was Jenks, the captain's steward. He had light hair, and watery blue eyes, and he looked like Jenks.

'From the third officer, sir,' he said, saluting.

He advanced with a note. The captain took it, and read it. He considered for a moment.

'Ask Mr Greene to stand by, Jenks,' said the captain. 'I'd like to see him in a few minutes.'

'Very good, sir,' answered the steward.

When they were alone again, the captain turned to his visitor.

'Rumours are dangerous things, Mr Holbrooke,' he remarked. 'You may remember that, during the early part of the war, there was a rumour of Russians passing through London. Take my advice, and pay no attention to this one.

Or, if you must, don't pass it on with additions from your own imagination. I think, if you don't mind, we will confine ourselves to facts rather than fancies, and get back to the facts of your own case. You suspect some particular enemy?'

'I didn't say that.'

'Then I'll put it another way. Has your successful business been of a kind to produce a special type of enemy?'

'I'm not sure that I rightly understand you.'

'I'm sorry. Perhaps it is time you did. You've asked me for special protection, Mr Holbrooke. You have been, if I may say so, unusually—persistent. You've asked me to make inquiries and to take precautions that could only be justified in a case of the most extreme urgency. When I ask for reasons, you give me general ones, and you call me slow and short-sighted when I do not organise an elaborate plan for circumventing a shadow. Materialise the shadow for me, and perhaps there will be something I can arrange to hit. But if you don't materialise the shadow, I can only conclude—' He paused, and his eyes fell vaguely on the note still in his hand. 'I can only conclude that you have some special reason for withholding the necessary information.'

'Such as?' demanded Mr Holbrooke.

'Well—I take it your success has depended on the failures of others?'

'All success does that.'

'Oh, no. Not necessarily.'

'Yes, sir. Necessarily. The pound I make, you lose.'

The captain bent forward.

'Not, Mr Holbrooke,' he suggested, 'if you give me full value for the pound.'

Mr Holbrooke took it well.

'I see,' he said. 'That's not too bad, captain. You're not as slow as I took you for. I get you.' He looked at his well-manicured finger-nails. 'Well, sir, I expect I've made a few people sore.'

'Quite a number, perhaps?'

'Sure thing.' All at once, as though humanised by the admission, Mr Holbrooke smiled. 'Business men aren't saints, and I make no claim to wings. I got some good knocks when I started out. Well, I've knocked back. Way of the world, isn't it? But I've never run foul of legislation. Barring Prohibition, of course, and that don't count.'

'I don't disbelieve you, Mr Holbrooke,' answered the captain, and now his tone lost a degree of its coldness. 'As you say, business is business. But, played in that spirit, it undoubtedly creates enemies—and I expect some of yours have sworn to get even with you?'

'Sworn black and blue,' nodded Mr Holbrooke. 'They've none of 'em done it yet, but the swearing just goes steadily on! Now, sit right down on your next question, because I guess I know it. Which particular enemies are on this ship? There I'm beaten. I don't know. There's too many! But I've had more threats lately than I've ever had before, and— darn it, sir—I've got my daughter on board with me, and I don't like it!' He didn't like admitting it, either. It wounded his pride. 'Darn it, this is supposed to be a pleasure trip for us!'

'About these threats,' said the captain. 'When did the last occur?'

Mr Holbrooke hesitated, then pulled a small sheet of paper from his pocket and handed it to the captain. 'Found it slipped under my door an hour ago,' he grunted shortly. 'This is really what brought me here.'

The paper bore the words, 'You're for it!'

'Does your business touch Chicago?' asked the captain, after a pause.

'*And* a few other places in the globe,' answered Mr Holbrooke.

But it was easy to see from his expression that the question stayed in his mind.

The captain waited a few seconds to see whether anything useful materialised from the expression. Nothing did. He rose, and took six slow paces to a window.

Gazing out, he caught a glimpse of a white-clad figure on the boat-deck. There were plenty of other figures about, but none more attractive. Mr Holbrooke's millions had done all that millions could do to produce a highly polished and highly finished article in daughters.

A young man was by the white-clad figure's side, and both were leaning over the rail, watching the waves.

Then the captain returned to his chair, and touched a button. Almost instantly, the steward Jenks appeared.

'Now I'll see Mr Greene,' said the captain. And added, as Mr Holbrooke rose, 'Don't go. Mr Greene is my third officer, and he's bringing some news that may be of interest to you.'

9

Cross-Examination

The third officer entered the captain's sanctum and saluted. He was a model of nautical smartness, and exuded duty and efficiency.

'So you've found a stowaway, Mr Greene,' began the captain.

'Yes, sir,' replied the third officer.

'Well, that's not an exceptional circumstance,' observed the captain, with a glance at Mr Holbrooke. The word 'stowaway' had acted on the American millionaire like an electric shock. 'Plenty of people like to get sea-trips for nothing. But we generally disappoint them.'

'How so, when the ship's under way?' inquired Mr Holbrooke.

'Make them work for their living,' answered the captain, and turned back to the third officer. 'Though I understand you may recommend stronger measures in this case?'

'The fellow's dangerous,' responded Greene.

'In what way?'

'Tell by the look of him, sir?'

'He put up a fight, eh?'

'Yes, sir,' said the third officer.

'Anything else?'

Greene hesitated. Then he answered quickly, as though to wipe out the hesitation.

'Yes, sir. He had a bottle of chloroform on him.'

'Hey, what's that?' exclaimed Mr Holbrooke, his eyes growing big.

The captain was equally interested in the information, but showed more composure.

'Chloroform, eh? Then I think I'd better see the man. Where is he now?'

'He's being looked after, sir. I didn't think it was necessary to trouble you to see him. I was going to suggest—'

'Yes, yes, never mind what you were going to suggest, Mr Greene,' interrupted the captain. 'Let us attend to what I suggest. Where was he found?'

'On one of the coal bunkers. Aft.'

'Well, bring him in. No, wait a minute. Have you got the bottle of chloroform?'

'Not on me, sir,' replied the third officer. 'I'll bring it when I come back.'

He turned, but the captain detained him with one more question.

'By the way, Mr Greene,' he said, 'I understand there's a rumour of a stoker who is supposed to have fallen into the water. Do you know anything about it?'

'No, sir,' answered the third officer promptly.

When they were alone again, the captain raised his eyebrows, and Mr Holbrooke burst out.

'Why, I got that rumour from two people,' he exclaimed,

indignantly. 'I should have thought your officers would have known of it!'

'*I* didn't know of it,' answered the captain; 'and my officers have too much to do to attend to rumours. May I know who the two people were?'

Mr Holbrooke reddened slightly. He didn't know who the two people were. As a matter of fact, now he came to think of it, he hadn't actually got it from them at all. He had overheard them talking about it. The captain shook his head rather sadly.

'And so wars begin, Mr Holbrooke,' he observed. 'However, I'll make inquiries.'

Then he fell into a silence, while his visitor stared gloomily at his bright finger-nails. He always got a peculiar satisfaction from his finger-nails.

And into this sombre atmosphere Ben entered a minute later, to continue the strange adventure on which Fate had launched him.

He did not cut a dignified figure. You can't, when your face has the memory of half a ton of coal upon it. His mind, too, was jerky. The transition from darkness to lightness, from the ship's stomach to the ship's brain had confused him, and he was also feeling the effects of many factors which worked against his efficiency. Item, lack of natural sleep. Item, superfluity of unnatural sleep. Item, a blow from a murderer. Item, a fall from a ladder. Item, having been off his nut. Item, an intense, abruptly born interest in a fellow-sufferer whose fate appeared to be in his hands. Item, a vast, empty space inside him that badly needed filling.

It was the fellow-sufferer, however, who confused him most. But for her, he could have gone straight ahead and seen what happened. But for her, he could have turned the tables on his captor, or made a definite attempt to. But what hit his captor would hit Faggis, and what hit Faggis might hit the girl, wherever she was. Yes, and where was she? And what was he to do? And why was he interesting himself in a wrong 'un, anyway, tell him that?

What he really needed, before tackling the difficult interview before him, was a week's holiday. With a hole inside and a bump outside, and things coming so fast one on top of another, what chance had a bloke? Well, there you were!

Chap in blue would be the old man. Who was the other chap? Gawd, there's a pair o' socks . . .

'Here he is,' said the third officer.

'Tha's right!' snorted Ben, as he was pushed forward. 'Shove me abart as if I was a pahnd o' cheese! We ain't 'uman beings, we ain't!'

'Better be careful,' the third officer warned him.

'Wot for?' he retorted. 'When yer dahn on the ground, yer can't fall.'

The captain interposed.

'All right, Mr Greene,' he said quietly. 'I'll talk to him. Perhaps he will be a little more polite to me.'

Ben turned his eyes towards the speaker. The amount of gold braid did increase the necessity for politeness. He decided to try it.

'I speaks proper, sir,' he said, 'when I'm spoke ter proper.'

'I see,' nodded the captain. 'A fifty-fifty arrangement. It isn't quite usual between a captain and a stowaway, but, as you're particular, we'll begin on those lines. What is your name?'

'Ben, sir.'

'And the rest of it?'

'There ain't no rest.'

'I dare say you'll find it, if you think.'

'I can't think.'

'Why not?'

'I got a bump.'

'So I see. How did you get it?'

''Oo?'

'How did you get your bump?'

'It's wot 'appens. When yer 'it.'

'Then what hit you?'

''Arf a dozin' ladders, a ton o' coal, the grahnd, and the third hofficer. Oh, and two hother blokes wot 'e chucks me ter when we comes hup.'

The third officer explained.

'He came quietly at first, sir,' he said; 'but he gave us a bit of trouble towards the end.'

'Well, they was tryin' ter force me 'ead between me legs or somethink,' Ben defended himself. 'It ain't nacheral.'

'I will see that you receive a proper apology from the Merchant Service,' commented the captain dryly. 'Meanwhile, let us return to essentials.'

'Where's that?'

'You say your name's Ben? Write it.'

A piece of paper and a pencil were handed to him. He wrote his autograph wonderingly. What did they want that for? The captain studied it, glanced at another piece of paper, looked at Mr Holbrooke and shook his head.

'What are you doing here?' the captain then asked.

'Eh?'

The captain's eyes grew a little colder. 'Answer me, my man,' he frowned. 'What are you doing here?'

'Oh, I see,' blinked Ben. ''E brought me 'ere.'

He jerked his thumb towards the third officer. The third officer glared angrily, but the captain remained patient.

'How did you get on the ship before he brought you here?' he asked.

'I come aboard.'

'The man's a lunatic, sir!' burst out the third officer.

'I'm not so darned sure!' added Mr Holbrooke, whose eyes were glued in a puzzled stare on Ben's.

'I'll judge,' said the captain. 'Give him a chair.'

What? Someone being nice to him?

'Go on!' murmured Ben, in surprise.

The chair was provided. Ben sank down in it. If the captain had judged that Ben needed the chair, he had judged right. All sorts of funny things were happening inside Ben.

'Now, then,' said the captain, beginning again, 'we're not going to have any more nonsense. I want you to tell me, without any prevarication—you know what prevarication means—?'

'Wobblin', ain't it?' guessed Ben.

'Well, that will do for our purpose,' agreed the captain, with a faint smile. 'Tell me, without any wobbling, what you are doing on board this ship, and why you came on board?'

Now for it! Ben hesitated. If he told the truth, he would entangle the girl. That was what she'd said, wasn't it? Well, he wasn't going to tell the truth. Not yet, anyway . . .

''Cos of me mother,' said Ben, as three pairs of eyes bored into him.

'Oh! And what about your mother?' asked the captain.

'Yus,' said Ben.

'Is she on board too?'

'Yus. No.'

'Which do you want?'

'No.'

'Where is she?'

'Where I wanter git ter. She sent me a letter, see? "Come an' see me," she ses, "'cos p'r'aps I won't be 'ere much longer." That's wot she ses.' Ben looked out of the corner of his eye to see how the story was going. What he saw wasn't very satisfactory. 'So 'ere I am,' he ended lamely.

'Have you got the letter on you?' inquired the captain.

'I never keeps letters,' he answered. 'I bin blackmailed afore.'

'Where was the letter sent?'

'Eh?'

'Didn't you hear?'

'Yus, sir.'

'Then answer me!'

'Well, I am hanswering yer, but yer goes so quick. I ain't feelin' well. The letter was sent ter—well, ter where I lives.'

'Where's that?'

'My 'ome.'

'Give me the address of your home?'

That was a nasty one. Ben hadn't had a home for years. He began to wish he'd made up another story.

'Popler Street,' he said.

'Popler Street where?'

'Popler.'

'Any particular number—or is the street all yours?'

'Eh? Number 22. Tha's it. Nummer 22 Popler Street, Popler, Lunnon.'

There was a pause. The three men looked at each other. Two were impatient, but the third, the captain, remained unperturbed. He knew what the other two men did not know—that anger would develop hysteria or its antithesis, numbness. He had read Ben's condition when he had offered him a chair.

'Twenty-two, Poplar Street, Poplar,' he repeated slowly. 'Well—admitting that for the moment—was there anything else on the envelope?'

'I tole yer,' replied Ben. 'Lunnon.'

'No name?'

''Corse there was a nime.'

'What name?'

Ben looked at the captain suspiciously.

'What name was on the envelope?' the captain pressed. 'Just "Ben, 22 Poplar Street, Poplar?"'

This was getting too complicated. Ben gave it up, and waited for the next. The next was even more complicated.

'Where did your mother write from?' inquired the captain.

'From where she is,' countered Ben.

'And where is she?'

'Well, where this boat's goin'.'

This was too much for the third officer.

'Yes, but where's the boat going?' he interposed angrily.

'If you don't know, you better sweep a crossin',' replied Ben.

The captain turned to the third officer.

'Mr Greene,' he said, 'we had better not have any interruptions.'

For a brief moment, the world became sweet again. Ben grinned.

'Tha's right, sir!' he chuckled. 'Tick 'im orf!'

The sweetness vanished. The captain was now frowning heavily at Ben.

'You'll be ticked off yourself, if you don't watch that tongue of yours!' he exclaimed.

Now it was the third officer who grinned. The reaction and the grin sent Ben suddenly off his balance. He heard himself shouting. Perhaps the bump also had something to do with it. It was a painful bump.

'I was born ticked orf!' came his hoarse complaint. 'Wot I was thinkin' of, comin' inter this world without fust askin' everybody's permishun, I'm sure I dunno! I'm a bit o' mud not fit ter wipe yer boots hon—'

'Say, do you allow this kind of language?' interposed Mr Holbrooke.

'Langwidge is like 'ens' heggs,' almost wept Ben. The room was growing misty. 'If it's comin, it'll come.'

Another silence followed this philosophy. When the heat had died down a little, the captain delivered his ultimatum.

'I think I have been patient,' he observed, 'and I am willing to remain patient for a minute or two longer, but I warn you, my man, that if there are any more outbursts this interview will come to an end, and you will not receive the benefit of very considerable doubts. Please remember that I am making every excuse for you, in view of your condition. Now, answer the rest of my questions quickly and plainly, and do not let us have any more foolery. Do you know where this ship is going?'

Ben gulped, and answered:

'No, sir.'

'Then did you just hope it would sail to the place where your mother is supposed to be—and where you have not yet told us she is?'

This needed consideration.

'Where is she?' rapped out the captain.

'In 'eaven, sir,' replied Ben. 'You've won.'

'I see,' said the captain slowly. 'You've been lying?'

'Yus, sir.'

'Why?'

'Well, yer 'ave ter say somethink, doncher?'

'Why not the truth?' suggested the captain, and then turned to the third officer. 'Mr Greene, will you kindly give me the article you found on this stowaway?' The third officer obeyed. 'Is *this* the reason why you find the truth a trifle awkward?' asked the captain, holding up a little green bottle.

Ben stared at the bottle. It seemed to contain the essence of the third officer's grin.

'That clorridgeform wasn't on me,' muttered Ben; 'and 'e knows it.'

'Where was it, then?'

'It was in his pocket, sir,' said the third officer.

'Lummy, there's a lie!' exclaimed Ben. 'It was on the grahnd! Pocket! That's good, that is! Orl I got in me pockets is 'oles! Heverythink helse goes right through!'

The third officer shrugged his shoulders.

'You deny that this is yours, then?' said the captain.

''Corse it ain't mine,' answered Ben. 'Wot'd I be doin' with clorridgeform?'

'You might have intended to use it on somebody?'

'Well, 'oo?'

'That would be for you to tell us.'

'Orl right. I bought it fer yer third officer. Now 'ang me.'

'It's a pity you can't realise that, if you've nothing to hide, the truth is the only thing that will help you,' observed the captain. 'If this chloroform is not yours, have you any idea whose it is?'

'No, sir.'

'You didn't get it for somebody else, for instance?'

'No, sir.'

'And nobody else gave it to you?'

'It ain't my birthday.'

'Where did you come on board?'

'Eh?'

'Tilbury?'

'No. Yus. No.'

'The no's seem to win. You *didn't* come on board at Tilbury?'

'Tha's right.'

'When, then?'

'Afore that.'

'How long before that? Be specific!'

''Oo?'

The captain repeated his question, and brought his hand down on his desk with the sound of a pistol shot. It was effective.

'Lunnon!' said Ben, flustered. 'Lunnon Docks. I'm telling yer, ain't I?'

'What were you doing at the docks?'

'Slipped in ter git a bit o' sleep, see?'

'Yes? And then?'

'Well, it weren't comfor'ble. So I wakes hup, see?'

'Go on.'

The captain's voice was still sharp. He had got Ben on the run.

'I'm goin' hon! I gits hup. I looks arahnd fer another spot. It was 'ard, see? And rats. And when I'm lookin' arahnd—well, I goes hon lookin' rahnd, and so I looks rahnd, like I'm tellin' yer—'

'*Will* you get on!'

'Give us a chance ter breathe! I looks rahnd, and I sees this 'ere ship. "'Allo!" I ses. "It's got its mouth open!" So in I slips, and presen'ly I falls dahn a ladder, an' tikes the count.' Ben closed his eyes, to add a touch of realism to his story. Then he opened them, and concluded, 'And when I comes ter meself, along comes yer third officer, picks hup the clorridgeform, ses it's in me pocket, and lugs me hup 'ere.'

The captain considered for a moment. Then he shot out a series of questions, and Ben felt as though he were dodging a maxim gun. The captain was learning that this was the only way to get him on the run.

'Were you unconscious from the moment you fell off the ladder till the moment you were found by my third officer?' he rapped out.

'Yus.'

'Do you know that's a long time?'

'It was a long fall. Besides, I've toljer, I ain't well.'

'What's the matter with you?'

'When anybody speaks sharp ter me, me hinside wobbles.'

'Perhaps that's because you didn't come quietly?'

'I did, till the third officer 'it me.'

'How do you know it was the third officer?'

'Ain't it hon 'is sleeve?'

'Oh; you can read gold braid?'

'Yus. This ain't the first time I bin on a ship.'

'Have you ever served on one?'

'Yus.'

'Name it.'

'*'Ilda.*'

'Is that all?'

'No. I was on a lot in the war.'

'How, a lot?'

'Well, you was blowed hup from one ter another, wasn't yer?'

There was a pause. The captain was giving Ben time to breathe. Then he asked, more slowly:

'Would you like to serve on a ship again? On the *Atalanta*?'

''Oo's that?'

'The *Atalanta* is the name of this ship.'

Ben blinked. The captain's keen grey eyes were on him. For one tiny instant, their souls seemed to meet—the one within its spotless cloth, the other within its cloth that was nothing but spot. And, as happens during these rare momentary meetings, Ben replied with the simple truth.

'Me 'eart's a bit funny,' he said; 'but I can polish brass.'

The captain nodded. Then he turned to the third officer.

'Take him away, Mr Greene,' he said, 'and see he doesn't get into mischief till I've decided what to do with him.'

'May I suggest the stokehold, sir?' answered the third officer. 'We've heard that weak heart story before.'

'I'll see,' replied the captain, and then shot his final question at Ben.

'One moment,' he said. 'Do you know anything about a stoker who is supposed to be missing?'

'No, sir,' replied Ben.

And the two souls drifted apart again.

Alone once more, the captain and Mr Holbrooke regarded each other speculatively.

'Well?' queried the captain. 'What do you make of it?'

'This,' answered Mr Holbrooke. 'That you ought to be

given a gold medal for patience! Why did you give the fellow all that rope?'

The captain shrugged his shoulders.

'Perhaps he interested me. He's got the imagination of a first-class journalist, but he wouldn't kill a fly unless he were driven to it. I'm some judge of character, Mr Holbrooke.'

'Ah, but s'pose he *was* driven to it?'

'I said a fly. If he killed a man, it would be an accident.'

The captain rose, and his visitor followed suit.

'Well, I'll tell you what *I* think, captain,' said Mr Holbrooke. 'You'll hear more of that fellow before you're many hours older.'

It was a true prediction. Before the captain was six hours older, he heard that the fellow had fallen overboard.

It was the third officer who brought him the information.

10

The Man with the Sack

If Ben had kept a diary, and it had been produced as evidence, it would have brought chaos to any police court. On rare occasions, his mind was as clear as yours or mine. He knew twice five was ten, he could tell you the time or the date, and he could say the alphabet backwards as far as X. But these *were* rare occasions; periods of unusual clarity; and the spaces between the occasions were vast and filmy. His brain functioned through a sort of smoke-screen.

He would have said, through the smoke-screen, that the kind word you spoke to him yesterday had been spoken a week ago, or that the kick he had received a week ago had been delivered last night. He passed through two minutes in a month, or a month in two minutes. Last Thursday week was next Tuesday fortnight. When clocks struck, if he didn't count carefully on his fingers, he couldn't say whether it was tea-time or cheese.

He had, nevertheless, a strange tenacity. Because of the fewness of his ideas (saving in the matter of repartee; God had vouchsafed him that one weapon), such ideas as came to him and were permitted to stay and settle grew into obsessions. He clung to them doggedly, ridiculously, often feeling that he would sink without them. There were two permanent ideas: cheese and cigarette ends. Others came and went in the confusing flow of time, shaping his thoughts and incentives.

As there were two permanent ideas, so now there were two temporary ones—though one of the temporary ones threatened to become permanent. Thus, Ben's life when he left the captain's presence was composed of the following four items: Cheese, cigarette ends, Faggis and the girl. His stomach wanted cheese, his lips wanted cigarette ends, his heart feared Faggis, and his soul ached for the girl. Not for the romance of her. Just for the comfort of her. Queer! Couldn't quite make it out. But there it was.

And why, after all, should he be so afraid of Faggis? This third officer, who was hauling him off, was a more immediate menace! But there it was again. Faggis stuck in his mind like a terrible shadow. Like the shadow, indeed, that casts itself before the event! . . .

'You got off light,' the third officer grunted.

'I feels light,' Ben murmured, and became momentarily practical. 'Does I git hennythink ter eat, or does I jest fade away, like?'

Apparently, since the third officer made no response, he was to fade away like, and the swaying of the deck reinforced this theory. It occurred to Ben that he really might be fading away. They were crossing the boat deck, and it wouldn't have surprised him if the boats had suddenly gone up like gas balloons.

He saw a bit of comfort on the heaving ground. He bent down to the ground, as the ground came up.

'Now, then!' came the third officer's sharp exclamation.

'Cigarette hend,' replied Ben. 'I saw it fust.'

Then he paused abruptly. The comfort was forgotten in a strange and disturbing sight.

A tall, white-haired man was approaching. He was walking with a buoyant, swinging step, and his face wore a smile. The smile was almost child-like in its satisfaction and self-sufficiency. It said, '*You* may live in your world, but *I* live in mine, and mine is the really sensible world.' In the sensible world, apparently, people strode along with sacks on their back.

'Yus, I'm fadin' away,' Ben told himself, as the man and the sack grew larger and closer. 'When 'e gits hup ter me, bet yer hennythink I goes pop!'

The only things that went pop, however, were his eyes. They remained popped while the white-haired man stopped and greeted the third officer.

'Aha, Mr Greene,' he boomed. 'When are you going to grow up to my size?'

'Taking your constitutional, sir?' replied Mr Greene amiably.

'Yes. And I've increased the weight again. Feel!'

The white-haired giant swung his sack down. Ben ducked, unnecessarily. As the third officer tested the weight of the sack, the white-haired giant turned to Ben, and his smile expanded.

'Now, the next time I want to increase the weight of my sack,' he exclaimed, 'you'd be just about the right size to put in!'

''Oo?' blinked Ben.

'You must lend him to me, Mr Greene, when you've done with him,' chuckled the white-haired giant. 'Before we touch land I've got to work my load up to eight or nine stone.'

'Well, you could have him now, Mr Sims, as far as I'm concerned,' replied the third officer callously. 'He's a stowaway.'

'Eh? What did you say?'

'Stowaway.'

'Indeed? A stowaway!' The white-haired giant's eyes again sought Ben's. 'Now, that's intensely interesting! What does one do with stowaways?'

Then he smiled at the third officer, and the third officer smiled at him, and he went on his way.

'Wot's 'e practisin' for?' asked Ben. 'A postman?'

It did not seem for a moment as though the third officer were going to answer. Then he changed his mind.

'One of those fresh-air, vegetarian, hygienic lunatics,' he said. 'He thinks that a straight back means a long life, and that a weight behind means a straight back. A sack a day keeps the doctor away.'

'Well, I'm blowed,' murmured Ben.

'Yes, quite mad,' nodded the third officer. 'Get a move on!'

Ben obeyed. Nasty, that man with a sack! Sims, the third officer had called him. Hadn't he heard the name before somewhere? Sims . . . Sims . . .

A girl near by turned her head, and nudged her companion.

'Say, look at that funny little man!' she said.

Her companion looked. He agreed he was a funny little man.

'But haven't we got better things to look at?' he suggested.

'I dare say,' replied the girl; 'but he kind of makes me want to cry.'

'He's a pitiable-looking object all right,' nodded her

companion, who looked himself the reverse of pitiable. His suit was a youthful grey. 'But what can we do about it?'

'He sure is,' said the girl, and raised her voice. 'Say, officer!'

Mr Greene halted politely. Ben became conscious that his bump was being stared at.

'I hope there's not been an accident?' asked the girl.

'No, miss. Just a stowaway,' answered Mr Greene. 'Nothing to worry about.'

'It's orl loverly,' added Ben.

Now he became conscious that she was staring at his eyes.

'But the poor fellow's hurt himself!' she exclaimed.

'We'll look after him,' the third officer assured her. 'There was a bit of a scrap.'

'Tha's right, nothink worth menshunin',' corroborated Ben. ''E on'y 'it me ninety times.'

'Get on!' growled the third officer. 'You're not supposed to chat with passengers!'

The girl's eyes followed the pair as they departed. Her companion smiled.

'Queer cove,' he commented. 'What about a game of shovel-board, Miss Holbrooke?'

Sims! Sims! Where *had* he heard the name before? Sims . . . Sims . . .

He thought about it while he was being taken to a small, confined space. He thought about it while he was eating a meagre meal that some semi-Christian provided for him. He thought about it while faces peeped in to have a squint at him, and winked at him. Some of the winks were unkind, but others were quite good-natured. Sims . . . Sims . . . One face said, 'Cheer up, old cock!' and when it disappeared Ben found a gasper in his hand. A whole gasper. He got a match from another face.

He went on thinking about it. Sims! It filled the time of waiting. His eyes drooped. The white-haired giant with the sack leapt into his vision, twelve times life-size. He opened his eyes quickly. The nasty vision vanished. Sims . . . Sims . . .

Minutes went by. Or hours. The man with the sack dodged in and out, a filmy figure leaping through the spaces of Ben's mind. Once the sack leapt through without the man.

'Oi!' gasped Ben.

That was 'orrible! He opened his eyes in terror, and saw the third officer looking at him. And, all at once, it occurred to him that the third officer wasn't any pleasanter than the white-haired giant with the sack.

'I hope you've enjoyed your snooze,' said the third officer sarcastically; 'but you haven't booked a bedroom for the trip, you know.'

'Wotcher mean?' replied Ben.

'That it's time you worked a bit for your living,' answered the third officer. 'Let's see if you can do that polishing you boasted about!'

Ben rubbed his eyes, and suddenly stared. It was dark out on the deck. How long had he been asleep?

'Wot—polishin' at night?' he muttered.

'Yes; at night,' responded the third officer. 'But you needn't be afraid of the dark. I shall be looking after you.'

In response to a prod, Ben rose. He stared out of the opening through which the third officer had come. Yes, it was certainly night . . .

Sims! Now he'd got it! Sims was the other name that had been mentioned in the conversation in the coal bunker. Sims! The man with the sack!

'Gawd, was *he* in it too?'

82

11

On the Boat Deck

Ben didn't like it. He tried to make a stand.

'Look 'ere,' he said, 'I wanter see the captain.'

'And, of course,' returned the third officer, 'the captain's just dying to see you!'

'Yus, but I'm seerious!'

'To do you justice, you *look* serious! What do you want to see the captain about?'

Ben couldn't tell the third officer that. He fell back upon generalities.

'I ain't bein' treated fair,' he muttered.

'It seems to me you've been treated with quite unusual fairness,' answered the third officer. 'You have been right to the fountain-head, and have had your case considered by the Old Man himself. You have not been put in chains. You have not been sent down to the stokehold. Instead, you are given a meal and a long sleep, and now you complain when I ask you to breathe on brass for a few minutes. I'm afraid I can't see your cause for grumbling.'

But then the third officer could not see his own face. It was really the third officer's face that was the trouble.

'I bin a fool!' Ben told himself, as he stared at the offending face and at the malignance with which it was saturated. 'I orter've tole the captain more'n I did while I 'ad the charnce.' Well, he would have to make another chance. Meanwhile, there seemed nothing to do but to obey the third officer.

'Where are we goin'?' asked Ben.

'I don't think that concerns you,' retorted the third officer, 'seeing you've no choice.'

'No 'arm in arskin', is there?'

'Not the slightest, if you don't expect answers. Now, then! Right turn! Quick march! And lift your feet!'

The final injunction came a moment too late. Ben tripped over a ledge, and went sprawling.

The third officer picked him up reprovingly.

'You know, if you're not more careful, you'll go overboard,' he observed. 'You wouldn't like that, would you?'

Ben did not reply. The remark, and the tone of it, chilled him.

They proceeded in silence. The sea churned darkly under a starry sky. The wind played its lonely night music. From somewhere in the distance, somewhere glowing with light, came other music. This other music was designed to destroy the loneliness of which the wind was chanting. The waltz from *Bitter Sweet* brought couples close in a miniature sanctuary of light and colour. Intimate smiles, whispered confidences, warm little pressures, flowed from the magic of the orchestra, combining to create the sweet illusions in which frightened humanity hides its head. But the song of the wind, rhythmless to finite ears, formless to finite minds, and designed by a fathomless need beyond human comprehension, told of the loneliness of oceans—the loneliness against which the other music fought—and of the might of space.

Ben, with each music in his ear, could not have described the separate messages. But he was conscious of them. He was conscious of the warmth of the one, and the coldness of the other.

They passed a few dim people. Some standing alone, some strolling or chatting in couples. Ben wanted to stop and talk to them, just to break up this horrible, silent journey with the third officer. But what could he have said? They were not of his world, or he of theirs.

"Ow much further?' he asked, at last.

'Up you go,' replied the third officer.

They ascended a companion to the boat deck. It was deserted. The boats were the only company. The third officer walked towards the boats. They hung from their davits in static expectancy, waiting for the crisis that never came. The crisis of a wreck, or of a man overboard. Ben's steps grew slower. He felt fingers on his sleeve. Not the firm, warm fingers of his little companion in the coal bunker. These were like the invisible fingers that had stretched towards him when he had been approaching dockland—the fingers that had drawn him through the opening in the wall, that had made him trip over the dead stoker, and shoot through the hole in the side of the ship. Only the fingers weren't invisible any longer. They belonged to a third officer, and protruded from a respectable sleeve with a gold line and a diamond . . .

'What's the matter?' asked the third officer.

Ben did not answer. The curve of one of the boats hung over their heads. Beyond the curve's outline, and below it, was a rail, and beyond the rail was the sea. The sea, and the wind, and the loneliness . . .

They were not walking any more. They were standing.

'So you want to see the captain,' said the third officer.

'Wot's that?' answered Ben.

The question surprised him, but only for an instant.

'If I take you to the captain—I might be able to manage it, you know—what will you tell him?'

'Wotcher mean, wot'll I tell 'im?' muttered Ben.

The third officer shrugged his shoulders, and waited. Ben noticed that the third officer's fingers were still gripping his sleeve.

'I ain't bein' treated fair, that's wot,' he said.

'It won't wash,' sighed the third officer. 'Really, old dear, it won't wash!' He shook his head. 'I suppose what you really want to see the captain for is to spin him some more lies about—that chloroform.'

'*Me*, lies?' burst out Ben. 'The lies was your'n!'

'Not quite so loud,' suggested the third officer, glancing round.

'Why not?' demanded Ben.

'After all, it doesn't really matter,' the third officer retracted. 'No one'll hear you. We're on the lee side. So—*I* told the lies, did I?'

'Yus. You sed the clorridgeform was in my pocket.'

'And wasn't it?'

'You knows it weren't.'

'In that case, where *was* it?'

'Wotcher gettin' at?'

'Well, you and I are trying to find out things, aren't we?

Tell me—where *was* the chloroform, if it wasn't in your pocket?'

'On the grahnd.'

'I see. And have you any idea how if got on the ground?'

And then Ben committed his blunder—the blunder he had been trying to avoid all this while.

'P'r'aps you'd come back ter look fer it,' he said.

His heart gave a leap the moment the words were out of his mouth. Now he'd done it! Lummy!

'Come back to look for it,' repeated the third officer slowly, and the point of his tongue appeared for a moment, as though to moisten suddenly dry lips. 'Come *back* to look for it?'

''Ere, lemme go!' exclaimed Ben, his anxiety growing. 'Wotcher keepin' 'old of me for? Yer gits me orl tied hup, and tha's a fack. 'Oo sed anythink abart comin' back? I ses p'r'aps yer 'd come ter look fer it—well, that don't mean nothink, does it, when a feller's bein' got at like a Spannish Hinniquisishun. Lemme go, or I'll 'it yer!'

To his surprise, the third officer let him go. The abrupt release gave the wind its chance, and sent him spinning towards the rail. He clutched it frantically.

'Now you can begin your polishing,' said the third officer, making no attempt to veil his sarcasm.

Polishing? Not it! It was clear by now, if it had not been all along, that Ben had not been brought to this deserted boat to do polishing. Then what had he been brought here for? The reason leapt at him with terrifying clarity. He had sensed it in his heart from the beginning, but had not known how to avoid it.

Ben's world was no longer cheese and cigarette ends and Faggis and the girl. It was not the white-haired man with the sack even. It was the third officer, standing over him with piercing eyes and the expression of a man who has been driven inexorably to a purpose.

He tried to run, but now his arm was gripped again, and this time with iron firmness. The third officer glared directly into his eyes, but still kept up his game of bluff, even though their two souls were naked to each other.

'Fool!' growled the third officer. 'What are you running for?'

Ben did not reply. What was the use?

'Trying to get to the captain still, eh?'

Just keep quiet, that was the ticket. Get him off his guard, and then hit him. Biff and bunk. Biff and bunk. Biff and . . .

'Tell me—how long had you been in that coal bunker before I found you, eh?' came the third officer's voice, like a low flaw in the wind. 'Let's have *the truth* this time!'

'When 'e gits 'is fice a bit closer,' thought Ben. 'Then 'e'll 'ave it!'

Of course, he could shout. He even prepared his throat at one moment to give the greatest bellow the world had ever known. But he knew his throat. It wasn't doing what he was trying to make it do. And he knew the ineffective squeak that came from his throat when it was disobedient. It sounded like a hen swallowing a lozenge before it meant to. And then there was the wind. Who'd hear a shout in this wind? If they'd been on the weather side, there might have been a chance, but Ben was an old sailor, and he knew where you couldn't spit.

The face was very close now. The words that came from it almost burnt.

'Won't answer, eh?'

'Yus, I will!' squeaked Ben, seeing red, green, blue, and every other colour. 'Yer a dirty wrong 'un, and, tike *that*!'

He struck wildly. He hit the face. It was a moment worth living for and dying for. Well—living for. When he found he was going to die for it he rebelled. He rebelled with his arms and his legs, and his head and his mouth. Discovering that all these were useless, he went on rebelling with his mind. He drew a great picture of himself smashing the third officer to bits. He seized the bits and threw them high into the air. There he went! Up, up, up! Down, down, down!

'Gawd—it ain't 'im—it's *me*!'

Realisation came back to him a blinding flash. He shot out his hands as space shrieked up to him.

12

Hanging over Space

By all the rules, Ben should have died. His ill-nourished body should have descended into the sea, and he should have passed on to whatever fate lies in store for human derelicts. But Ben did not respond to rules. If unexpected things were constantly happening to him, he constantly did unexpected things back. And he did one of the unexpected things now. He flung out his hands; and his fingers, instead of coiling round ungraspable wind, coiled round a thin wisp of solidarity.

Of course, it was ridiculous to imagine that the thin wisp would hold. In mental experience, you were already in the water before your fingers grasped the wisp. You had left your yellow penknife to your next-of-kin, you had come up three times, you had failed to come up the fourth time, you had drowned, and you had woken up in a little golden bed with angels standing all around you with plates of illuminated cheese. But here was this thin wisp bumping into Time and sending it backwards again. Time's engine had been travelling at six thousand miles an hour, and now it had met another engine on the same track, had had a head-on collision with it, and had been shot back to the station it had started from. And here was Ben, clinging dizzily to one of the pieces!

'Then I ain't dead?' he reflected.

It seemed not. The discovery, however, was not as consoling as it ought to have been. It brought new terror—or, rather, it revived the old. Had he been dead, life would have been over and done with. Now death lay still ahead of him, with all its pulverising horror.

The wisp he was clinging to was a rope. It was looping somewhere or other along the side of the ship, and it was below the level of the boat deck. Ben's head, therefore, was also below the level of the boat deck, and he appeared to be facing a vast wall. He could not say what his legs were doing.

Well, there was only one course to pursue. That was to hang on. The vital question was, would the rope also hang on? Every moment Ben expected it to give way, and to accompany him on the postponed descent.

The rope did not give way. Evidently, he was doomed to remain suspended until he gave way himself. His strength was decreasing every instant, and he knew he would not have long to wait. The swaying of the boat too, did its best to shorten the time, bringing the wall towards him at one second, and then carrying it away the next. Now he was pressing too hard against the side, now he was rudely separated from it, and wanting it. Push . . . pull . . . push . . . pull. Like a lift that had toppled over and was breathing sideways. No comfort anywhere.

And then there was the wind. That often took a hand, as though it wanted a little of the credit for dislodging him. When the wall bore towards him and down upon him, he was sheltered, but when it bore away the sheltering roof disappeared, and the wind poured upon him, determined to be in at the death.

Oddly, the idea of shouting did not occur to him for some while. When it did occur, there seemed little hope in it. His shout would probably bring the third officer's face over the rail above him, and the rope that separated Ben from eternity would be speedily loosened or cut. But as his fingers began at last to slip and slide, and his shoulders scarcely seemed any longer to be connected with his arms, a cry rose from his clenched lips. He was beyond adhering to any policy by now, for he was almost beyond adhering to the rope . . .

There came a blank, and then a moment of queer clarity. 'All hover!' he muttered, and said good-bye to the world. The world waved back. It ought to have been a handkerchief. That was what you generally waved with, wasn't it? Well, then, why *wasn't* this a handkerchief? Why was it another bit of rope?

The new bit of rope was undoubtedly waving to him. There it was, waving above his head, as his fingers on the old rope grew looser and looser. Backwards and forwards, backwards and forwards, now swooping down on him, now jerking up away from him, now swirling round him, like a seagull gone mad. All at once, through the glaze of Ben's mind, dawned the glimmer of a purpose. Yes, the rope seemed to have a purpose. It wasn't merely waving to him. It was trying to speak to him. 'Don't you see, I'm a loop!' it was gasping. 'A loop, man! A loop!'

Gawd, so it was! And the loop was descending lower and lower in its mad dance around him. For one insane second Ben thought it was a halo being lowered to him by God. Then a more earthly theory bounded into his mind. The loop was no longer gasping. It was shouting. 'Get in me, man! Get in me, man! *Get in!* GET IN!'

His fingers on the other rope gave way, and opened wide. At the same moment, the loop of rope also opened wide, and swam down over his head. A convulsion occurred in space. A human knot writhed against the laws of gravitation and of logic. Had Einstein observed the human knot, he might have evolved an entirely new theory . . . And then something tightened round Ben's waist, and his fingers found a new anchorage.

He no longer swayed in and out. He revolved round and round. Sometimes the wall came forward and hit him, but he didn't mind. He just hung, letting whatever happened happen. It occurred to him presently that he was rising slightly. He wondered if he had turned into a tide. Then something else occurred to him. He realised that, by jerks and wriggles, he could assist the rising tide he seemed to be.

And with this realisation came hope and all its madness. When you know, for a certainty, that you have been dead, it is not easy to keep your wits about you. In a frenzy Ben clawed at the rope that gripped him, pulled on it, lurched up at it, jumped up with it, rose higher and higher with it. He began to laugh. His laughter was noiseless, for it was only in his mind. Higher and higher . . . higher and higher . . .

Now his hand was gripping something else. Something hard. Something soothingly unbendable. And now something was gripping him. Something he vaguely recognised. What was it? Something warm.

Ben sprawled over the hard thing and lay flat. The warm thing bent over him.

'Quick!' it whispered. 'For God's sake, quick . . . *The boat!*'

13

Grim Preparations

If ever you meet Ben and ask him to talk about his unexpected trip abroad, he will tell you of many things. He will tell you of ladders and of coal, of corpses and of sacks, of eyes that frightened him and of other eyes that comforted him—as, for instance, the brown eyes that looked down at his own dazed ones while he lay on deck sprawling back to life. He will tell you of an amazing journey in a small boat, and of an even more amazing journey on land that followed it, a journey through terrifying mountain tracks and haunted woods.

But he will not be able to tell you how he got into the small boat. That, to him, will ever be an impenetrable mystery.

He remembers the exhortation, 'For God's sake, quick! The boat!' He remembers the conviction that somebody was asking him to achieve the impossible. Might as well ask him to jump over the moon! He would require at least a month before he could get back enough strength to move an inch from where he lay soaking the boards beneath him like a full sponge. The tiniest pressure on him produced a waterfall . . . And then, his next recollection is of lying in the boat, and of somehow having achieved the impossible!

He was on his back, staring up at stuffy, dark canvas. His mouth was wide open, and he was gasping like a caught fish. Of course, the achievement was not really his. The credit belonged to the owner of the brown eyes, who had prodded a dormant body into miraculous activity, and had assisted it, with only a few seconds to spare, into cover.

Now they lay side by side, eyes fixed unmovingly on the protective canvas, and ears alert for what was going on outside. The canvas covered them completely, making a low, tent-like roof. Ben's companion was thoroughly efficient, and no opening had been left to mark the spot where they had entered . . .

Footsteps fell upon their ears. Ben often wondered why God had created footsteps. Life was much happier without them. The footsteps drew nearer, and stopped almost beneath the little boat. They stopped on the very spot where, only a few minutes earlier, Ben had stood with the third officer. Then low voices rose from the spot.

'Here,' said one of the voices. The third officer's.

'H'm! Made a bit of a splash, didn't he?' answered the other voice. Sims's! The man with the sack!

There was a pause. Ben's heart pumped, while he visualised the two speakers staring at the little lake he had made. He hoped there were other little lakes, to reduce the significance of his own.

'Well, there's been a bit of spray,' remarked the third officer. 'I don't suppose he splashed quite as high as this.'

'Probably not, probably not,' said Sims. 'Poor fellow! Fancy his falling in like that. What's your theory? Suicide?'

A soft chuckle followed the suggestion, and an oath from the third officer followed the chuckle.

'Shut that!' the officer growled. 'He toppled over. Working on the rail, you know.'

'Yes, exactly,' said Sims. 'Exactly. And you weren't quite in time to save him. Or perhaps you weren't there at the unfortunate moment? What do you think? You'd come to see me about something perhaps, eh?'

'Trot out what *you* think,' retorted the third officer, rather irritably. 'Let's stop being funny, and have your opinion.'

There was another pause. When Sims resumed the conversation, his tone had altered slightly.

'I'll tell you my opinion, Greene,' he said. 'My opinion is that if you *were* present when our poor friend toppled over into the sea, your first duty would be to report the matter. You wouldn't waste time chatting with a passenger, would you?'

'Yes, but for our purpose he needn't have fallen into the sea just *yet*,' rasped the third officer.

'That's true,' replied Sims. 'He *mustn't* have fallen into the sea just yet.'

''E 'asn't,' thought Ben.

A slight pressure of the body beside him implied that his thought was shared.

'But his absence will have to be explained in due course,' continued Sims, 'and what we've got to do is to ensure that the explanation helps and doesn't hinder us. And, by the way, I haven't told you *all* of my opinion yet.'

'P'r'aps I don't want any more of it,' interposed the third officer, smarting under the other's sarcastic tone.

'You're going to have some more of it, just the same,' answered Sims. 'My opinion is that you're a bungler, Greene, that we're in our present nasty situation through your bungling—'

'Here! Watch your tongue—'

'. . . And that it is entirely due to your bungling that we shall be forced to alter the details of our scheme, and to act before we are quite ready to. In fact, Greene; through you we shall have to act now. *Now!*'

'Well, and why not?' demanded the third officer. 'The position's all right geographically. We're across the bay.'

'And any port in a storm, eh?' said Sims. 'It won't be the particular port we'd decided on, you know.'

'It won't be the port we *finally* decided on,' the third officer corrected him; 'but we always had this one as an alternative—'

'If things went wrong!'

'Bah! Things *haven't* gone wrong! North Spain's as good as South. Don't make difficulties! And, look here, Sims, you're pretty glib with your criticisms! How have I bungled? Tell me that?'

'How *haven't* you bungled?' retorted Sims. 'That would be the difficult question to answer! In the first place, you bungled with the first stoker you selected to assist us. Why didn't you wait? You should have waited till Tilbury. Then you'd have had my brain to add to the thing you call yours. But, instead, you show yourself a bad judge of character, dangle your prize before the wrong sort of man— and also before it was necessary—'

'Well, I didn't want to leave anything to chance, you fool!' interrupted the third officer.

'. . . And put the wind up him by asking him to help

you in a job that now won't have to be carried out at all! Because, obviously, we won't be making use of the coal bunker now, will we?'

'Obviously not. Or of your sack.'

'The sack? Ah, there I'm not sure. We'll come to that.'

'What about coming to it now?'

'No, not for a few moments, Greene,' said the owner of the sack. 'I've got to impress you first with a sense of your inefficiency, so that, when we do discuss the sack, you won't interfere with the project of a better brain.'

'I've had enough of this, Sims! Do you want to join our friend and help him feed the fishes?'

'To continue with the story of your bungling,' the other went on calmly; 'you allowed the stoker to escape. He'd never have *wanted* to escape if you hadn't followed up your unsuccessful persuasions with bullying and threats. No wonder the fellow got scared!'

'I was afraid he'd split—'

'Finesse, Greene, finesse. Subtlety. Tact. The third officer of the *Atalanta* should be a master of them. But you don't begin to understand them. And therefore you frightened this man, and he escaped from the ship to run about wild with a story he'd blurt out to the first policeman—'

'You seem to forget, his mouth was closed rather effectively a minute or two after he escaped!'

'Through no credit of yours. Having dodged you, he meets another man on the dock; imagines the other man is after him; the other man, who has just committed a murder in Hammersmith, imagines the same; there is a tussle, and the Hammersmith murderer commits his second murder in twelve hours.'

'And I was a fool, I suppose, to seize a perfectly obvious

opportunity?' rasped the third officer, while Ben, a few feet away, revisualised the incidents at the dock, this time in all their correct detail. 'Here was this other man—this fellow Faggis—wanting to quit the country; and here was I, wanting just such a fellow as Faggis! Terrible bungling that, wasn't it?'

But the third officer's sarcasm had no effect upon his critic.

'The idea was all right, if you hadn't rushed it,' replied Sims. His voice, at moments, was like hard steel. 'If you'd tested the position first—'

'Oh, yes! Of course! If I'd known that Faggis's damned accomplice was on board—which he didn't know himself, mind you!—if I'd had second sight—' He paused, and emitted an oath. '*That's* what's done us, Sims! The girl! That's why Faggis has got in this stew and why he's trying to apply pressure! His seeing her in the coal bunker when he went back like a fool that second time, and her giving him the slip and saying she was going to the captain! God, I wish I knew where she was at this moment—I'd like to wring her beastly little neck!'

Ben felt a little movement at his side. He tried to pat it, but missed.

'Yes, where *is* she now?' asked Sims icily.

'How the devil do I know?'

'Of course, you don't know! You don't know anything. You didn't know that the girl and the stowaway overheard your conversation with Faggis in the coal bunker.'

'Well, I've got rid of the stowaway, haven't I?'

'You don't know that Faggis has got hold of a knife, and that he's ready to use it on you or on me if we don't get him out of his fix damn quick. You don't even know how to hold on to a bottle of chloroform without dropping it. *That* was a pretty bit of bungling if you like!'

'And *you* don't know that, if we've got to do something damn quick, going round and round the mulberry bush won't help us!' exclaimed the third officer. 'Suppose you stop pretending you're the Prime Minister of the world, and get down to business?'

'I'm going to get down to business,' replied Sims, dropping his voice slightly, 'and shall *continue* to be the Prime Minister, Greene, of *our* little world. Now, then. What's the time?'

'Ten to eleven.'

'I thought you fellows spoke in bells?'

'So we do, to fellows who understand them.'

'Ten to eleven. That means ten minutes to "lights out." Ten minutes to "God Save the King," eh?'

'You're quite a mathematician!'

'And how long, after "lights out," before passengers are snug in their bunks? Half an hour?'

'The majority, I should say.'

'An hour, the lot?'

'About that.'

'Midnight. Well, Greene, we'll make it midnight.'

'I suppose it would give you a pain to speak plainly?'

'I apologise. I forgot I was talking to someone who couldn't see through an open door.'

'*You* don't know when the blasted door's open or shut! See here, Sims, is it quite necessary for us to go on loving each other like this? This mutual affection is becoming positively cloying!' The third officer's voice rose querulously. 'You're known on board as the Lunatic. I'm beginning to think the title fits. Tell me your ideas, or maybe I'll lose my temper and see you to the devil! The service for which I'm being paid doesn't include listening to insults.'

'At midnight,' said Sims, 'your stowaway will fall overboard.'

'Where's he in the meanwhile?'

'I suggest that you have him under lock and key.'

'That sounds all right.'

'You can arrange things to support that suggestion?'

'Easily. He gave trouble, and I locked him up. O.K.'

'Good. Be sure you get all your details tidy, in case you're questioned closely—'

'Oh, leave that to me! You talk as if I was a two-year old. The point we've got to get tidy is how he happened to be on the boat-deck at all after I'd locked him up?'

'You went to say good-night to him.'

'I see. And he did a bunk?'

'Exactly. Slipped past you and made a dash for it.'

'O.K. And—yes, while I'm chasing him, he blunders on to the boat-deck, gets too near the rails, and topples over.'

'Right again.'

'Well, that deals with *him*! But then what happens?'

'I happen.'

'What do you mean?'

'I happen to be on the boat-deck.'

'In that case, wouldn't you have given me a hand?'

'Of course. I was giving you a hand when the poor stowaway went overboard. It was, I imagine, because the odds were two to one against him that he grew so desperate.'

'I get you.'

'I doubt it.'

'What do you mean?'

'What I say, which is what I generally mean. I doubt whether you get me. You aren't half subtle enough. If you get me, what do I do next? Tell me that. After the stowaway has fallen into the sea?'

There was a short pause. The third officer was clearly anxious to prove that he could be as subtle as anybody, if he really put his mind to it.

'It's obvious,' he said at last. 'You come along with me to report the matter, and corroborate my story.'

'Idiot!' retorted Sims. 'Why should your story need corroborating if—as you say—you tidy up all the details?'

'Hell! Then what *do* you do?' barked the third officer.

'I dive in after our poor friend,' said Sims. 'Theoretically, of course.'

'What!'

'Thereby proving the theory that I actually *am* a lunatic.'

'Yes, but—'

'Why do I do that? For this reason, Greene. I've got to be got off the ship somehow or other, haven't I? Tell me a better way?'

'A theoretical dive won't do it,' murmured Greene.

'Yes, it will, when we're only trying to establish theories,' Sims pointed out. 'And then there's another thing. If a passenger is in the water, as well as a stowaway, the captain is far more likely to stop the ship, isn't he?'

'Wrong there—he'd stop it anyway.'

'Perhaps. But it will make for more confusion and excitement, which is what we want.'

'Yes, but where will you *really* be, Sims, while people are trying to spot your head bobbing up and down in the water?'

'Here, Greene, here. In the boat we are standing under at this moment.'

He rapped the outside of the boat softly as he spoke, and the sound of his rapping was not louder than the sound of two hearts beating only a few inches away from his knuckles.

'Somebody else will also be in the boat,' Sims went on, with a quiet chuckle. 'Oh, we shall be a merry little party! My sack? I'm not sure. I doubt if I shall have to use it now. This new arrangement alters things. But you look after *your* details, Greene, and you may be sure I shall look after mine. For a short while, you and I will have to separate and act independently of each other. But when you come along to lower the boat to search the black seas for me, then we will meet again . . . and the black seas will swallow us up. Now do you get me, Greene, eh? *Now* do you get me?'

He chuckled again, and the chuckle was followed by a silence longer than any that had preceded it. Greene was thinking hard and furiously. Personalities were forgotten. The grim business in hand had his undivided attention.

And, while he thought, the atmosphere beneath the canvas covering of the little boat became increasingly hot, and Ben turned his eyes from the stuffy roof to find out what the other eyes were doing. But all he could see from his cramped position in the dimness was the bottom of a little nose and the vague impression of two little lips pressed very firmly together.

'It's a damn risk,' muttered the third officer, at last.

'It is certainly a damn risk,' agreed Sims. 'It always was a damn risk, and it is now a greater damn risk than ever. The stowaway and the girl have added to the damn risk.

103

Faggis is a damn risk. *I* am a damn risk. Don't forget *that*, Greene! But aren't you going to get a damn price for the damn risk if all goes properly to plan?'

'Who, exactly, will be in the boat?' asked Greene.

'Me and my gal,' answered Sims unpleasantly. 'There will also be Faggis. He, certainly, won't expect to be left behind. And I shall need his presence in my little boat just as much as you'll need his absence on your big one. I suppose my little boat has a sail?'

'Of course.'

'Would it be too much to expect you to find me a couple of extra ruffians to augment my crew? Stokeholds provide all types, don't they? And there'd be—fifty quid apiece for each of the ruffians at the end of the trip.'

'It might be done.'

'It had better be done. The ruffians will go down in history, of course, as noble volunteers. And, with you to lead them—'

'The devil, I don't lead them!' exclaimed Greene.

'The devil you do, Greene. How are they to set off otherwise? You will be the chief hero of the moment. Everything will be prepared in advance, naturally—those preparations are among your details—but when the boat actually descends to join in the search, it will appear to descend on your sudden impulse, and the crew will be our picked volunteers who will respond to your impulse.'

'Suppose I can't get the volunteers? It's doubtful.'

'Then we shall have to do without them.'

'And suppose I get into trouble for my impulse?'

'You will! It will be a most unfortunate impulse. The boat will capsize. You will return to the mother ship, sopping, with a grim story explaining why the boat you set out in can never return. But, if you are dismissed the service, you'll have won enough to retire on, so why worry?'

'Thanks! But why am I sopping? Are you telling me that I've got to jump out of the boat?'

'You needn't jump. You can let yourself down into the water quite slowly and gently the moment we connect with the surface, provided you do not report yourself until we have disappeared into the night. Have I thought of everything?'

Then Greene laughed.

'By God, you haven't!' he said. 'How is our little impromptu rescue party going to be engineered with crowds all round us? Who's the darned fool now?'

'You are, as ever,' responded Sims. 'The crowds will be on the other side of the ship—the side over which the stowaway and I have supposedly jumped. On *this* side, the side from which *we* go, there will only be just enough hands to help with the launching. It will be among your details to collect them, Greene, and to see that none get into the boat who are not wanted there.'

'God!' muttered Greene. 'You're expecting a lot!'

'And you're going to get a lot for supplying what I expect,' retorted Sims, tartly. 'Any more questions?'

'Yes, one,' answered the third officer. 'Faggis's girl. You'll be gone, and Faggis will be gone, and—and *your* girl will be gone, but *I'll still be here*! How do I deal with Faggis's girl, if she turns up and gets nasty?'

'My dear Mr Greene,' said Sims, and his voice bore a note of finality. 'If, after so many of his troubles have been removed, an experienced third officer cannot deal with a chit of a girl whose character is not likely to tell in her favour, his brain cannot be superior to that of the green scum that populated the world in the Protozoic Period. Faggis's girl, Greene, will be another of the details you will have to settle. If she presents a difficult detail, it may console you to remember that I myself will be surrounded by them.'

He paused. From a distant brilliantly lit saloon came the strains of 'God Save the King.'

'Lights out,' murmured Sims. 'The good ship *Atalanta* is going to bed. Make the most of your hour, Mr Greene.'

'What are you going to do, during *your* hour?' inquired the third officer.

'As it will be the last peaceful hour I am likely to know for a considerable time,' answered Sims, 'I shall stay just where I am, by the boat, this interesting little boat I shall soon know so much better, and smoke.'

14

Re-enter Faggis

The voices ceased. The dark world outside the little boat in which Ben and his companion lay grew silent, apart from the discord of the wind which had now dropped to a low moan. The third officer had departed to attend to his unsavoury details. The man with the sack—for so Ben invariably thought of him—remained, to ponder over his.

What now? Ben's muddy mind groped around for a solution. Probably the far clearer mind illuminating the small warm body beside him was also groping, but there was no way of getting into touch with it, no way of effecting a union. If they whispered, even, the grim figure standing so still beside the boat would stir, raise his head, and listen. And then—anything might happen!

'Tork abart bein' cornered!' thought Ben miserably. That was another thing. It wasn't easy even to *think*. You see, your head was going round and round. But for the comfort of companionship, Ben felt he would have gone off his blooming nut and blubbered.

But, of course, he mustn't blubber. He'd *got* to think. So he started, and it went like this:

'We gotter git aht of the boat. Yus, but we can't. All right. We can't git aht of the boat. But we gotter.'

This not being helpful, he wiped it out, and began afresh:

'Nah, then. 'Ere we are. Wot are we goin' ter do? That's wot we gotter decide, like. And, when we've decided, like, we'll 'ave ter do it.'

He felt this was an improvement. There seemed some sense of order about it. But a disturbing question, arising directly out of his weak condition, came along to upset his faint serenity.

'Yus, but 'ow are we going ter do it?'

And then another question, more complicated still:

'And, any 'ow, wot is it?'

That was terribly dashing. It seemed to extinguish all incentive. For what was the use of working a bursting brain to find out what one knew one couldn't do?

On a clean slate, he now wrote this:

'We're 'ere. While that chap's there, we gotter stay 'ere. Orl right.'

He closed his eyes. He really did feel pretty awful. Then he opened them in a panic. Where was the girl?

Something tickling his ear warmly, told him that she was still beside him. It was her breath. She was gently prodding him, too. It was the combination of the prodding and the breath that had made him open his eyes. How long had they been closed . . .

'Don't go to sleep,' said the tickle.

'Was I?' he whispered back, so low that he couldn't hear it himself.

'Began to snore,' said the tickle.

He worked his fingers up to his eyes and held them open. Snoring, was he? Lummy! He'd give himself away when he was dead!

Presently he felt the tickle again. It was wonderfully comforting, even though it did make his ear feel like a bath with the warm tap turned on.

'Hear anything?' asked the tickle.

Ben shook his ear. It was all he dared. If you speak with your stomach jumping, you never know what sound will come out.

'I think he's gone,' said the tickle.

'Gawd, 'as 'e?' cried Ben.

'Sh-h!' hissed the tickle.

'Was that me?' thought Ben.

Evidently Sims *had* gone, or he would undoubtedly have heard Ben's shout. But he had only gone for an instant. The girl's sharp ears soon caught the sound of returning footsteps, and, seizing Ben's arm, she pressed it violently. The next moment, Sim's voice sounded below them.

'What are you doing here?' demanded the voice.

'I'm not taking orders from anybody,' came the gruff response. 'Let's know what's happening?'

Ben recognised the second voice with a shudder. It was the voice of the man who had a couple of murders to his credit, and who suggested by his tone that he was quite ready to add to the number, if necessary.

'Get back!' ordered Sims sharply. 'If anybody sees you, you're done for!'

'And if that girl sees the captain, I'm done for,' retorted Faggis. 'Think I'm going to sit still all night and wait for it?'

'You won't have to wait all night, if you're sensible.'

'What's *happening*, then? Darnation, I want to know!'

'Greene's not told you yet, then?'

'Greene!'

'Haven't you seen him?'

'No.'

'Perhaps you didn't stay where we left you?'

'I'm not staying anywhere unless I want to! And, see here, if there's going to be any double-crossing, you needn't think you're going to get away with it.'

'If there is any double-crossing, Faggis, we shall *none* of us get away with it. Put back that knife. I don't need to be reminded that you've got it. *You* need to be reminded that I've got a revolver, and that when I'm really annoyed I can be just as troublesome as you can.'

'Talk!'

'Is it? Why, my dear fellow, if I shot you at this moment, who'd blame me? I'd merely have shot a murderer.'

'Then why don't you shoot me?'

'Because I need you, just as you need me. Not brotherly love, my darling. So get back, and stay back till you're wanted.'

'When's that?'

'Midnight.'

'Definite?'

'Quite definite. At midnight you can come here—to this spot—and you'll find the get-away all nicely arranged.'

'What do we get away in?'

'In this little boat.'

'Oh, so that's it?'

'That is it.'

'Anything to prevent my hopping in the little boat now, and waiting there? No one'd find me, and I'd be on the spot.'

'Why, that's quite a good idea, Faggis,' said Sims, after a moment's consideration. 'Yes, quite a good idea.'

'Then I'll act upon it. Help me in.'

'By all means.'

Ben did not hear the little gasp behind him. It was muffled by his own big gasp. Gawd! Now it was coming!

He clenched his fists, though without any hope of being able to put them into action. When you are lying helpless on your back, and are discovered by two giants, one with a knife and the other with a revolver . . .

The canvas roof shivered. Fingers were touching an edge of it outside. Ben suddenly discovered that the grip on his arm was hurting him.

'Hallo—someone seems to have started already on this cord,' came Sims's voice, closer than it had ever been before.

'Who'd have done that?' answered Faggis's voice, nearer still.

'Oh, Greene, I expect,' said Sims. 'Come along! Be quick!'

Ben heard himself talking hard.

'Nah, listen, miss!' he was saying. 'Soon as we sees 'em, I 'ollers. Not a hordinary 'oller. A 'oller like the Zoo. They jumps back, see? Then you jumps hup, see? And then, while I'm still 'ollerin', you nip aht and leg it ter the capting.'

It was a sound plan, if any plan could be sound in such an extremity as theirs. But there was just one flaw in it. He didn't say it. He only thought it. With the fluttering canvas immediately above him, and the knowledge that at any moment a gap would appear somewhere containing a couple of murderous heads, he couldn't get his lips to move at all.

'For God's sake, be *quick*!' muttered Faggis.

'In you go,' replied Sims. The fluttering canvas sagged.

111

But the next instant it became taut and motionless. 'Hey—someone's coming!' whispered Sims. 'There's no time! Walk away carelessly—quick, man, quick!—and stand over by the rail there till they've gone.'

Something was collapsing at Ben's side. Only the knowledge of another's extremity prevented him from collapsing also. He found himself holding the collapsing thing tight, striving to comfort it.

'It's orl right, it's orl right, they ain't comin', it's orl right,' he tried to whisper.

But again his lips refused to translate the message into words. Two terrified people shivered in each others arms.

Meanwhile, outside the little boat, the quick instruction of Sims was obeyed, and the newcomers emerged out of the dimness of the boat deck.

One was a young man in a dinner-jacket. The other was a beautiful girl in a pale green evening frock, with a cloak of darker green thrown loosely across her bare shoulders.

'Good-evening, Miss Holbrooke,' said the voice of Mr Sims.

15

Death Tries Again

The young people paused in their stroll. The man unwillingly.

'I'm glad the weather hasn't interfered with my advice of a constitutional before turning in,' observed Sims pleasantly.

'Your advice was very definite,' replied Miss Holbrooke, 'and so I'm keeping my promise.'

'Very charming of you. And tonight, I see, you have a companion—'

'Who wasn't quite so keen on her keeping her promise,' interposed the companion, rather curtly. 'After the heat of the ballroom, it's dashed cold.'

'But the wind's dropping,' retorted the girl.

'And I see she has wisely put on a wrap,' added Sims, 'so she will come to no harm. Hygiene before all things, sir. That's my motto. And if it were yours too, Mr Carter, you'd expand inches.'

'Thanks, but I don't think I'm worrying about my expansion,' answered Carter, and turned to the girl impatiently. 'Better not stand here, really.'

She hesitated, and Sims shook his head reprovingly.

'Young man,' he remarked, 'you are not going the right way about it. You ought to realise that Miss America is too independent to take orders from Mr England.'

'Sure!' laughed Miss America. 'Or from anybody. I guess you've sized me up, Mr Sims.'

'Oh, do come on!' urged the young man who was trying unsuccessfully to give the orders. 'You'll catch your death!'

Something in Sims's attitude was making him irritable. Sims was quite aware of the fact. His capacity to irritate had produced many a situation after his own heart.

'You can go on, Mr Carter, if you want to,' suggested Miss Holbrooke.

'Now, that's a plan!' exclaimed Sims. 'Honour an old man, Miss Holbrooke, by exchanging escorts for once! Mr Carter, I promise, shall have you for the rest of the trip!'

There was a short, awkward silence. It was the young man who ended it.

'I never intrude,' he grunted, and moved away.

'Good-night!' called Miss Holbrooke after him. 'See you in the morning!'

But then she proved that she didn't like orders even when they were subtle ones.

'Sorry, Mr Sims,' she said, in a low voice, 'and thanks for the thrill! But I guess you were joking—I'd better go after him.'

'As you like,' nodded Sims. 'But I wasn't joking.'

'What! Do you really feel romantic?'

'Romance wouldn't have been my subject.'

'What would it have been?'

'Your father.'

Miss Holbrooke caught her breath. She had been on the

114

point of running after her lost cavalier, but now she postponed the impulse.

'What about my father?' she demanded. 'Do *you* know
anything?'

'Do you?' he countered. Then, while she stared at him,
he added quickly, 'I see by your face that he's taken you
into his confidence. Well, I'll take you into mine. You see,
Miss Holbrooke, I'm a detective, and I've stumbled upon
some information that will put you wise to the whole
thing. Tell me, have you said goodnight to your father?'

'Yes. He went in early.'

'I hope he took the sleeping draught I advised?'

'I think he did.'

'And what will you do when you leave me? Go straight
to your state-room?'

'Certainly.'

'But—Mr Carter—?'

'I've said good-night to him too. You heard me.'

'And you'll stay in your state-room till morning?'

'Of course. Why—'

'Yes, of course. Your father's enemies had counted on
that. They reckoned that, after you had gone to your state-
room, no inquiries would be made about you until
tomorrow—and by tomorrow you were to be many miles
away. Kidnapping, that was their game. To kidnap you,
and to hold you until they got a huge ransom for your
return.'

'But—why?' demanded Miss Holbrooke, her eyes flashing
angrily.

Indignation mingled with her fear. Sims looked at her
with sudden admiration.

'You're taking it well,' he replied. 'Showing the true

American spirit! You ask why? Well, I've found that out too. It's a Chicago ring. Your father did them a dirty trick once—that is, they considered it a dirty trick. Held on to a document he'd got hold of—made 'em pay through the nose for it—and froze them out of a fortune. Well, now they want the fortune back. And they were going to use *you*, Miss Holbrooke, as your father had used their bit of paper. What do you know about that? Pretty damn blackguards, eh? Or—do you see their point?'

Miss Holbrooke did not answer for several seconds. She *was* taking it well. The best pluck of America ran through her veins. But she was fighting a spell of dizziness, and she suddenly caught hold of her informant's sleeve for support.

'Say, I feel funny—in our elegant language, you've spilt a mouthful, you know,' she muttered. 'I don't think I've quite got on to it yet! How did they propose to kidnap me on board a ship?'

'Their first idea was to bundle you away to a coal bunker,' he informed her, 'and to pretend you'd fallen overboard. But things went wrong—I may have been one of the things, eh?—and so they changed the idea.'

'What to?'

'Not quite so loud, Miss Holbrooke. See that figure over there by that rail?'

A swift rustle followed, and another gasp.

'He's one of them.'

'Then me for the captain, right now!' she whispered.

'Yes, but don't you see, *I'm another of them*,' replied Sims.

And, after that, there was a silence.

It was this silence—sudden, unrevealing, sinister—that awakened Ben out of his numbness. While the voices had continued, he had listened dazed. So, apparently, had his companion. Words had fallen upon unreceptive senses, situations had evolved, changed and gone, without intelligently registering themselves. Recalling these situations afterwards, Ben wondered why he had not taken advantage of them. The advent of the two young people temporarily altered the balance of power, and nothing had been done about it. Instead, the two frightened listeners had lain perfectly still, incapacitated by shock and not daring to move. 'And, any'ow,' argued Ben subsequently, in defence of his inactivity, 'there was my little gal, wasn't there? If I'd shouted, it'd 'ave put 'er in the soup!'

But, in this terrifying silence, the inactivity became a nightmare, and he lost his head. At one moment, Miss Holbrooke's vivid voice, pulsing with youth and life—at the next, utter stillness. Not even a cry! Not even a protest! Not even the tiniest gasp! Just stillness, and . . . yes, surely, a faint aroma of chloroform!

What was happening outside the little boat? What was being done to the girl who had become so abruptly silent? It was more than brain could bear, and Ben forgot the girl inside for the sake of the girl outside. His head rose up against the canvas, convulsing it into violent movement, and he roared.

Then followed events that were swift and tumultuous. A face appeared. It seemed to shoot down on Ben from the sky. Another face followed. This one seemed to be rushing at him out of a long tunnel. He struck at both. He missed both. Both struck at him. Neither missed.

One hit him like a hammer. The other, like a sharp-pointed corkscrew. The corkscrew entered him and tried to pull some part of him out. He objected violently, but an enormous black man, after having extinguished him with his bulk, informed him that all the best people were subjected to such treatment. 'You must certainly let me pull your chest out,' said the black man.

'Yus, but wot'll I do, goin' abart without no chest?' argued Ben. 'I'd look funny.'

'If you like, I'll take your head instead,' suggested the black man.

He twisted the corkscrew into Ben's head, and pulled. Ben continued to object. 'Look 'ere,' he begged, 'can't I die like wot I did larst time? There was hangels then, and cheese. 'Ow'll I eat, if yer tikes me 'ead?'

But the black man gave such a violent pull that the head came off, and after that Ben had to give up and just float. He floated rather peacefully at first. In the distance, about ten thousand miles away, people were murmuring. They appeared to be troubled, but Ben wasn't troubled, and it was nice to be out of it all. Then, however, the floating became less peaceful. He began to heave and toss, like a boat. Perhaps he *was* a boat? You never knew.

A strange sensation came to him. He felt as though history were repeating itself, and as though he were over the ship's side again, still hanging to the rope. An idea dawned. 'I've got it,' he thought. 'I'm still 'ere!' It was the only solution, for he was certainly swaying, and the wind was playing on his skin.

The voices, though! He couldn't account for *them*! Sometimes close to him, sometimes ten thousand miles away. Near—far. Near—far. Swing—sway! Swing—sway! Down—down! Down—down! Down . . . down . . . down . . .

'Well, I ain't worryin',' thought Ben. 'This is where I meets the hangels, ain't it?'

118

Now the sea was all around him. Black, inky sea. Swelling, heaving sea. He could hear it. He could smell it. You always know sea. Good-bye . . .

But when he opened his eyes, angels were not gathered around him. Instead, he found himself staring up at the faces of Sims and Faggis

16

Six in a Boat

Ben was not born to be a prime minister, but he had his subtlety. As reality swept back upon him in a form just as terrifying as that in which he had left it, he knew it would find him wanting unless he became, to some extent, both strengthened and acclimatised. He knew the lunacy of coming to grips with reality yet awhile and of attempting, in his condition, to battle against those cruel staring faces. So he very quickly closed his eyes again, and lay quite still, hoping that the momentary opening would not be interpreted as a return to consciousness, but as a sort of inverse wink.

God did not hear many of Ben's prayers, but he evidently heard this one. Beyond a sensation that the two faces advanced a little closer for an instant—and that may have been imagination—nothing happened. Ben was left to breathe in earnest imitation of a man totally unconscious.

'Wunner if I ought ter groan a bit?' he reflected. 'I got enough pains ter.'

He had any number of pains. He tried to count them,

from the head downwards, but gave up at his waist. He was never good at arithmetic.

'Yus, I better groan,' he decided. 'It's unnacherel not ter.'

On the point of groaning, however, he changed his policy.

''Corse I mustn't groan,' he remembered. 'I'm unconshus, and don't feel nothink. Gawd, I wish I was!'

It was his head that pained him most. If the black man had come along now, he could have had it with a pound of tea.

Well, he couldn't waste time thinking of his bumps. What he had to do was to find out the position, or as much of the position as a man could find out with his eyes tightly closed.

One thing was clear. He was still in the little boat, and the little boat was no longer swinging on its davits. It was sailing on the water. He could hear the water lapping against the sides as it swished through, and he had caught a glimpse of the sail during that momentary opening of his eyes. You can tell when you're low down too. Everything seems high up, like. When you're high up, everything seems low down, like. No doubt about it. The little boat had left the big boat, and was proceeding on a voyage all its own.

Another thing had been revealed by that momentary glimpse. It was no longer dark. The sky had been fish-grey. It had smelt of dawn. The air, also, smelt of dawn. Something stirring and whipping in it that was not merely the breeze. Trust an old sailor's nose! Yes, the sun would soon be up, revealing all the crests and undulations of the heaving surface in a million points of gold.

Small boat sailing. Good-bye, *Atalanta*. Night over. Well, what next?

The only other definite thing Ben's glimpse had discovered for him was the presence of Sims and Faggis. But they could not be the sole occupants of the boat in addition to himself? There must be others. What others?

He must get another glimpse somehow. The answer to this last question was too important. Too much hung upon it. Perhaps, if he tried one eye at a time, and opened it a quarter, he might learn things without at the same time giving things away.

He opened his right eye a quarter. All he saw were his own eyelashes. He closed the eye again, took a quiet breath, and opened it half. Half seemed terribly daring.

This time he saw more than his own eyelashes. He saw a bit of a leg. A knee, frankly exposed. Beige. With a ladder. He recognised the ladder; and the sun that was shortly to bring joy to the world could bring joy no greater than the joy brought to Ben by that humble little ladder in a girl's beige stocking.

The intense comfort of this discovery satisfied him for several moments. The girl—the one that was his—was in the boat. They hadn't strangled her, or tipped her into the water. 'And they ain't tipped *me* into the water too,' reflected Ben suddenly. 'That's funny! There wouldn't 'ave bin no question in Parlyment!'

One thing puzzled him about the leg, though. Shouldn't it have been straight out, like? It was up and down, like. Ben himself was straight out, like.

Then his mind began to wonder about other matters, and he tried his left eye. Again the quarter-measure merely revealed his own lashes, plus this time a bit of his nose. The left side had always bulged out a bit more than the right since a wallop he'd received in a cellar two years

122

ago. But when he opened the eye a full half, he found himself staring at something green. Smooth and green. What was it? He was a bit too close to make out.

Very gingerly, he shifted his head a fraction. It took him five minutes. There weren't going to be any silly risks this trip! If the sort of statistician who calculates how long it would take a toad or a snail or a growing finger-nail to get from London to York had brought his mathematics to bear on the rate of Ben's head, the journey would probably have worked out at three and a half billion years. Fortunately, however, the head did not have to travel so far to discover what the smooth green thing was. It was a bit of a flimsy evening cloak.

A little farther away than the cloak, and partially covered by it, was a bare arm. A small portion of the arm was also covered by two or three loops of thick cord. The loops of thick cord added a lugubrious touch to the tiny picture within Ben's limited range. So did an edge of some coarse brown material that appeared to be doing duty as a more complete covering. It was the sort of material out of which sacks are made.

The form beneath the sacking was not up and down, like. It was straight out, like.

'Gawd!' thought Ben. 'Then they reely got 'er!'

While he had been knocked out and had been passing through a series of horrible nightmares, Sims and Faggis and the third officer had carried out their scheme. Had it been carried out all according to plan? Had Ben's roar precipitated it? Had Ben's companion done anything to interfere with the scheme, or had she also been overpowered immediately—chloroformed like Miss Holbrooke, in fact—and lain helpless during the whole mad gamble? To these questions, Ben could supply no answers. Whatever had happened, here they were in the boat, and all he could do was to lie quietly until something else happened.

He lay for a long while. Part of the time (though he would have denied it, had you taxed him) he slept. The sun rose, sending its illusion of beauty across the water and spreading its golden carpet that led to nowhere. The sea became blue, concealing its tragedies. The sky, no longer haunted by shadowy spectres and secret thoughts, expanded into its gracious dome. And beneath the gracious dome, and journeying through the fickle warmth of external beauty, went the little boat with its cargo of strangely assorted hearts.

Voices murmured above Ben. Sometimes they rose sharply. Limbs moved around him. He received more than one kick. But he paid no attention. He told himself that he was being very clever, and was secretly getting back his strength.

At last he came out of a doze with a jerk. The jerk was evoked by a crab, thirty feet tall, that insisted on trying to blow Ben's nose with a potato sack. 'Git orf me!' yelled Ben. 'Think I don't know 'ow?' He flung himself at the nearest object for support. It was a leg encased in a beige stocking with a ladder, and it seemed to press towards him as he seized it, as though implying that it was on his side against the crab. For the second time in the boat, Ben opened his eyes, and found faces staring at him.

'Hallo! Ivor Novello's woken up at last,' said one of the faces.

It was the third officer's face. That wasn't right, was it? What was *he* doing here?

'I thort you was stayin' be'ind!' mumbled Ben.

It was an odd remark to come back to the world with, and a laugh greeted it.

'You see, he knew all about it,' grinned the third officer. 'Just as well we brought him along with us.'

'Just as well if we'd given him to the fishes, as I wanted to!' added Faggis, now shoving his own face forward. 'Now he's awake he'll make a fuss when we do it.'

'Only you *won't* do it!' came a voice above the leg Ben found he was still hugging. 'We've had enough of that talk!'

'There's more coming,' snarled Faggis. 'See here, you fellers, what's the use? Why not get rid of them both, and start clear?'

Then Sims spoke up from the stern. He had hold of the sheet.

'How many times am I to remind you, Faggis,' he said, 'that I am in command of this little expedition, and that my word goes? If I have agreed—for the time being—to spare his life, for the sake of getting the girl's assistance—'

'Who wants her assistance?' interrupted Faggis.

'It may be more valuable than you imagine,' retorted Sims, 'and, don't forget, we're *paying* according to value. We've got a journey after we land, and since it's necessary to keep one lady in good health—don't forget that, Faggis—another lady may come in quite handy to help us with the job.'

'And, of course, the other lady, with her record, wouldn't dream of double-crossing us, would she?' suggested Faggis, sarcastically.

Then the other lady chipped in.

'With my record,' she exclaimed, 'I'd do a lot of good to myself double-crossing! Think I'm anxious to chum up with the police?'

She spoke vigorously. Clearly, whatever time she had passed through, it did not compare with the time Ben had passed through. Or else she had an amazing faculty for recovery. Ben rejoiced in her spirit, though her actual words rather surprised him; and the thought that ran through his mind was given words the next moment by Faggis.

'Of course, you're not anxious to chum up with the police,' he replied; 'but you were going to chum up with the captain!'

'You're a fool, Faggis! That was to scare you!'

'Oh, just to scare him, was it?' murmured the third mate, considering the theory.

'And even if it *hadn't* been,' the girl ran on, 'the golden bait came along *afterwards*, didn't it? Think I'm a saint? I want money, same as anybody. And now I know where I stand, and have got some others to look after my interests, Faggis, and see *you* don't stick a knife in me, I'm in this the same as you are, and just as keen on making my little bit!'

Ben's eyes opened wide. He wasn't sure that he liked the way things were shaping. Of course, all this spelt safety for the girl. Still . . .

'You've got your answer, Faggis,' said Sims, 'and it's a good one. Our lady accomplice, by the way, has she a name?'

'Lots,' replied the lady accomplice. 'Molly Smith'll do for this trip.'

'Well, Molly Smith is implicated in the crimes of murder and abduction, and it's hardly in her interest to double-cross us. And, anyway, Faggis,' he went on, his voice hardening, '*I'm* looking after that, and the sooner you recognise who is the leader of this party, the safer *you'll* be. So now drop interrupting, please, and let me get on with business.'

The business, evidently, was Ben. Handing over the sheet to the third officer, he left the stern and subjected Ben to a searching scrutiny.

'Feeling better, eh?' he asked.

'Like Kid Berg,' responded Ben. 'And 'ow are *you* feelin'?'

'Shall we say—Carnera?' suggested Sims.

'If yer like,' answered Ben. ''E got beat once.'

Sims smiled. Most people got angry when Ben cheeked them, but Sims didn't seem to mind at all. His complacency was rather uncanny. The third officer, for instance, got in a wax the moment you opened your mouth.

'Do you know, you're quite interesting,' remarked Sims.

'So are you,' returned Ben. 'Can't think wot the Brighton Aquarium's doin' without yer.'

'But, of course, I can't let you do *all* the talking.'

''Corse, yer can't. Yer might 'ear some things yer didn't like.'

Something pressed gently against his arm. It was the beige stocking with the ladder in it. 'It's torkin' ter me,' thought Ben. 'Wot's it sayin'?'

'Yes, that is certainly possible,' observed Sims, after a little pause, during which his scrutiny grew more searching still. 'You're not very fond of me, are you?' Ben did not reply. The beige stocking was pressing him again. 'And that's a pity, because people who aren't fond of me get into all sorts of trouble.'

On the point of retorting, Ben suddenly realised what the beige stocking was talking about. Lummy, what a fool he'd been—or nearly been!

'Look 'ere!' he exclaimed, raising his voice querulously, 'wot 'ave yer done ter *mike* me fond of yer? Give me a charnce, and p'r'aps I'll love yer like stickin' plaster!'

The outburst had its effect.

'What sort of a chance?' inquired Sims, delaying the axe.

'Think *I* wouldn't rather earn a bit o' money,' responded Ben, 'instead o' bein' shoved hoverboard ter feed the sardines?'

'S.O.S.,' murmured the third officer, and Faggis laughed. The implication, intended to queer Ben's pitch, had the reverse effect. The white-haired leader of the party was taking advice from nobody.

'And what could *you* do, to earn some money?' asked Sims.

'Hennythink.'

'But what?'

'"Oo?'

'That doesn't seem to answer the question.'

'Oh! Well, wotcher want me ter do?'

'I'm asking what you *can* do?'

'Oh! Well, fer one thing, I can keep me marth shut.'

'Yes, but *we* could keep your mouth shut—for nothing.'

'Yer'd 'ave the Hadmerality arter yer if yer did. I'm standin' by fer the next war.'

'Really,' smiled Sims. 'That's interesting. I should have imagined we could have lost the next war quite easily without you. So you've nothing else to offer—'

'Yus, I 'ave,' interrupted Ben, deciding that he must make a serious effort. 'Do yer remember that bloke wot was fahnd bound and gagged on Noomarket 'Eath? It was me wot done that.'

The information was received with various degrees of incredulity. The third officer snorted, Faggis laughed blatantly, and Molly Smith's mouth twitched. It seemed to be endeavouring not to smile.

'I see. So you're a killer,' queried Sims politely.

His expression, alone, remained unchanged.

'Bound and gagged, I sed,' Ben corrected him. 'But I did kill a feller once. 'E missed me, and went hover the cliff. And then I can whistle when a copper's comin'. And we're goin' ter Spain, ain't we? Well, I knows the Spanish fer "Yus."'

'You really do seem quite accomplished,' murmured Sims. 'Anything more?'

'Yus,' answered Ben. 'If things is goin' bad, I can sing "Three Sailors o' Bristol City," and cheer yer hup.'

This was too much for the third officer.

'How much longer are you going to listen to that darned idiot?' he cried.

'Personally I find him rather amusing, Greene,' replied Sims. 'Too amusing, anyhow, to lose at the moment. We'll postpone the execution, I think, and take him along with us. I've a little plan into which he will fit quite nicely. Naturally, he won't live for ever. Unfortunately, none of us do that, eh? But, till death claims him, I like to hear the sound of his voice. And, of course, before he dies, we must certainly hear him sing "Three Sailors of Bristol City."'

'I wunner if I've won?' thought Ben.

17

The End of the Voyage

Thus Ben became, pro tem, an accepted member of a gang of kidnappers; and, such being the case, he sat up and began to take notice.

One thing he noticed, as the little boat slipped along through the deep blue water on an eastward course, was that the white-haired Mr Sims was very definitely the leader of the party. There was something in his personality, an indication of impervious purpose and of cynical callousness to details, that raised him executively, if not morally, above his companions. The companions might bicker and argue. They were totally unable to dictate. The moment the bickering ceased to amuse their chief he came down upon it like a cold steel hammer, and it ended.

Who was second-in-command? Opinions were divided. Faggis thought he was, and Greene thought he was. This division of opinion caused most of the bickering.

But what was Greene doing in the boat, anyway? It had been decided that the third officer was to stay behind on the *Atalanta*. Ben remembered that bit. He was to start off in the boat, and after that he was to jump into the water and pretend the boat had capsized. Yet here he was, deserting the mother ship with the rest!

'What are *you* doin' 'ere?' asked Ben suddenly. 'Funk the cold barth?'

'Mind your own business!' retorted the third officer.

'It is my business,' said Ben. 'Ain't I one of yer? And why doncher keep 'er bit closer ter the wind?'

The third officer growled, but Sims smiled.

'So you know how to sail a boat?' he remarked.

''Corse, I does,' answered Ben. 'See me at 'Ampstead 'Eath pond!'

'Excellent,' nodded Sims. 'Perhaps I'll make you take your turn at the sheet.'

Encouraged, Ben put another question.

'Where we makin' for?' he inquired.

'Land,' replied Sims.

The encouragement evaporating, Ben continued with his cogitations.

Sims, Green, Faggis—he'd got *them* sized up. Now what about the girl? The girl whose name for this trip was Molly Smith? Well, he reckoned he'd got her sized up too. Playing a game, she was! The same game she'd prompted *him* to play! And they'd have to continue the game, to save their skins, as long as they were in the boat. But when they touched land . . .

'Yus, wot 'appens when we git ter the land?' wondered Ben.

It would be a foreign land. A land full of strangers. For all the use the strangers would be, it might as well be a land full of monkeys! How would they be made to understand the position? The only Spanish word Ben knew was 'Yus,' and, now he came to think of it, that was Italian.

You bet, Sims knew the lingo! That would give him the whip hand. And, even if he didn't, what could Ben and Molly Smith do against three hefty men, a knife and a revolver, and goodness knew what else besides?

Revolver! Lummy, there was an idea! Revolver! Where was it kept?

Ben shifted his eyes cautiously south-east till they rested on Sim's middle. His eyes searched the middle for a bulge. But it was the front middle, and he wanted the behind middle. Or, strictly speaking, a little lower down than the middle. That was where you kept 'em, wasn't it?

Well, there was plenty of time. Night would come. And then . . .

Meanwhile, there was the sixth of the party to think about. The most important member, and the silentest. With sudden apprehension Ben turned to the figure covered by the sack, or nearly covered by it. A portion of the soft green cloak was still visible—the cloak that had made such a pretty splash of colour in the ballroom of the *Atalanta*, but that gleamed now with such grim incongruity. A glimpse too, of the bare arm, with the tight cord pressing into the skin. Travelling along the arm to the shoulder, and from the shoulder to the head, Ben's anxious glance revealed the fact that Miss Holbrooke's eyes were closed.

Asleep . . . or drugged?

Suddenly Ben became very still. Instinct told him that, just as he was gazing at Miss Holbrooke, someone was gazing at him. Was he looking too sympathetic, he wondered? He tried to change gear quietly into another expression, and to look baleful. Then, holding on to the balefulness and struggling not to let it slip—it was not an emotion that sat easily on his features—he turned his head so that he could get a glimpse of the watcher out of the corner of his eye.

He discovered it was Molly Smith, and the reaction of the discovery sent him into a bath of perspiration.

Molly was not looking in the least baleful. Her eyes were full of tense sympathy. They were speaking to him. She seemed to be able to speak with every part of her anatomy. She was saying, 'Well done! Well done! Stick to it! The blackguards! Oh, the blackguards! For God's sake, stick to it!'

'You bet I will!' he thought back. But his eyes did not express the thought. Transition of expression was not his forte.

Then Ben noticed another thing. Sims and Faggis were staring across the vast expanses of water. They seemed to be searching the horizon, and it was not difficult to guess what they were searching for. Sims was using binoculars.

'Are we being follered?' he asked.

Receiving no answer, he tried another tack.

'When do we eat?' he inquired.

He was ignored again. He grew indignant.

'I knoo a 'ungry man once,' he declared, 'wot hupset a boat!'

'*Must* you talk!' came the third officer's voice from behind him.

'Not when me marth's full,' he retorted.

A hand shot out towards him. 'Oi!' he cried. But the hand for once was not menacing. It contained a hunk of bread.

'Well, I'm blowed!' blinked Ben. 'Tork abart Haladdin's lamp!'

He took the bread, and set his teeth in it. Or, rather attempted to.

'Lummy, the baker didn't leave this 'ere larst night!' he muttered. ''Ow long 'ave we bin on this bloomin' boat? A year?'

Sims removed his eyes from the binoculars for an instant to answer him.

'I think it is time you learned,' he said cuttingly, 'that we are not interested in your conversation.'

'Well, that's a good thing,' replied Ben, ''cos there won't be no conversashun while I'm gittin' this block o' granit dahn!'

He chewed in silence. Silence, at least, apart from the chew. Then he demanded a drink. After all, one had to live.

'What'll you have?' jeered the third officer. 'Champagne or a cocktail?'

'Cocktail,' he answered. 'Greene Gargle.'

A cup of water was handed to him. It was better than any cocktail. He drank it slowly, to enjoy its full trickle down his dry throat. Then, his meal over, he settled down to wait patiently for the next.

The breeze freshened. It struck them favourably from the north-west. The boat gathered speed, and raced over the rhythmic swell. Once, in response to a sudden command from Sims, they swung round and changed their course to south. ''E's seed somethink!' thought Ben. But twenty minutes later they were going east again, this time with a touch of north in it.

Behind them, the sun climbed down towards the horizon. They had been sailing for many hours, and still Miss Holbrooke lay motionless in the bottom of the boat. Many times Ben glanced at her, to make sure that the sack beneath which she lay was going up and down. If it stopped, he swore he would hit things. Even while watching the movement, he once nearly saw red.

'Gawd!' he swore to himself. 'Some'un'll pay!'

He saw Molly's eyes on him warningly. She could read thoughts as well as convey them. She was guessing Ben's oath.

'Clorridgeform, miss?' he asked.

There was no harm in asking that, was there?

She shook her head, and touched her arm.

'Oh, I see,' muttered Ben. 'Interjecshun.'

And while he swore another oath, Sims lowered his field-glasses, and reported land.

18

The Landing

The theory that the world was not, after all, bounded everywhere by water became a fact. Into the eastern line that separated the sea from the sky entered a vague disturbance. It looked at first like a long, low cloud, darkish at the base and light at the upper edge; the upper edge, however, did not possess the gracious sweeps and curves of vapour, but the jagged points and angles of solidarity. Gradually it became the serrated ridge of a mountain range, its peaks glowing in the low rays of the western sun; glowing and growing as the little boat drew nearer. The darkish base turned into foliage, mystic and silent, forming a green shadow beyond the rocks of the shore. Had the little boat contained an artist, his eyes would have glowed at the picture unfolding before him and he would have attempted to remember it for the walls of Burlington House.

But there was no artist in the little boat, no heart to beat æsthetically. As the water narrowed between the boat and the land, becoming breadth instead of length, hearts beat with very different emotions, each emotion an earthly one. Ben's heart, with which we are mainly concerned, beat loudest. The sight of the advancing land brought with it a sudden sense of renewed responsibility. In the little boat, all had been conjecture and theory. On land, there would have to be action!

What sort of action? What would happen immediately after the boat was beached? Ben had no idea. All he knew was that, in some queer way, he had become the squire of two dames, and if things didn't come out all right for them, then, lummy, it didn't matter if things didn't come out all right for him, either.

'Gawd, I'm the 'ero!' he thought in sudden amazement.

It looked like it. But he didn't know yet whether he was going to be the hero of a comedy or a tragedy.

The mountains were now very high, and even some of the rocks reared above them. They had entered a small bay, and the third officer was steering towards the best landing point. The shore was deserted. Beyond the shore and a space of tumbled boulders rose the fringe of a forest.

Ben looked at Sims. He discovered that Sims was looking at him. Sims had put away his binoculars, and was holding a revolver. He smiled, as their eyes met.

'Nearly there,' said Sims.

''Ooray,' replied Ben.

The sail came down. Ben was ordered to take an oar. A few seconds later the boat touched bottom, and ran up an incline of moist shingle. Obeying a long-dormant instinct, he jumped out, and began to assist in the beaching of the boat; but he fell away almost at once, and stood still, panting.

'What's the matter?' asked Sims, toying with his revolver.

The leader was not doing any work. He was directing operations. Apparently, he did not trust anybody.

'Miggerams,' murmured Ben.

'What?' said Sims.

'Got 'em,' answered Ben. 'Me 'ead's a blinkin' maypole.'

'Then sit down,' conceded Sims, 'and don't get up till you're told to.'

Ben sat down on a boulder. The sudden exertion of rowing had told upon him. He remembered that he wasn't well.

Someone sat down beside him. It was Molly. She stared straight ahead of her, as though intent on the beaching of the boat, but her lips moved almost imperceptibly, and the words she spoke slipped sideways. Just as far as Ben, and no farther.

'Get your strength back first,' she said.

Adopting the same process, he responded:

'Wot abart you?'

He felt like a crab that had discovered how to talk.

'O.K.,' she said. 'Are you game?'

Their eyes were on the boat. Faggis and the third officer were lifting the captive out.

'Fer murder,' murmured Ben.

Now the three men were holding a consultation. There seemed to be another argument on, but Sims, as usual, was winning. This was obvious by his unruffled attitude, and also by the manner in which he toyed with his revolver.

'Got any idea?' asked Molly, continuing the sideways conversation.

'Yus,' replied Ben.

'What?'

'Git 'er away from them.'

138

'Of course. But how?'

'Ah, now yer arskin',' said Ben.

Sims had won the argument. The third officer, covered by the revolver, was turning out his pockets.

'Wot's that for?' wondered Ben.

'He's taking no chances,' whispered Molly.

Faggis followed suit. His pockets revealed a knife. Sims relieved him of it.

'Now 'e's got 'em both,' muttered Ben. 'Pistol and sticker. Wunner wot 'e'd sell 'em for?'

'*Cave*,' the girl warned him. 'He's coming!'

Sims approached. His feet crunched on the beach with almost hypnotic composure. Did nothing ever worry him?

'Now, you,' he said to Ben. 'Got anything dangerous on you?'

'On'y me gold tooth-pick,' replied Ben.

'Turn out your pockets.'

Ben did so. They were empty.

'Well, I'm blowed!' he said. 'Where's my acid drop?'

Sims turned to Molly. His eyes seemed to go right through her, but she stood the scrutiny well.

'You won't search *me*!' she declared.

'It isn't necessary,' answered Sims. 'I can see there's nothing inside your dress beyond your figure.'

''Ere, that's rude!' objected Ben.

But the lady he was defending didn't seem to mind.

'People like us weren't born polite,' she remarked, with a faint smile. 'Anyway, the rude one needn't worry. I know which side my bread's buttered. Well, what's the next step? Do we look round for a hotel, or what?'

'You'll see,' replied Sims, and moved away again.

He rejoined the others, and they consulted a map. The next step, evidently, depended upon the map.

'Wish they'd start quarrellin' agine,' murmured Ben. 'That's wot we want, ain't it?'

'Yes, but not a chance,' answered Molly. 'There'll be no big quarrel, unfortunately. You see, they know which side *their* bread's buttered too. Sims is the only one who can lead them into safety—and if they don't keep in with him, they get no pay.'

'P'r'aps they won't git no pay no'ow!'

'They will, if the game goes right.'

''Owjer know?'

'Oh, we've got our code. Have to have it, or we couldn't carry on.'

'Yus, but wot abart *your* code?'

'Mine?'

'Yus. You're double-crossin', ain'tcher?'

'Oh, I see what you mean.' She paused. 'Yes, I'm double-crossing. But then you know why *that* is.'

'I've fergot.'

'I told you, this kind of game's too gory for me.'

'So yer did. And that lets yer aht, like. I git yer. But, look 'ere, miss. Wot mide yer come in on it at all? You was goin' ter the capting, wasn't yer?'

'I was! But a nice chance I had after you shouted, didn't I, when the whole world tumbled on top of us in that boat? You were dead to the wide. And if I'd cried out, like you did, goodness knows *what* would have happened! I expect you'd have gone overboard again, for one thing—and I wouldn't have been able to fish you back again *that* trip!'

'Lummy! That's right! I ain't fergot wot yer done fer me. And arter that, I s'p'ose they got away with it?'

She did not answer at once, and Ben looked at her suddenly.

'Here, don't do that!' she whispered sharply. 'Look down at your toes again!'

Ben obeyed. She was sharp, this kid! If they got through this safely, it wouldn't be Ben's fault, it would be hers.

'I'm not sure,' said Molly, after a pause. Her voice was very low now. Scarcely audible. Her lips would have been envied by a ventriloquist. 'They got away—as you see—but, have they got away with it?'

'Well, ain't they?'

'We don't know what happened after we left the ship.'

'They'll think we gorn dahn.'

'We don't *know*, I say! They won't have found the upturned boat. And Greene didn't go back and tell them.'

'So 'e didn't,' blinked Ben. 'Why didn't 'e? Funk, like wot I sed?'

'Wind up of some sort, yes. But not of the wetting.'

'Wot was it, then?'

'Questions, I'd say. Didn't like the idea of a cross-examination. You see, everything wasn't quite tidy. He might have been caught on a loose end.'

'Yus, when 'is finish comes 'e'll be caught in a *tight* hend! Wot time did we shove orf, miss? Soon as I was knocked aht, or midnight, wot they sed.'

'Later still. Nearer one. Look out!'

'Wot?'

'All right.' He raised his head. 'Now it's down again. They made it later because it would be quieter.'

'Yus, but I thort—seemed as if we was goin' dahn jest arter I went unconshus.'

'If you were unconscious, how would you know?'

'That's got me! On'y part of the time I hexpeck I was on'y 'arf an' 'arf, you know. But, look 'ere, was we all lyin' there orl that time? Me an' you an'—'er?'

'And Faggis. All covered up like good children! God, I could have screamed! Don't ask me what happened when the game started! I've an idea it didn't all go right, and that they changed their plans to fit. But the whole thing's a blur! I'm almost as vague as you are. But I did *one* thing . . . Steady! They're coming again!'

'Yus, I likes 'em that way too,' said Ben loudly. 'Baked in their skins.'

'Oh, my God!' muttered the girl. 'Don't try and be subtle!' A few moments later, Sims's long shadow fell across them.

'I'm sorry to interfere with your tête-à-tête,' he said; 'but we've got a four-mile walk ahead of us, and as it won't be an easy walk and we shall be racing the sun, we must start at once.'

'Then you've found the hotel?' queried Molly.

'Oh, yes. Quite a charming one. Four walls and a roof, run by a man with a mule.' He smiled as he added, 'Our rooms were already engaged provisionally, you know, in advance, and it was just a question of finding the best way to the hotel from this spot.'

'Rather lucky, aren't we, that it's only four miles?' suggested the girl.

'Exceedingly lucky,' admitted Sims. 'It might have been forty miles. Let us hope the luck will continue. Now, you, Ben—'

''Ere!' interrupted Ben. 'You ain't bort me nime!'

'No. I got it free from Mr Greene. You, Ben, will carry the food, which has been packed in the sack while you've

142

been recovering your strength. Do you think you can manage it?'

'Wot, *food*?' replied Ben. 'Don't be silly!'

'But no eating on the way, Ben.'

'That's orl right, Albert.'

'I beg your pardon?'

'Granted. But, look 'ere—ain't them hothers goin' ter carry nothink?'

Sims nodded grimly.

'Their load is somewhat heavier than yours,' he remarked, 'and they will take turns at it.'

He turned his head as he spoke. Faggis and Greene were already marching towards the forest. Faggis was carrying Miss Holbrooke across his shoulders.

'Look here, Mr Sims,' exclaimed Molly suddenly. 'There's one thing I've got to get clear right now.'

'*Got* to?' frowned Sims, swinging back abruptly.

'*Got* to!' repeated Molly firmly. 'That girl—how much longer is she to remain in—in that condition?'

'Until we get to the hotel,' answered Sims. 'Then she will receive every attention, till we move on to our next hotel. This is only a temporary one. And, meanwhile, as you can see, she has been unbound. If we meet any strangers—which is highly unlikely—she has had an accident.'

'I see.'

'And you're satisfied?'

'Quite. I'm not squeamish. I'm in on this. But, don't forget—I bar the rough stuff.'

'I am entirely in sympathy with you, Miss Smith. There shall be no rough stuff—*unless it becomes necessary*.' He emphasised the last four words.

'Yus, but now *I* got somethink ter say too,' interposed

143

Ben. 'I'm ter carry the sack, and they're ter carry—'er. Wot are *you* carryin'?'

'This,' said Mr Sims, and wagged his revolver.

Then he began to walk away.

'Well, there's one thing 'e's fergot!' muttered Ben. 'The boat. S'p'ose that's discovered?'

'The boat will be attended to later,' remarked Sims over his shoulder; 'but our first job is to race the sun. Pick up that sack over there, and come along.'

Ben's forehead was moist as he turned to Molly Smith.

'Gawd, 'e's got ears, ain't 'e?' he murmured. ''E wasn't s'p'osed ter 'ear that! Yus, but I was orl right about them baked-in-their-skins,' he added, to console himself. 'You 'eard wot 'e sed abart hinter'uptin' our tater-taters.'

'Oh goodness, come on!' gasped Molly, seizing his arm. 'When you talk, I honestly don't know whether to laugh or cry!'

'Laughin's best, miss,' he assured her. 'I does it hevery time I dies.' A thought struck him. 'P'r'aps that's why I ain't dead yet? They wants yer ter come serious.' Then another thought struck him. 'I say, miss. Wot was that thing you was sayin' yer did when 'e come hup? Not wot yer did when 'e come hup, but wot yer sed yer did—well, when 'e come hup. I can't 'elp it, miss—my 'ead's still funny.'

'I scribbled something on a piece of paper, and dropped it on the boat deck.'

'Well, I'm blowed!' murmured Ben, and prayed that the piece of paper hadn't been lost. 'Wot was it yer wrote?'

'Something I overheard,' whispered the girl. '*The name of the second hotel we're going to!*'

19

The Mountain Track

The name of the second hotel they were going to? The name of the . . . Ben stared. But before his face could register the emotion that was going on behind it, his companion issued a swift instruction.

'Pick up the sack!' she muttered. 'Quick!'

They were under observation again. Sims was glancing back over his shoulder. Ben bent down in a flurry, slipped, and clasped the sack. But he went on thinking—you can think in any position. Name of the second hotel, eh? The second place they were making for? Why, that would mean . . . No, would it? . . . Well, it might, you know, if . . .

'Is he dying?' came Sim's voice from the distance.

Ben leapt up, rising as quickly as he had descended. The sack was on his back. He didn't know how it had got there. He staggered forward with it, in the direction of the calling voice.

'Manage it?' asked the girl at his side.

'Yus,' murmured Ben.

'If you get tired, I can lend you a hand,' she suggested.

'Wot, a gal?' he objected. 'Go hon!'

'Go on yourself!' she retorted. 'This isn't a question of politeness. It's just a question of whether you can last out.'

'Last hout? When there's trouble arahnd, I'm always last hout and fust hin.'

'I believe you'd joke on your deathbed!'

''Corse! Ain't I jest toljer? It's the on'y way ter stop yerself wobblin'.'

She looked at him, hesitating. Then she turned her head, and stared at the three men who were in advance. Faggis and Greene had paused, and were addressing Sims as he reached them.

'Something's worrying them,' frowned the girl. 'I expect it's us. I'm going on ahead, if you don't mind, or they'll think we're getting too thick.'

'That's right,' agreed Ben. 'The blasted orficer's comin' back for yer.'

'And then there's Miss Holbrooke,' she whispered. 'I'd better be near her, in case she comes to. She may need help.'

'So may you,' he said. 'If yer does, give us a shart.'

She smiled, and went forward to meet the third officer, while Ben trudged behind with the sack.

Ben himself was now the man with the sack! The thought come to him uncomfortably. The sack he was carrying contained food and other necessary odds and ends. What had it been originally designed to contain? He glanced at Sims, who was leading the party with Faggis a few paces to the rear. Sims had just reached the first trees of the gloomy forest. Ben shuddered.

Now he, too, was entering the forest. They were following a narrow, winding track. It wound gently upwards for a while, and the trees became thicker as they ascended. The

146

trees seemed to be crowded nearer and nearer, as though anxious to watch the little procession go by. 'We're a reg'lar Lord Mayor's Show for 'em, ain't we?' thought Ben. Of course, when you looked at the trees, they stood very straight and still. It was only when you caught them out of the corner of your eye that you found them moving, and advancing, and whispering.

The sky became blotted out. Ahead were dark green shadows through which the ascending path wound like a small, too venturesome child. Behind, also, were dark green shadows. A door seemed to have been closed between them and the beach. Ben fought a sudden longing for the beach. It had been clear and sunny there. If something came at you, there was space to run. And then, bordering the beach was the water, on some invisible part of which the *Atalanta* sailed, with its sense of orderliness and security. True, Ben had not experienced any of the security. He had experienced all the *Atalanta*'s most insecure and uncomfortable places. But there had been law-abiding folk within hail, and even the throb-throb of the engines had been the pulse of organised, civilised work. Here, in this forest, too thick even for the sun to pierce, there were nothing but ghosts or murderous solidarity. 'Yus, there's three murderers 'ere,' thought Ben, 'and a couple o' gals, one drugged, and me!' A pretty gruesome Lord Mayor's Show!

The path grew steeper. They were now beginning to ascend a definite slope. Not a nice, wide slope, but a narrowing slope, with great dark blobs on each side denoting cavities. The procession halted. Greene took Faggis's load. Ben shifted his own from one shoulder to another. As he did so, he suddenly found Sims a yard away, watching him.

147

'Like the view?' inquired Sims.

'It's better when its back's turned,' answered Ben.

'I think I must try your own back view,' said Sims. 'It may help you to get a move on.'

''Oo's goin' ter git a move on hup this mounting?' demanded Ben.

'We all are,' replied Sims. 'You included. We've some way to go yet, and I've given orders in front to mend the pace.'

'I can't go no quicker, not with this sack.'

'You can, and you will.'

''Ow?'

'I've a simple little device that will make you.'

He drew a step nearer and poked his revolver in Ben's back.

'Yer know,' said Ben, 'barrin' the Kaiser, yer the nicest man I hever met.'

The journey continued. Sims, adhering to his new policy, remained in the rear. Several times Ben felt the point of the revolver between his shoulder blades, and accelerated materially. As the path grew steeper, the acceleration grew harder, but the point of the revolver was ruthless, and kept him on.

'Wot would you say if I was ter drop dahn dead?' puffed Ben once, as he felt a particularly hard jab.

'If you stop to talk, you will undoubtedly drop down dead,' replied Sims.

But five minutes later, Ben risked conversation again. The climb was beating him. He tripped on loose stones, and once fell flat. His breath was going, and also his nerve. They were now emerging from the thick forest and their track was bordered by chasms and dizzy depths.

"Ow much longer?' he panted.

'If it's more than fifteen minutes longer,' replied the voice behind him, 'we shall be going over this ridge without the sun to help us.'

The sun had greeted them again as they rose out of the forest, but it was now very low indeed, and their shadows were grotesquely elongated. Ben noticed, with something of a shock, that his own shadow ended at the waist some twenty feet away, and that his head was over the side of the road, probably a thousand feet below!

'Well, I'm done in, any'ow,' said Ben; 'so yer might as well know it.'

The revolver touched his back again.

'I tell yer, it's no *good*,' gasped Ben, almost blubbering. 'If yer feels 'ow yer feels, yer can't 'elp 'ow yer feels.'

The revolver pressed harder. Ben dropped his sack.

'I shall count three,' warned Sims.

'One, two, three!' said Ben. 'Now I done it for yer.'

He closed his eyes and opened his mouth and waited. Nothing happened. When he opened his eyes, he saw Greene clambering back towards them. Sims had summoned him, and Greene looked surly.

'Pick it up, Greene,' ordered Sims, 'and be slippy.'

'Bah! The fellow's only shamming,' growled Greene. 'Think *I'm* so damned fresh?'

'Damned fresh,' returned Sims. 'If the fellow were shamming I'd know it!' His voice rose suddenly to a bark. 'Do you hear me, Greene, or don't you?'

The third officer scowled, and glanced at the revolver. Then he glanced ahead. Faggis was now carrying Miss Holbrooke, and Molly Smith was walking beside him.

'Oh, all right,' muttered Greene; 'but if you're not using

him as a pack horse, why you don't tip the fool over the mountain beats me hollow!'

He picked up the bag, turned, and made after the others. Sims paused before continuing himself, and gazed at Ben speculatively.

'I wonder if he's right,' he mused. 'Shall I tip you over, my man?'

'If yer does,' answered Ben, 'I'll call a bobby.'

'You know, Ben,' observed Sims, drawing an inch nearer, 'you don't quite believe in me yet, do you?'

'Wot's that?'

'Faggis has two murders to his credit, and Greene goes about with chloroform and injection needles. It was Greene who gave Miss Holbrooke her present injection, you may like to know. Then Greene tried to murder you, also, didn't he? But, so far, you haven't seen any of my own activities. So you still imagine that when I poke you behind with my revolver it won't go off—that when I consider tipping you over into a precipice there is no chance that I will actually do it—'

He seized Ben's coat collar as he spoke, and jerked him towards the edge.

'. . . And that, behind my talk, I am really quite an amiable old man, whose favourite occupations are Ludo and stamp collecting!'

Ben found himself staring over the edge, looking down at the tops of trees twenty thousand miles below.

'Fer Gawd's sake, git on with it!' he squeaked.

'I will,' replied Sims, and pushed him.

Ben jerked out over space. There was nothing but space between him and those infinitely distant tree-tops. The alarm-bell rang in Heaven and Hell, and all the inhabitants left their occupations hurriedly to receive him. 'Ben'll be here in a minute,' rang the cry. 'He's only got to hit those trees.' 'Nonsense—he'll die through loss of breath on the way down!' cried another theorist. 'Don't you worry,' cried a third. 'He's dying of fright before he starts!' Then the question arose as to which was to have him. A red devil thrust out two arms holding a large sack. An angel held out a golden fishing rod. 'Go away!' hissed the red devil. 'He's coming down, and Hell's always at the bottom.' 'But I can pull him up,' retorted the angel, 'and I know he'd prefer to go to Heaven. He's begging me at this moment. Can't you hear him?' 'He told a lie to the captain about his mother.' 'Yes, but he says he's sorry.' 'Well, what about that old man he bound and gagged on Newmarket Heath?' 'Don't be silly! You know that wasn't true! He's got a soft heart, and he cries if you look at him. He's crying now. And, if he'd lived, he'd have helped these two poor girls—' 'Go away! Here he comes! Here he comes! Right into my sack . . .'

Bong! A violent jerk! Space disappeared. Hard ground was under him again.

'And, if there's any more nonsense,' said Mr Sims, 'the next time I *will* drop you!'

A foot away was the small stump of a withered tree that had been struck a year ago by lightning. Ben stretched his arms forward and put them round it.

'Get up,' ordered Mr Sims.

'Can't fer a mo', guv'nor,' replied Ben. 'I'm goin' ter be sick.'

20

Arrival at the 'First Hotel'

Sims had expended two valuable minutes on Ben. This was partly due to his knowledge that, unless Ben received some stimulant (such as being held over a precipice) he would walk slower and slower until he stopped, and there was genuine need for acceleration, and partly to the natural malice that lay like poison behind his usually unruffled exterior. He had implied the truth to Ben when he had suggested that he was just as capable of killing as were Greene and Faggis. If, when necessity pressed, he did not kill, it was only because he found somebody else to do the job and take the risk for him, and the thwarted homicidal instinct went inwards to burst out in such impulses as that which had caused him to seize Ben and hold him over space.

Sims's heart knew that Ben feared him mortally. Sims's pride, however, was worried by Ben's refusal to yield permanently to the fear, and by the cheeky humour and badinage that ran so doggedly through it. And because, for the sake of wider policies, Sims accepted the cheeky humour and the badinage with imperturbability, his thwarted impulse again went inwards, gathering venomous force for its ultimate expression.

The wider policies could not be interfered with for such small fry as Ben; but if, without interfering with them, a process of torturing the small fry could be developed, this would make a most entertaining hobby, a very agreeable sauce to go with the main dish.

That was why Sims did not drop Ben on to the tree-tops a thousand feet below—and how he came to make his cardinal mistake.

For a quarter of an hour the journey continued, while the valleys filled with deepening shadows and the pools of blackness rose up to them. Soon they would themselves be drowned in the advancing tide of the night, and there would be nothing to tell their eyes whether the next step would descend on solid ground or a precipice. But, at the moment, the dropping sun still sent its final slanting rays upwards to the ridge on which they walked—a ridge that would have been a dream to any beholders from below, but that was a nightmare to some of those who were actually upon it.

The ridge widened, assisting the process of acceleration. Now the yawning chasms lay only on their left, fresh heights appearing on their right to deride their achievement and reduce their pride. 'You think you know anything about climbing?' they jeered. 'Try *us*!' Fortunately for weary feet, there was no need to try them. The track wound along their base, possessing its own goal. And the goal was now very close.

All at once, Sims paused, and called on those ahead to halt. They halted obediently. Ben's were not the only feet

that were tired, nor was his the only oppressed spirit. The
mountain heights towered over anxious souls, and Sims
alone appeared to consider himself their equal. He stared
up at a peak now. His boots were in shadow, but the sun
illuminated his white hair. Then he lowered his eyes and
rested them on a little clump of pine trees. There were five
pine trees. Like Sims, they rose out of the shadows and
glowed only at their tops.

'Dead beat?'

It was Molly Smith's voice. She stood by Ben, and was
regarding him quietly.

'Ain't you?' answered Ben.

'Bit of a climb,' she said; 'but I've not had anything to
carry. Well, we'll soon be at our first hotel!'

'That's right,' murmured Ben. 'Growvenner 'Ouse,
ain't it?'

Sims was studying his map. Molly glanced towards him
for an instant, then turned back to Ben and went on in a
low voice:

'There's a man and a mule at Grosvenor House.'

'And six donkeys jest arrivin'.'

'Listen! The man's been told to look out for us.'

''As 'e?'

'Yes. There were two places we might have landed at,
and this is one of them. The man was told to stand by in
case we turned up.'

'Then 'e won't 'elp us!'

'No, but the mule may!'

'Go on!'

'Suppose,' she whispered, 'suppose we could get hold of
the mule!'

Ben's brain was muzzy, and it took him a few seconds

before the full beauty of this plan dawned upon him. Then he realised its possibilities. Lummy! Get hold of the mule, eh? Get hold of it, and jump upon its back . . .

'Yus, but 'ow many does a mule 'old?' he asked. 'We'd want a halligater.'

'*Cave!*' muttered the girl.

Sims raised his eyes from the map and looked towards them. The sunlight had left his hair, and he was now a tall, dim figure fast merging into the background. Near him squatted the dim figures of Greene and Faggis. Thus shortened, they might have been the gnomes that haunted Rip Van Winkle in the Catskill Mountains.

'Stay here, all of you,' ordered Sims. 'I'm going ahead to investigate.'

'How long'll you be?' inquired the third officer.

'How do I know?' replied Sims.

'As you like,' grunted the third officer; 'but if you get into trouble don't blame us for not sending a search party.'

Sims considered the point. Then he nodded, implying that it was a sound one.

'Say, ten minutes,' he said. 'If I'm longer than that, you can begin to wonder.'

'Right,' answered the third officer. 'In ten minutes we'll ring up the fire brigade.'

Sims smiled. Something glinted in his hand. The next moment, he was gone.

Slowly the minutes ticked away. Greene timed them by a wrist-watch, but Ben watched them pass by fixing his eyes on the highest peak on which the sun still played. The shadows went upwards like spreading ink, and Ben calculated that the ink would spread to the top by the time the ten minutes had run their course.

The first minute passed in utter silence, save for the striking of a match. By the light of the match two faces became successively illuminated, each making a little momentary cameo in the darkness. When the match went out, only two points of light were left, like evilly glowing eyes.

In the second minute, inspired by the incidents of the first, Ben made a discovery. He found a third of a cigarette in a pocket. It had escaped him for days. But he did not forget his manners, even a thousand feet up a Spanish mountain.

''Ave one, miss?' he asked, holding the cigarette end out. She shook her head. 'It's orl right,' he assured her. 'Picked it hup in Bond Street.'

He remembered the nob who'd dropped it. Spats. But she still shook her head, so he placed the precious fragment between his lips.

In the third minute he made another discovery. He hadn't a match. The cigarette end returned to his pocket. They often had to wait.

In the fourth minute, Faggis made a remark,

'What do we do if he pitches down a precipice?'

'Pitch a few more down a precipice,' replied the third officer.

In the fifth minute, Ben made a remark.

''Arf way,' he said, with his eyes on the ascending shadow.

The sixth minute passed in silence. In the seventh there was a little rustle. Molly Smith was drawing an inch or two closer to Ben. In the eighth, Greene got up.

'What the hell's happening?' he exclaimed. 'I don't like it!'

'P'r'aps he's done a bunk?' answered Faggis.

'When we've got the girl?' retorted Greene. 'Don't be a lunatic!'

'And, if you want to live to ninety,' said Faggis, 'don't call names.'

In the ninth minute, Faggis got up. Greene had left his boulder, and had gone a few paces along the track.

In the tenth minute, the shadow above them reached the highest solid point, extinguished it, and continued invisibly into space.

'Good-bye,' murmured Ben.

A little night breeze rose. Or perhaps it was only now that they noticed it. It came to them from the direction in which Sims had vanished, and whispered a thousand horrors in its fluttering sigh. Faggis and Greene looked at each other.

'What about it?' asked Faggis.

'We'd better push on,' replied Greene.

'Suppose we find something we don't like?' suggested Faggis.

'Are we finding anything especially attractive *here*?' rasped Greene. 'I'm not keen to die of exposure, if you are!'

'P'r'aps you're right.'

'I'm damn well right. Pick her up, and come along.'

'Pick her up, eh?' There was a pause. Then Faggis suddenly shot out, 'Why?'

'Faggis,' said the third officer, 'you objected a minute ago when I called you a lunatic. Why must you prove yourself one? That girl means money to us, and security. If we lose her, we lose everything. Oh, for God's sake, stop staring, and get on with it! It's getting so damned dark that in another minute we shan't dare move a step!'

'All right, all right,' drawled Faggis, stooping. 'You'll get paid for compliments later.' Then he paused again. 'What about the others?'

'They'd better come too,' growled Greene.

'You bet, we're coming too,' remarked Molly Smith quietly. 'We're just as interested in Miss Holbrooke as you are.'

Without more words, the procession resumed its way. The little breeze rose to a sudden hilarious shriek to meet them, and then dropped dead. All they now heard were their own footsteps, crunching over the almost invisible track.

'This is narsty,' thought Ben.

They had proceeded about a hundred yards, taking each step with exaggerated caution, and pausing a dozen times at imagined sounds, when something definite caused them to halt. A streak of yellow light streamed out from some unseen point on their right, and lay with incongruous brilliance across their path.

'What's that?' whispered Greene.

'Home, probably,' answered Faggis. 'If we go on, we'll see.'

He trudged on again as he spoke. He seemed anxious to get it over. The others followed. Round an angle, the source of the light was revealed. A lamp on a wooden table, shining out through the open window of a small, dark building.

The lamp was not the only thing visible through the window. On the floor of the room, near the farther wall, lay a prone figure.

21

The Conference in the Hut

'God! They've done him!' gasped Greene, staring numbly at the outstretched form.

But Faggis suddenly woke up.

'*Have* they?' he muttered; and, swiftly laying his burden down, he darted towards the hut. A door at the side stood open.

Greene hesitated. As a rule, he managed to dominate Faggis, but for once he found himself less alert. Possibly he realised more intelligently what the loss of a leader meant, and was momentarily stunned by the swiftness of the message from his brain. He did not move for two or three seconds after Faggis had darted forward, but continued to stare through the open window, as though waiting for the figure lying there to move. But the figure did not move. The lanky form lay, face downwards, obviously dead.

Then, while he stared, Greene suddenly gave an exclamation. It came at the moment Faggis appeared in the room bringing movement into the grim picture illuminated by the lamp. It was not the sight of Faggis, however, that produced the third officer's cry, and sent him dashing also towards the hut.

'Gawd!' gulped Ben.

This was the only thought that came to him at such moments. It covered everything—emotion, impotence, and prayer.

Greene was now in the room with Faggis, and Faggis was bending over the body. As Greene advanced, Faggis rose, and stared past Greene at the door.

'Any'ow, it makes one less, miss!' muttered Ben.

Receiving no reply, and considering that the situation demanded one, he turned to Molly Smith, and found there was no Molly Smith to turn to. That made him one less, also, and he didn't like it.

'Oi!' he whispered hoarsely.

A figure began to grow out of the shadows.

'Thort you'd gorn,' gasped Ben.

'No, I've not gone,' replied the voice of Mr Sims. 'I'm still here.'

Ben sat down upon the ground. He did not remember doing it, but as he was on the ground he supposed he must have. A dozen Mr Simses seemed to be dancing all around him.

'Beg pardon,' he mumbled weakly, to the one who looked the most distinct; 'but are you dead or am I?'

'We are both alive—at the moment,' replied the most distinct Mr Sims.

'Then—'oo's the bloke in there?'

'Ah! *He* is undoubtedly dead!'

'And ain't 'e you?'

'I imagine not. I also imagine, from what I have observed, that he was temporarily taken for me, probably on account of our similarity in build and the fact that he was lying on his face.'

'Oh! That was it, was it?' murmured Ben. 'But—'oo deaded 'im?'

Sims considered the question for an instant.

'He was tired of life, Ben,' said Sims, 'and, taking a knife, he killed himself.'

Ben offered no comment. But Faggis did. He had emerged from the cottage, and had overheard the last remark. Greene was still in the room, examining the dead man.

'That's the way *I* always try to work it too, Sims,' he observed sarcastically. 'Suicide covers a multitude of sins, eh?'

'It has its uses, Faggis.'

'P'r'aps one day *you'll* commit suicide?'

'We might make a pact?'

'Sure! Meantime, let's hear the truth of that nasty mess inside there.'

'Sure! Pick up Miss Holbrooke, get her into the hut—there's an upper room with a bed in it—put her there—and you shall hear the story.'

Faggis obeyed, and they walked towards the hut. Suddenly Ben wondered why no one had noticed the absence of Molly Smith. The solution was at his elbow.

'I've discovered something!' whispered Molly. '*The mule!*'

Lummy! For slippiness, eels weren't in it!

They reached the hut. Greene was standing anxiously in the doorway. He stared at Sims venomously, divided between gratification and anger at the sight.

'How many more have we got to kill?' he demanded.

'I can only think of four,' replied Sims. 'I exclude of course Miss Holbrooke. Take her up, Faggis, and then come down again.'

A minute later, Miss Holbrooke was lying on the bed in the little upper room, and the rest of the party had gathered in the parlour immediately below to hear their leader's story.

It was gruesome, and it was short. When Sims had reached the cottage, he had found the wrong man waiting for him. The meeting had involved a joint surprise, for the wrong man seemed unprepared, and was, according to Sims, wholly lacking in tact. The result was that antagonism developed rather swiftly, and the swiftness of the development necessitated a swift solution.

'And the solution, gentlemen, lies at our feet,' said Sims.

'You mean—he was a detective?' asked Greene bluntly.

'To tell you the truth,' admitted Sims, rather sadly, 'we hardly had time to find out very much about each other. He may have been a detective.'

'Nothing to show it on him,' said Greene.

'There wouldn't be, if he was a good detective,' replied Sims. 'But, if he was a detective, he was a very bad one. As I have implied, he had no tact. He seemed quite incapable of fencing. He also had no sense of self-protection. Would a detective have arranged to meet so considerable an army as ours without a bit of an army himself? It's not likely—no, it's not likely.'

'Then, darnation, who *was* he?' demanded Faggis. 'And how do you know he wasn't the proper feller, after all?'

'Because I do not happen to be a fool, Faggis,' answered Sims, 'and do not give responsible jobs to strangers. This man was a stranger to me. He may have got inside knowledge in some way—there has never been a scheme so watertight that leakage was impossible—and he may have been working for a rival party.'

'More likely he was working on his own,' suggested Greene.

'Much more likely,' agreed Sims. 'It would explain, perhaps, his nerviness—his lack of assurance. If he had had friends near by, or shortly arriving, he'd surely have used his wits to hold the situation. On the contrary, he lost his head—and I did not lose mine.'

'He lost more than his head,' said Greene.

'Yes, exactly. And we must see that we do not lose our own heads, and we must not bank on theories. He *may* have been playing a lone hand. He may have been one of a gang. Or he may even have been a detective—a very bad detective. Only in the first of these three alternatives have we nothing to fear. Do you understand?'

'We're not babes-in-arms,' remarked Faggis.

'Thank you, Faggis. I will make a note of it. And, as we're not babes-in-arms, we must act on the assumption that the worst is possible. The worst being that this man has friends, either inside or outside the police force, who may come and look for him.'

There was a short silence. Minds were busy. But they all waited on Sims's mind.

'In addition to general vigilance and absolute unity,' said Sims, at last, 'there are three immediate things to be done. But let us settle the vigilance and the unity first. Is it agreed, without the remotest dissent, that I am your leader to be obeyed instantly and without question in all things?'

'That's obvious, isn't it?' replied Molly, addressing the conference for the first time.

'I'm glad to hear you say so,' answered Sims, his voice giving no indication as to whether he believed her or not. 'What about the others?'

'O.K., for me,' said Greene.

'What's this about?' said Faggis. 'Who's objecting?'

'And you, Ben?' asked Sims, turning to the least effective member of the party with a cynical smile.

''Oo?' blinked Ben.

'Have I anything to fear from you?' inquired Sims.

'Fear from me, is it?' responded Ben. 'Oh, yus! I look like I could knock anybody dahn, doesn't I? If yer was ter put me hup agin a week-old chicken wot 'ad bin rode hover by a motor bus, I couldn't pull its beak!'

'But if the flesh were not weak, what would the spirit be?' pressed Sims.

'Yus or no,' retorted Ben, 'whichever one yer tryin' for.'

'That's generous. Well, I don't think there's anything wrong with our unity, when my revolver and my knife—'

'*My* knife,' corrected Faggis.

'. . . The knife that used to belong to Mr Faggis but that now belongs to me—are added. Now, how about the vigilance? Suppose you station yourself at the window, Greene, and keep a look out?'

'And stop the first bullet?'

'We'll lower the lamp. Then you won't be such a mark.' He lowered the wick as he spoke. 'Now I think you'll be safe, Greene. Do you mind?'

'Delighted! But I can't think why I'm honoured?'

'A third officer has to pass a vision test. Your sight is keener than ours.'

'Hear that, Faggis? A compliment! The Eighth Wonder! Well, here goes to make myself a target.' He crossed to the window. 'And now what about those three immediate things we've got to do?'

'One is to get rid of this fellow at our feet.'

'Agreed. But where do we put him?'

'Somewhere where he won't be found until the year 1990. I've no doubt you two can stow him away safely.'

'Us, of course!'

'You, of course. Then we've got to have another look for another body.'

'Ain't this cheerful?' said Ben.

'Shut up, you fool!' exclaimed Faggis. And then asked Sims, 'What other body? And what other look?'

'The body of the man who *ought* to have been here,' replied Sims. 'It's my opinion he hasn't been long dead. Maybe he isn't dead at all. That would explain the flurry of the fool I've just had to kill myself.'

'I see,' murmured Greene, and he gazed more intensely out of the window. 'Yes, that might explain it. You've had one look already, then?'

'I was searching when you came along.'

'Well? And Number Three?'

'Ah, yes. Number Three,' said Sims, 'is the boat.'

'What about the boat?' exclaimed Faggis.

Greene, also, seemed rather surprised.

'This about the boat,' answered Sims. 'If the boat is found—and there may be folk around to find it—it will almost inevitably lead to us. On the other hand, if it is hidden away, it may be useful should we suddenly need it.'

'That's right,' nodded Ben. 'If some 'un comes along, you on'y got to jump four miles!'

'Will you shut up!' cried Faggis.

'All the same, he's right this time,' remarked Greene. 'How's the boat going to help us in an emergency?'

'If one knew in advance all the points affecting an emergency,' said Sims dryly, 'there wouldn't be an emergency. I know you've had a long day, Greene, but try to keep your brain awake. That boat has got to be hidden away somewhere, and it's got to be hidden in a place where we can get hold of it quickly and launch it if we want to.'

'Brain awake! By Jiminy, that's comic!' rasped Greene, smarting and indignant. 'How the devil d'you suppose we're going to make the beach in the darkness?'

'It won't be in the darkness,' replied Sims calmly. 'You forget, there'll be a moon.'

'That's true,' reflected Faggis. 'And no clouds, as there were last night, to obscure it. Yes, but talking of brains,' he added, 'where were yours when you let us leave the boat in the open before coming along here? Couldn't we have stowed it away then?'

There were two reasons why Sims had not stowed the boat away then, but he only explained one of them. The other they learned later.

'I think my brain can even stand that question, Faggis,' said Sims. 'We had one hour for this journey, and the light was failing. There wasn't time. Any more questions?'

'Yes, I've got one,' interposed Molly, 'and it comes before any of the others, or I drop out. You've got to bring Miss Holbrooke round!'

Mr Sims shook his head in mock despair.

'Dear, dear!' he murmured. 'This young lady is very persistent.'

'And she's going to get more so.'

'Then my hand is forced. As a matter of fact, I had wished to see to Miss Holbrooke first, but I anticipated trouble from other quarters.'

He glanced towards Greene and Faggis, and Greene asked curtly what that meant.

'Well,' explained Sims, 'if I bring Miss Holbrooke round, she will have to be looked after, and I shall not be able to leave the hut myself.'

'But I'll look after her,' said Molly. 'That's what I'm here for, isn't it?'

'Ah, but who will look after *you,* Miss Smith?' queried Sims. 'And Ben? However, let us have a show of hands, just to prove that I am not invariably an autocrat. Who votes for immediate attention to Miss Holbrooke?'

Three hands went up. The hands of Molly, Ben and Sims.

'Three to two,' announced Sims. 'The ayes win. Then our arrangements are as follows. Miss Holbrooke will be attended to in the room above our heads. Miss Smith will remain with Miss Holbrooke, and read nursery rhymes to her. You, Greene, and you, Faggis, will get rid of our quiet friend on the ground—you can do that while I am being Miss Holbrooke's doctor—and after that, if the moon is not up, we can poke round for any sign of the late manager of this hotel—or of the enemy.'

'We shan't find much till the moon's up,' commented Greene. 'It's almost pitch black out there.'

'And, when the moon is up,' replied Sims, 'you and Faggis will set off immediately for the boat.'

'I'm not so sure about that,' said Greene suddenly.

'I am,' answered Sims. 'I'd shoot you where you stand without the slightest hesitation, if it suited my purpose.'

Greene frowned uneasily, and Faggis took up the objection where Greene dropped it.

'There's two of us,' Faggis reminded him.

'I can count,' responded Sims. 'But, even if, while I killed Greene, you killed me, Faggis, or if while I killed you, Greene killed me, the survivor would be utterly helpless and

167

discredited and moneyless in a strange country. No money. No language—saving in the decorative sense. No future prospects. A black past. And, just incidentally, I happen to belong to a little organisation that would be very curious if anything happened to me. You don't suppose all of this could have been planned and carried out if my friends hadn't been pretty useful, do you? No, Faggis. No, Greene. If I'm dead, *you'll* never make a cent out of Miss Holbrooke. You'll just swing for her.'

He paused. Greene shifted a little way from the window, and glanced quickly at Faggis.

'I wouldn't lose a hell of a lot if I *did* shoot you both this instant,' said Sims.

Faggis had been sitting on the edge of the table. He rose carelessly.

'Why don't you?' he asked.

'Well, I'm rather tender-hearted,' replied Sims, quietly watching every movement, 'and my friends rather like me to stick to my word, just as they insist that others shall stick to theirs. If you're good dogs, I expect you'll still be worth your keep.'

'If we're good dogs,' said Faggis, lounging a step nearer.

'Very good dogs,' repeated Sims, and covered Faggis.

Faggis smiled, and shrugged his shoulders.

'We'll play square, if you do,' he said, and sat down again. 'There's just one thing I want to ask, though, and you can stick down your cannon while I'm asking, if you like.'

'I don't like,' answered Sims, 'until I hear what the question is.'

'Quite a simple one, Sims,' said Faggis. 'What do *you* do, exactly, while Greene and I are seeing to the boat?'

'Yes, that's quite a simple one,' agreed Sims. 'While you're seeing to your end, I'm seeing to mine. Miss Smith will be watching Miss Holbrooke. I will be watching Miss Smith—'

'What's that?' interposed Molly. 'Watching me?'

'Of course. With Faggis and Greene away, I must see that our two latest recruits do not suddenly get it into their heads to jump upon me.'

'A lot of good that would do us!' retorted Molly. 'You think us mugs, don't you?'

'You would certainly be mugs to jump upon me.'

'Well, you can put that out of your mind!'

'I mean to. While you are spending the night upstairs, the key of your room will be in my pocket.'

Molly swung round angrily.

'You're going to lock me in?' she cried.

'There! You see!' answered Sims. 'You rouse my suspicions at once! Why shouldn't you be locked in? Will it make any difference to your plans?'

'Not a cent's worth,' retorted Molly. 'That's why it's so damn silly. Still, have it your own way. You're the boss, aren't you?'

'I am,' admitted Sims.

'And wotcher goin' ter do ter me?' asked Ben. 'Lock me hin too?'

Mr Sims removed his eyes from Molly, and fixed them on Ben.

'Don't be impatient, Ben.' He smiled. 'You'll learn all in good time.'

'You're not going to hurt him?' exclaimed Molly.

'Hurt him, Miss Smith? I love him like a son!' He raised his head suddenly. 'Do I hear a movement upstairs? Run

169

up to Miss Holbrooke quickly, please. I'll follow you immediately.'

She hesitated.

'I said, "quickly,"' repeated Sims. 'I meant it.'

'Well, no monkey tricks!' She frowned, and left the room.

'And now bind that idiot and gag him,' said Sims. 'Good and tight!'

22

The Binding of Ben

Sims had once charged the third officer with lack of subtlety.
He was himself a master of the art, and it was largely due
to his realisation of this fact that he often permitted himself
the luxury of the cat playing with a mouse. He enjoyed long
speeches, when he knew the end of them. He enjoyed toying
with time when there did not appear much time to toy
with. He enjoyed the impatience and anxieties of lesser
men. Perhaps his only weakness lay in this indulgence, with
its ever-present danger of excess. Perhaps, being an adven-
turer as well as a criminal (it is the combination that makes
for genius in the underworld), he knew of the weakness,
and derived a certain thrill from the very danger it imposed.

His subtlety during the conference now ended was proved
by its conclusion. He had laid his plans and set his stage
exactly as he required. He had egged his second lieutenants
to the edge of rebellion, and had delayed them with his
revolver. Now, substituting astuteness for force, he had
quelled them by throwing limelight on a common enemy.
The order to bind Ben was a master move.

He did not even stay to see it done. He went upstairs to lock the other members of the party in. After all, provided Greene and Faggis carried out his instructions, which seemed reasonable enough in general if not entirely so in detail, was he not showing his confidence in them, and leaving them alone?

The sense of this argument drifted through the minds of Greene and Faggis as the door of the parlour closed and as Sims's footsteps were heard ascending wooden stairs to the floor above. It became even more apparent as they looked at Ben, whose mouth was still gaping with the unpleasant news he had just heard. Here was the definite victim! Why not cease to regard themselves as such?

'Well?' said the third officer.

Faggis nodded.

'Let's get on with it,' he replied. 'Where's some rope?'

Then Ben found his voice.

'Tie me hup, is it?' he cried. 'Jest you come near me, if yer wants a wollup!'

He sprang away as he spoke. The spring took him back to a chair. He swung round and lunged at it. It went down for the count.

'Did you ever see such a damned fool!' grinned Greene.

'Some farmer ought to buy him for a windmill,' grinned Faggis.

Ben's arms were revolving sixty to the minute. The chair was *hors de combat*, but he was still fighting it.

'Yus, you come near the windmill!' he roared, now swinging back to the more upright enemy. 'And see wot yer'll git!'

'Do you know, I think I will,' said Greene.

He came near, and he got it. The windmill whirled forward upon him, and he staggered to the ground.

'Peel the blighter off me!' he cried, amazed and indignant. 'He's biting!'

Ben felt himself peeled off, and hung limp in the encircling arms of Faggis. But the third officer's hand was bleeding. There was still a little savour left in life.

'Would you believe it!' fumed Greene, rising.

'Yes, I would,' laughed Faggis, 'because he bit me in just the same way on London docks! Hey, keep clear of his legs—*they're* beginning to go round now!'

Greene drew away, then approached gingerly. He seized the revolving legs, and Ben was pinioned at all his moveable points. A moment later he felt his belt being slipped from his middle. Its tightness evaporated, to reappear again a few inches higher up in a slightly larger circumference, this time including his two arms.

'Well, there's a dirty trick!' he thought. 'This is the larst belt *I'll* ever wear! Yer can bust braces!'

Next, his feet. They found a bit of rope from somewhere. They tied him with it to the chair he had maltreated, and stuck him in a corner. Then they stood away from him and regarded him.

'Wotcher think I am?' muttered Ben. 'The Pershun Hexibishun?'

'What about the gag?' asked Greene.

'He may make a noise,' answered Faggis.

'Gawd, ain't yer goin' ter leave me even me marth?' demanded Ben.

'Afraid we can't trust it,' sighed Greene.

'Wot for?' persisted Ben. He longed for his mouth. 'Arter yer gorn, there won't be nothink 'ere ter bite.'

'You might shout,' suggested Faggis.

'So I might,' he agreed, and did so.

Many things had happened in that lonely hut on a Spanish mountain. A murder had been committed there, thieves had shared their spoils there, a deserter had starved there, and lovers had met there. Its memories were both bitter and sweet. But when Ben shouted, he created fresh history. Never before had its wooden walls contained such sound. For an instant, while it filled the room and tried to burst it, Greene and Faggis stood still, incapacitated by a totally new experience. Upstairs, Molly Smith gasped, Sims raised his head, and the girl on the bed over whom he had been bending opened her eyes and murmured, very faintly, 'What's that?'

Then the sound ceased, as abruptly as it had started. A handkerchief was clapped over its source, and a second handkerchief was tied round to secure it.

'Well, any'ow,' thought Ben, driven back to man's last extremity, 'they'll be done in, both of 'em, when they wants ter blow their noses.'

They had bound his arms. They had bound his legs. They had bound his mouth. Only his thoughts were free.

By the light of the grudging lamp, he watched his oppressors conclude their work in the room. The body on the ground was dragged towards the door. Not liking the sight, Ben closed his eyes, but the dragging sound so exaggerated the vision that he opened his eyes again almost immediately to disprove his imagination. In his imagination, the corpse had jumped up and started a horn-pipe.

'This is all very well,' said Greene, at the door; 'but where are we going to put him?'

'Shove him over a cliff,' proposed Faggis. 'Sad Climbing Fatality!'

'Yes, but s'p'ose we shove ourselves over the cliff in

this darkness?' answered Greene. 'Then it'd be a sadder climbing fatality!'

'That's true.'

'Why not wait till the moon?'

'And leave him here?'

'Can't see the objection.'

'Nor can I. Just a question of—'

'Of what?'

'Carrying out Sims's orders, that's all.'

'Sims be blasted!'

'One day, yes. We'll blast him together—eh, Greene? And then blast each other! But, just at the moment, I think we'd better keep in with the old man.'

'Growing to love him, eh?'

'Growing to love his money! Once I get hold of that—'

He paused. His eyes went up towards the ceiling. Soft footsteps sounded above.

'Yes; once we get hold of the money!' murmured Greene, nodding. 'Meanwhile, we pull together. But that doesn't mean scrapping every shred of our native intelligence, and I'm not going to risk lugging this fellow over a mountainside in the dark. Besides, Faggis, we want to be free while we poke around out there. Lean him against the wall. He'll look pretty that way, and can keep our mummy company.'

Faggis laughed, and propped the dead man up. Then he turned to Ben.

'If he asks any questions,' he said, 'give him our love, won't you?'

After that they left the room, taking the lamp with them. In the darkness, Ben heard their steps receding. But, overhead, soft sounds still went backwards and forwards across the floor.

23

The Chamber of Horrors

Comparatively few of us go through the experience of being bound and, gagged. Outside the region of definite physical agony, this is probably the most uncomfortable condition one can endure, and the definite physical agony will certainly accompany the condition if it is endured too long, if the binding is so tight that it impedes circulation, or if the gagging covers nose as well as mouth.

Fortunately Ben's gag was limited to the lower feature, through accident rather than kindness, and he was able to breathe. How he thanked God for having designed man with an alternative breathing device! Two ears, two eyes, and a couple of breathers. Never before had he felt so grateful to his nose! There was nothing else he could feel grateful to, however. He had not even the blessing of solitude in the darkness. Sharing the room with him, and leaning unseen against a wall, was a dead man.

'Yer know, somethink's wrong with me,' he reflected. 'I ain't goin' mad!'

It really wasn't reasonable. It made him a little anxious

about himself. He *ought* to have been going mad. Any sane man would. He ought to have been laughing like one of them yiheenas and raving like what he'd heard. But, instead, his senses were almost glaringly alert and his mind was painfully clear. Panic was somewhere in the middle of him, but it was sitting perfectly still, waiting to spring— sitting still in the darkness of Ben, as Ben was sitting still in the darkness of the room.

'I know why I ain't bein' mad,' thought Ben suddenly. 'I gorn beyond, like.'

In this uncomfortable beyondness, he listened for sounds. For sounds above him. For sounds outside the hut. For sounds—least desired of all—from the wall against which the dead man was propped.

''Allo, Charlie!' he tried to say. When dead, all people became Charlie to Ben. 'Wot's it like?'

But the attempt at friendliness was abortive. Neither Charlie's ears nor Ben's mouth were functioning. This made conversation difficult.

The footsteps of Greene and Faggis had died away, but sounds continued to come from the ceiling. Faint, stealthy sounds. Those would be Sims. Quick, definite sounds. Those would be Molly. Vague murmurings. Couldn't say anything about those. Too indistinct. Too like the murmuring of wind. Perhaps it *was* the wind? The wind had begun to rise a little. It was moaning round the hut like a lost soul . . . Yes, but *was* it the wind? Gawd! 'Ow did one know? . . . Now, silence again. Ben prayed for sound. The sound restarted. He prayed for silence. Nasty sound, this time. Louder, like. Lummy, *that* moaning wasn't the wind! Someone had cried out . . .

Things grew rather unbearable in the little parlour. That cry had been particularly unpleasant. He tried to blot it out by recalling happy memories. A pound of cheddar. A gold-tipped cigarette end. A bath he'd got out of taking. A kindly bobby who had given him fourpence. And, once, the Prince of Wales had hit him with his smile. The Prince of Wales did him a lot of good. You can hang on to the Prince of Wales! That smile of his—it tacks princes and paupers together, and could even join Edward and Ben in a kind of a love knot. You just thought of the Prince's smile, and hung on to it . . .

Thud!

The Prince of Wales vanished.

The silence that followed the thud seemed ten minutes long. Actually, it was one minute. At the end of it a key clicked in a door above, and footsteps resounded on the stairs. Not quick, definite ones. Faint, stealthy ones.

The steps reached the ground level. They halted. Ben felt, rather than saw, the parlour door being pushed open. He also felt, rather than saw, somebody standing in the dim aperture.

'Feeling comfortable?' inquired the soft voice of Sims.

For the first time in their association, Ben made no retort. Sims remarked upon it.

'I miss your humour,' he said; 'but sometimes the lesser good has to be sacrificed to the greater. You, on this occasion, are the lesser good.'

'This ain't fair,' thought Ben.

'I suppose there's nothing I can do for you before I go?' came the ironic request.

'Yer could scratch a tickle,' thought Ben.

'Because, Ben, as you've probably realised by now,' concluded the voice of Mr Sims, 'you have reached the end of your journey.'

The door closed. Sim's footsteps sounded again outside, then vanished into the void.

The end of the journey? . . .

Now there was utter stillness in the hut. No sounds overhead. No sounds on the stairs. No sound in the parlour. But, oddly enough, it was not the silence that dominated Ben's thoughts just now, nor was it Sims's parting threat. It was the growing sensation on his nose that he had voicelessly invited his tormentor to scratch.

At first it had been the merest baby of a tickle. The sort of tickle that, if caught young, could be dislodged with a rapid wrinkling of the nose itself. But it was a baby no longer. It had grown up before Ben had seriously noticed it, and like an ignored disease now demanded drastic treatment. Becoming more and more intense, it expanded and spread. It spread through his entire body till he became one vast tickle. It spread beyond him. It filled the room, till the room seemed to prick and hum with it. Surely, if this went on, the whole of Spain would soon be up scratching! The thought was so arresting that, for an instant, the agony was suspended. 'Lummy, I'm sort of ticklin'-in!' thought Ben. He pictured Spain scratching itself. 'I know that's silly, but it's jest ter git me mind orf!' he told himself, while his eyes streamed. But *he* couldn't scratch. He hung limply on his cords, in Chinese agony. Even the Prince of Wales could not assist him now.

Then, from an incredible source, help came. It came swishing along the wall, with a sound that froze. A limb flung out, swept Ben's face, and completed its downward course on the floor. Salvation had come from the dead.

Several minutes later, Ben came out of a blackness deeper than the blackness of his wooden prison. He came out of

179

it sweating, while a thousand cold hands relinquished him grudgingly to slip back into a vanishing nightmare.

'Now I *'ave* bin mad,' he blubbered in his mind. 'But, o' corse, I'm orl right now.'

He tried to blink his tears away. He *must* be all right now! Lummy, wasn't he *forgetting*? The girl upstairs . . . the girl upstairs . . .

He managed to raise his head, and to stare upwards. Still no sound! Surely Molly Smith would have given him the comfort of a signal, if she had been able to? And, if she was not able to, why wasn't she? If only he could have shouted! He was lost without his 'Oi!' He tried to blow, but his mouth was blocked up, and you can't aim at the ceiling with your nose.

Suddenly he became conscious of a new thing in the room. It was small and dazzlingly white, and it was on the floor. It gave him a start. How could new things appear in rooms unless somebody entered to put them there? Lummy! *Had* somebody entered? That thought gave him another start. Perhaps, while he had been mad, somebody had come into the room and placed the white thing there!

Then he found out what it was. It was a little spot of moonlight.

He concentrated on it. It was something to do. He watched it grow less intense and expand, then become a point again, then vanish, then reappear. Clouds in the night sky have no knowledge of the queer antics they play in rooms! Presently the spot of light expanded definitely, painting the whole floor silver with a rapid brush. The brush swept from the window to the back wall. It illuminated, crudely and callously, Ben's silent companion. For the first time Ben saw the features in all their distinctness.

Face down, the dead man had borne some vague resemblance to the fellow-being who had killed him. Face up, he looked quite different. Not so old. Not so large boned. Not so expressive of rugged strength. Yet there was a certain similarity, even face up, that bothered Ben for a while. Something joined them together. Something linked them. And, all at once, Ben got it. It was criminality.

''E wasn't no detective,' he thought. 'Wrong 'uns, the pair of 'em!'

As he stared at the moonlit form, a shadow suddenly passed over it. Not, this time, the vague shadow of a distant cloud, but the distinct shadow of something infinitely closer. Something immediately outside the window, in fact.

The shadow paused. A second shadow joined it, making two long black strips over the head and body of the corpse.

Ben did not turn his head. He knew well enough whose the shadows were. The owner of one of them laughed, confirming the knowledge.

'Pretty picture, isn't it?' came Greene's voice outside the window.

'It's got Madame Tussaud's beaten to a frazzle!' came Faggis's response. 'Talk about the Chamber of Horrors!'

'Yer right,' agreed Ben, in the silence of his thoughts. 'If I was ter see meself lookin' like I do, my 'eart wouldn't stand it.'

'Think he's dead yet?' queried Greene.

'Fancy he must be,' answered Faggis. 'Let's go in and poke him.'

'What for?'

'Just to see. If he's not, we could raise his gag a bit to cover his nose.'

There was a pause. Ben kept his bulging eyes glued

on the shadows. When they moved, which way would it be? Towards him or away from him?

They moved towards him. Ben's heart leapt. Lummy, yer've *gotter* 'ave yer nose! But the footsteps died away instead of coming closer, and then he realised that shadows sometimes played dirty tricks on you like that. He'd hit one once that was a mile off.

'They've gorn ter the boat,' he thought. 'When the moon come up they was goin' ter, wasn't they?'

And now there was only Sims. But Sims was worse than a dozen Greenes and Faggises. Sims was the one you really needed out of the way . . .

Another shadow fell upon the moonlit corpse. Ben was so used to the corpse by now that he hardly noticed it. He was using the corpse as a mirror, or as a cinema screen across which moving silhouettes flitted. The new silhouette was as unmistakable as the departed ones had been. It was Sims's silhouette. And he was chuckling. As the others had. But Sims's chuckle was softer and infinitely more unpleasant. It was the chuckle of a mind that moved in a much larger circle.

'Git hon, git hon,' thought Ben, as Sims's shadow paused.

'Still comfortable?' inquired the shadow.

'I'm dead,' decided Ben.

'Pretend, by all means, if it amuses you,' said the shadow. 'The real thing will come along in good time. It never spoils by anticipation.'

The shadow slipped along the corpse's form, slid off the head, and disappeared. Ben put a question direct to God.

'Why ain't people nice ter me?' he asked. 'Did yer tell 'em not ter be?'

Sims's footsteps did not vanish with his shadow. They

entered the hut, paused at the parlour door, and then began ascending the creaking wooden stairs to the floor above. The soft chuckle accompanied them.

'Yer know,' Ben told himself suddenly, 'I don't think I can stick no more.'

As he came to this decision, a new head appeared at the window.

24

Spain Intervenes

The new head was different from any of the other heads. It was small, and it had beady eyes, and it was scrubby. A month's tangle concealed the lower portion, and two lips an inch apart were only visible because Nature had originally designed them to protrude. Such complexion as was discernible was pasty yellow. Above the beady eyes were bushy eyebrows which, like the lips, protruded in obedience to a mistaken theory that the world needed to see them. And above the eyebrows was an orange handkerchief, more sensibly concealing whatever lay behind.

Ben saw this head direct, not first in its shadowed form, for he had removed his gaze from the corpse and had been staring at the window when it appeared.

If Ben thought the head looked terrible, the head returned the compliment. The protruding lips increased the space between them to two inches, and in the process revealed three yellow teeth. The beady eyes swelled like pop-corn. The bushy eyebrows rose into a loose flap of the orange handkerchief and stayed there. But whatever spectacle Ben presented to that astounded gaze, it did not outdo the spectacle presented by the gazer himself. 'Gawd, 'e's worse 'n me!' thought Ben aghast, and he was right. The Chamber of Horrors was now outside the window.

For several seconds the two faces stared at each other, transfixed and motionless. Then the face outside the window disappeared. The thing to do was to pretend that it had never really been there at all, and Ben was pretending hard when it came back again for a second look.

It had come suddenly before. Now it came slowly, a bit at a time. It stopped half-way, revealing only one yellow cheek and one beady eye; and so it remained. Something had impeded its hesitating rematerialisation.

The something was not outside. It was in the room. The single eye had caught sight of the second inmate lying on the ground. The sight of the second inmate evidently created as much astonishment as the sight of the first. For two seconds the eye hung there. Then it dropped abruptly below the level of the window frame, like an over-ripe plum from a tree.

It was no good pretending any more. Ben fell back upon another device. 'P'r'aps I'm dead,' he thought, 'and this is the fust thing yer see.' If this were so, then death was vastly overrated.

Would the apparition appear a third time? Yes, it did. But not now at the window. It appeared at the door. The shock of this caused Ben's heart to loop the loop, because he had still been staring at the window and had not heard a single sound. How had the man slipped into the house without a sound? Didn't Spaniards 'ave no feet? 'Now 'e'll throw 'is sirocco at me,' thought Ben, 'and that'll hend it.'

He forgot that he had decided he was already dead.

The face in the doorway topped a body no bigger than Ben's own. The orange handkerchief glowed quite low in the aperture. Probably the man was bending, which would reduce his height, but, even so, the dimly-seen figure was obviously not that of a giant. 'Why don't 'e chuck 'is sirocco, or come in?' wondered Ben. 'I thort Spanish blokes was quick, but this 'un's a local—stop at orl stashuns—'

The next instant the local proved that it could be an express when it tried. It was in the room in a flash, and the door was closed. Footsteps resounded on the ceiling above.

The footsteps crossed the ceiling. A door above was opened, and gently closed. The figure by the parlour door leaned against it, with sudden weariness. It seemed to be trembling.

The footsteps descended the creaking stairs. They came slowly and rather heavily. The significance of this did not dawn upon Ben till later. All he could think of at the moment was, 'Will they stop at the bottom, or will they go on?' The figure leaning against the door was evidently thinking the same thing.

They did not stop at the bottom. They crossed the small space of passage, and left the house. 'Is that good, or ain't it?' wondered Ben. He tossed up in his mind, and the coin came down heads. But he had forgotten to call.

The man by the door evidently thought it was good. A faint sigh came from him, and as he moved away from the door Ben realised for the first time the man's condition. He was almost collapsing, and a dark stain on the orange handkerchief, unnoticed till now, gave an index to the reason.

''Corse—this is the bloke wot *orter've* bin 'ere when *we*

come 'ere!' Ben thought in an illuminating flash; 'but the feller on the grahnd comes along first, afore us, and give 'im one, and then 'e 'ops it, and nah 'e's back agine, wonderin' wot's wot!'

Yes, that seemed to fit it. But in that case why was this fellow afraid of Sims? Sims would be his pal. The answer to the question came in another illuminating flash.

'If 'e don't know wot's wot, then 'e don't know 'oo's 'oo! And that's why 'e's kep' aht o' the way!'

Working on this theory, Ben watched the newcomer closely. Watched him pause as he reached the figure on the ground. Watched him stoop. Watched the look of mingled fear and ferocity that sprang into the ugly face, displacing for an instant its bewilderment. Watched him suddenly rise erect, and lean against the wall, and close his eyes. Watched him open them again to stare at the silent watcher.

'Now 'e's tryin' ter figure *me* hout,' thought Ben. 'P'r'aps 'e thinks *I* done the dead bloke in—and then some'ow got tied hup like this arterwards.'

Strewth! Here was an idea! The fellow who had killed the man on the ground would be on the side of the newcomer. If Ben pretended he was that fellow, he would get the newcomer on his side. And if he pretended that he had got tied up by the man who had just left the hut—that was, Sims—then the newcomer would think Sims was on the side of the man on the ground, and might help Ben against him!

But how was he going to pretend all that in Spanish? It was hard enough to know what it meant in plain English!

He began by nodding his head up and down, and rolling his eyes towards the corpse. The newcomer blinked at him, and suddenly shot out:

'*Quein? . . .*'

Ben nodded harder, to imply that he absolutely agreed. The man seemed vaguely impressed. He raised his hand to his forehead, and spoke again.

'*Que debo hacer?*'

Ben nodded harder still. He meant, 'Certainly, with knobs on.' The man drew a little closer, and suddenly pointed to the figure on the floor. Now Ben nodded so hard that his head nearly came off. Then he stopped and sniffed. The sniff meant, 'This is orl I can do, you durned idjit! Carn't you see? Ain't yer got no brains?'

The man proved he had. He came close to Ben, peered into his face, fumbled with the gag, and loosened it.

The emotion of finding his mouth free was temporarily incapacitating. Ben tried to speak, but failed. His mouth seemed to have forgotten what mouths did. After swallowing twenty-four times, however, at first singly and then in couples, he felt that he had cleared his throat for action, and he muttered:

'Thankeo!'

His deliverer shook his head. Ben tried 'Thanki-vitch,' but it went no better, and his deliverer still shook his head.

'*No comprendo,*' he mumbled.

'Sime 'ere,' whispered Ben; 'but 'ave a shot at this. Undo me armeo!'

'*Espero—*'

'Yus, we'll tork abart that later! Undo me armeo! Rahnd me middleo. Fer Gawd's sake, espero me belteo.'

Something got across. The Spaniard's fingers began fumbling again, while Ben suddenly looked towards the window. If Sims's figure were to pass that little space of light . . .

188

'Mike 'asteo!' muttered Ben anxiously. 'Wot's the matteo?'

Something was clearly the matter. The Spaniard's fingers were very weak. All at once, Ben forgot his own sorrows and became acutely conscious of the Spaniard's. Lummy, he did look ill! Tottering, he was! . . .

The belt grew looser.

'*Esta asi bien?*' gasped the Spaniard.

'Nigi novi novgrod,' replied Ben, trying to be matey.

Then next moment he had slipped his arms out of the belt, and the Spaniard had sunk down on to the floor.

''Ere, stick ter it, me lad!' whispered Ben. 'I'll be with yer in a miniteo. I'll bet yer ain't as badeo as yer lookeo. Got a knife?'

The Spaniard did not reply.

'Oi!' muttered Ben. 'Knifeo! Wotcher call it—sirocco? Thing yer cuts cheeseo! Oi!'

But the Spaniard was not interested. Something had happened in his throat. He lay quite motionless.

'Gawd, I b'leeve 'e's gorn!' thought Ben.

He fought a sudden emotion. It was silly, of course. The fellow was ugly and a wrong 'un . . . But it's funny how, sometimes, it gets you.

25

How Mr Sims Killed Ben

There was no doubt about it. The little, ugly faced Spaniard was dead. After being attacked he had remained hidden away somewhere, and now he had staggered back to perform a last strange service to a fellow-sufferer before answering his final call. His life had not been too good. But neither had it been too easy. Our worst acts are generally the sum of our greatest difficulties, and possibly Fate in a kindly mood had sent him tottering back to commit an act that might stand in his stead when his case was being considered.

But what happens after we are silent and still is beyond our knowledge today, as it was beyond Hamlet's. All we know is what happens before. Ben, in his ignorance of the future and of its value, regarded the ugly faced Spaniard who had loosened his cords and then died with exonerating sympathy. Your nature goes with your face, and you didn't make your face. Well, there you are! Who's to blame?

Suddenly Ben realised, in a panic, that he was doing

nothing. He must get busy! Sims might return any minute! Feverishly he began to struggle out of his cords, and while he struggled he was visited by some strange thoughts. He did not let the thoughts interfere with his progress; this formed a sort of running accompaniment.

One strange thought was this. He was in a room with two dead men, and both of them had helped him. It almost seemed as though people were born on condition that they did not assist Ben while they were alive, but as soon as they died and the oath no longer held, they did what they could. One dead man had freed his arms and the other had scratched his nose. 'Wunner if I'll 'elp hennybody arter *I'm* gorn?' wondered Ben. 'Barrin' worms!'

Another strange thought came in the form of a tune. Ben only knew three tunes well. One was 'Three Sailors of Bristol City.' Another was 'Three Blind Mice.' He liked that one; it seemed to go with cheese. (Of course, you don't count 'God Save the King'.) The tune that came to him now was 'Ten Little Indians.' At first he didn't know why. Then the reason dawned upon him lugubriously. The ten little victims grew less and less. His own little deader boys were growing more and more!

'I 'opes they stop at two,' he thought.

And hastily set aside the reflection that things generally went in threes.

He was free now all but his feet. There were some knots there he didn't seem able to manage. He didn't know whether it was because they were difficult knots, or because his fingers seemed all thumbs.

'Afore yer died, Charlie,' he murmured to the Spaniard, 'I arst yer if yer 'ad a knife. Mind if I look?'

He bent down. He could do that. His hands played

gingerly over the limp form and suddenly yelped. He thought the form had pinched him.

But it wasn't a pinch, it was a prick. With hopefully thumping heart, he felt about for the safe end. He found it, and drew slowly from the tumbled clothing a gleaming thing.

'Strewth! 'Is sirocco!' he blinked.

It was a bit of all right!

'Seems as if yer carn't do enuff fer me, Charlie,' he muttered. He did not realise how much more Charlie was going to do for him in a few minutes. 'I like you better'n the hother one, and that's a fack. Charles II's the lad fer me!'

He had to go on talking. It was the only way to prevent himself from fainting.

He cut the final cords with Charles II's 'sirocco'. Now he was free! He lifted a leg in triumph, and the other gave way under him.

He had hardly recovered from this shock before he received another. There was a sound outside the window, and Sims went by.

Ben had been sitting. Now he went flat. If Sims turned his head and, looked in, it would be the end! The two dead men *would* be augmented to three! Fortunately, Sims did not turn his head. His mind happened to be in the room immediately above. But when he had passed the window, and was turning into the hut, Ben suddenly came into his mind, and he walked to the parlour door.

Ben, on the other side of the door, fought a violent desire to bellow with fear. He remembered that he couldn't always control the desire when it came, and he found himself hugging Charles II as though for protection.

The door handle rattled, but the door did not open. Only Sims's voice entered.

'I've not forgotten you, Ben,' purred the voice. 'I'll be down in two or three minutes—and then I'll look in and say good-bye.'

What was that? Look in and say good-bye? . . .

The footsteps resounded again. Up the creaking stairs. Into the room above. Half-way across the ceiling. Pause . . .

'I gotter *do* somethink,' thought Ben.

He disengaged himself from Charles II with scarcely a shudder. Queer how one got used to dead people! A little more of this, and he'd qualify for a grave digger. Live people were much more trouble . . . The steps began to resound above again.

'Wot abart standin' by the door,' thought Ben; 'and stickin' the sirocco in 'im as 'e hopens it?'

He visualised the operation. It wasn't nice. Besides, he felt so groggy he doubted whether he could be quick and strong enough for it.

'Wot abart pertendin' ter be dead, and then, when 'e bends hover me, gettin' 'im hunder the chin?'

That didn't seem nice, either.

And then came the staggering idea. It was so staggering that, for quite five seconds, Ben just sat frozen with it. And they were not ordinary seconds, such as you are passing while you read. Each second carried life or death. When they had gone, Ben rose, and turned towards the dead Spaniard. The idea still froze him, but his limbs had begun to respond to it because his brain could not find any flaw in it. Will-power followed brain and ignored emotion. Hardly realising that he was doing more than working out a stupendous theory in his mind, he raised the body of the Spaniard, and began to draw it upwards towards the chair.

Somehow he got it into the chair. He never knew how. He swore, when considering the matter in retrospect, that the body helped him, and in reference to this astonishing claim it must be recalled that Ben was developing a theory that men only assisted him to live after they themselves were dead. You and I—receiving perhaps more assistance in life—cannot accept Ben's theory. It is probable that Ben got the dead Spaniard into the chair because, when men are desperate, they often confound all logic. What is your best pace for the mile? Put a hungry tiger behind you, and you will beat it.

Once the Spaniard was in the chair, the rest was comparatively easy. While the footsteps still resounded in the room above, Ben tied the helpless limbs, and gagged the mouth that was already beyond the power of speech. "Ope yer don't mind, Charlie!' he mumbled once, partly in response to an unnecessarily worried conscience, and partly because the Spaniard's spirit, now escaped from the useless flesh, might be lurking in some dark corner with disapproval.

Well, if it was, the risk had to be taken. The Spaniard's spirit was less of a menace than Mr Sims's flesh! Working feverishly, Ben completed his gruesome job, the final act of which was to pull off the orange handkerchief that had bound the hanging head.

And, as he did so, the footsteps above crossed the ceiling for the last time, and began, slowly and heavily, to descend.

Ben dived for the table, and crept under it.

The footsteps on the stairs grew nearer and nearer. Twice they paused, and if Ben had been in a condition to wonder about anything save his own skin he might have wondered why these pauses occurred, and why the steps were so slow and ponderous. Yet, after all, the cause of the second pause seemed obvious enough, for this pause occurred when the bottom of the stairs had been reached.

But why was it so long?

It seemed interminable. Once or twice there was a faint sound, as though something were being put down or moved; but to Ben, quaking under the table, the sound was indecipherable, and it was not till later that he divined its cause.

'P'r'aps 'e's fergot me,' thought Ben.

The next instant, the thought was proved wrong. The door began to open.

Ben watched the bottom of the door. This was all he could see. It came towards him, opening inwards, till the advancing corner was only about three feet away. Then two boots appeared. Large boots, covered with dust. And the bottoms of the trousers, chopped off just below the knees by the edge of the table.

The moment that followed was agonising. Sims, standing in the doorway, was looking at Ben's substitute. The chair to which the substitute was bound stood in shadow, for the moonlight had not yet reached that corner of the room, but the sharp silver line that marked the boundary of the moon's progress on the floor was only a few inches away from the chair legs, and if Sims waited he would see the Spaniard revealed, like a statue unveiled . . .

'Dead, Ben?' inquired Sims's voice.

Ben's heart thundered in reply.

'From your position, I'm inclined to believe that you are!' went on Sims. 'You're a crafty fellow, Ben, but if you were alive I doubt whether you could hang your head in such a realistic fashion. And they seem to have knocked your head about a bit, too. Very rough of them, very rough! I'd speak to them about it if I were seeing them again. But, unfortunately, I won't be seeing them again. Meetings and partings, eh? Life is made up of them.'

He paused. Ben kept his eyes fixed on the boots, imploring them mutely to turn and disappear. They did not turn. They came forward a step.

'I wonder, Ben, whether I've told you too much?' said Sims. 'Perhaps I have. And perhaps, when Greene and Faggis return, you may pass on what I've told you to them? Yes, I think I'd better make quite *sure* you're dead, eh?'

The boots advanced again. They were now up to the table. Impulsively, Ben raised his knife a few inches.

'Another step, and I'll pin yer ter the grahnd with me sirocco!' he thought, trembling violently.

The boots continued to move. He stretched forward to strike. Then the boots grew dim as a cloud began to cross the moon's surface. The floor became heavy and shadowy once more.

'On second thoughts, I don't think I'll go too near you, Ben,' murmured Sims. 'Now that the moon has gone in I can't see you very distinctly, but that rope round your legs doesn't look too good to me. Suppose you're not properly bound, and are waiting till I reach you to spring up at me? I've had that trick played on me before. No, I'll shoot you, instead. From here. It'll be safer.'

Ben laid his knife down and raised his moist hands to his ears. He was sweating hard, and he did not think he could bear to hear himself shot.

There was no sound, however. Sims worked quietly and with quiet weapons. A sudden flutter of the already limp form in the chair was the only sign that a bullet had post-humously entered it.

'Good-night, Ben,' said Mr Sims.

A moment later, the bottom of the door swung to again, and Ben was alone.

He lay quite flat for two minutes, while perspiration ran all over him. He was as still and as limp as the Spaniard who had just performed his last service for him. Then, suddenly, he raised his head.

Hoofs! Hoofs on the road! Growing fainter and fainter and fainter!

26

Life Grows Worse and Worse

The sound of the hoofs brought Ben out of his lethargy. Forgetting he was under a table he sprang to his feet, and the resulting impact produced another form of oblivion. When he recovered, the hoofs were no longer audible.

Now he crawled out, and stood up carefully. Speed was vital, but so was caution. Another knock like that and he wouldn't have any head left—and now, if ever, was the time he wanted it!

He walked dizzily to the door. The moon emerged from the clouds again as he opened it, and a little patch of light streamed through a small window in the passage. It revealed the emptiness of the passage, and the bottom stair. Ben took a breath, and turned towards the bottom stair.

There should have been no need to take that breath. Five people who might have murdered him, three of whom had actually attempted to do so, no longer threatened him. Sims, Greene and Faggis were out of the house, and the other two were out of the world. But stairs, particularly if they were wooden and uncarpeted, always had an unnerving effect upon Ben. They were in the same category as corners and cupboards, and just as liable to spring surprises. And then these were foreign stairs. You couldn't trust anything foreign, never mind what it was!

There was another reason, however, why Ben took that breath, and why he ascended with such palpitations. The memory of the slow, heavy steps he had heard upon them twice seemed to fit somehow into the sound of the hoofs, like pieces of a jig-saw puzzle, and he didn't like the picture they made.

On every stair he told himself that he would find everything all right in the upper room towards which he was ascending. On every stair he believed he was wrong. And when at last he reached the top, found the door of the room ajar, and poked his head in, he discovered his worst fears justified. The room was empty.

''E got 'em both dahn,' thought Ben, 'and now 'e's gorn orf with 'em!'

Yes, that was obvious. The tumbled little bed showed that it had lately had an occupant. The occupant's form could almost be discerned in outline. But now the occupant had been carted away, and also the girl who had been deputed to sit by her and look after her.

And neither of them had offered any audible protest! That fact impressed itself upon Ben with all its sinister implications.

Subconsciously Ben pieced together the probable movements of Sims after Greene and Faggis had started for the beach. He had found and harnessed the mule. To a little cart, very likely. He had returned to the hut and ascended the stairs—light, soft steps—and had descended with one of the girls—slow, heavy steps—occasionally pausing to shift the burden, or open a door, or listen. Twice he had made this journey, and each time the girl he had brought down had uttered no sound. And now they were being driven away to . . . where?

As the question rose miserably in Ben's mind, his eye fell upon a little piece of paper lying under a chair. It was the chair by the bed, upon which Molly Smith had presumably sat. He lurched towards it eagerly, stooped, toppled, and picked the paper up sitting. On it was written:

'*Don Manuel. Villabanzos.*'

Ben stared at it with almost tearful gratitude. 'It's fer me,' he thought. 'The nime of the second 'otel! Doncher worry, miss—I'll be there!'

He clambered up from the floor, and sat on the side of the bed. He resisted a nearly overwhelming desire to lie on the bed. He knew that, if he gave way to the desire, he would close his weary eyes and would not open them again until he saw Greene and Faggis bending over him. Yes, lummy! Greene and Faggis! He must leave before *they* got back! He had a double reason for continuing on his way with as little delay as possible.

Sims would be ahead of him, and they would be behind him. As usual, his mission was to be the middle of the sandwich!

Still, there were one or two small matters to be attended to before he left the hut with all its gloomy associations. The first was food. He wanted a bit in his stomach and a bit in his pocket. Descending the stairs, he hunted around, but he couldn't find a crumb. Sims had taken the sack, and had evidently cleared out the larder as well.

Next, weapons. 'I've got me sirocco,' he thought; 'but if there's hennything helse knockin' abart, I might as well 'ave it.' He found a hammer, and put it in his pocket with satisfaction. It went right through the pocket on to the floor, so he picked it up and tried the other pocket. This proved all right for hammers.

Lastly, the two dead men. Answering an odd impulse for which he could not account, he paid a final visit to the room in which they awaited some final ministration from the living. There was not much Ben could do, and there was no call for him to do anything; but somehow he hated the idea of leaving the Spaniard bound, and he loosened the cords that secured him and then eased the body to the floor.

The two bodies now lay side by side. It gave Ben a funny feeling to look at them. Had they truly, only a short while ago, been at each other's throats? Rapacity and life had divided them. Peace and death brought them together again, destroying their quarrel and their menace. 'Good luck ter yer,' muttered Ben. And shoved the table-cloth over them.

Then, rather ashamed of himself, he left the hut, gave an anxious glance westwards in the direction of the coast, and turned his face eastwards.

He had used several minutes in these preliminaries to departure, but two of the preliminaries had been practical, and only the third sentimental; and even the sentimental preliminary had been necessary for his peace of mind. If he had left the little Spaniard bound in the chair, the vision would have haunted him horribly. It was much pleasanter to think of the poor, ugly fellow lying quietly under the table-cloth, next to his old foe . . .

The moon was high, and the track, as Ben stepped out

upon it from the shadows of the cottage, was dazzlingly clear. If the moonlight showed up the dizzy valleys and gorges as well as the track, and made the mountain-tops look like great white ghosts, it was nevertheless welcome. In darkness, this journey would have been impossible.

After all, you could keep clear of the gorges if you walked straight and didn't wobble, and you needn't look at the ghostly mountain peaks, not if you didn't want to! And you didn't want to. One of the peaks was like a sword point, and another was like a witch's face, and another was like a crocodile's open mouth. And no matter how fast you walked, they all seemed to be walking along with you, telling you that you weren't going to get away from them and so you needn't think it!

'Funny thing abart mountins,' reflected Ben. 'Yer can pass a 'ouse in a tick and 'ave done with it, but a mountin sticks ter yer like. Wunner why it is?'

But he soon stopped wunnering. The mountains were on his right and, the valleys were on his left, and his reflective mood had brought him too near the valleys. He veered away swiftly, and, as though in response, a valley suddenly darted towards him, seeming to slash his road in two with a vast black knife.

A deep gully ran in southwards from the left, stabbing the mountainside which had gradually crept forward from the right to the very edge of the track. The gully ended in a point, and was perhaps more like a black arrow than a knife, an arrow that had been shot by some invisible giant from the north and had wounded sheer rock. A hundred yards ahead of the spot where Ben paused and gasped at space was another spot where, presumably, he had to get to. He could see the track gleaming as it emerged from the dark gash in the mountainside. Before the giant had sent this shattering arrow, the road had probably run straight across this great dividing gap, but now one had to turn sharply to the right, and creep round the wound.

'Well,' murmured Ben, 'wot I ses is, wot yer gotter, yer gotter, and I gotter!'

So he turned to the right, and crept.

On one side, sheer rock. On the other, sheer precipice. Immediately beneath, a narrow, rough track that was sometimes not more than nine feet across. Nine feet from rock to precipice. And a precipice, you understand, that to look over was almost to fall over. Its carpet, surely, was in another world!

Ben began erect. Then he found himself stooping. In that position you could hit the mountain more quickly if it came too close, or dart away from the precipice if it advanced too near. Then, when the precipice insisted on advancing too near, and the mountain refused to go back, he found himself crawling. After all, nobody was looking.

Crawling, he neared the extremity of the incision. He wasn't looking at it, but he was conscious of it, because the precipice was narrowing and the wall of cliff on the opposite side was looming closer and closer. It seemed to be pressing down upon him. Trying to prevent him from breathing. The silence became more intense. Not that he had heard anything before, but sound, as a theory, had existed. Here, in this appalling, suffocating vastness—not the vastness one escaped in but the vastness that squeezed one into nothingness—even the theory of sound ceased to be.

'Gawd! Where's me 'eart!' thought Ben.

Not even that!

Then, with a sharp crack, the theory of sound swept back.

'Oi!' thought Ben. 'Some 'un's shootin' me!'

He tried to lie flat, but couldn't, because he was. The cracking continued, then a little dribble, as of a dancing stone. The stone danced during a second of freedom after a century of captivity. *Plop!* The swansong rose from the depths, where the stone had reached captivity again for yet another century.

Thus Ben's crawling body influenced the history of geology.

''Ere it is agine,' thought Ben.

His heart had returned, and was thumping the ground like a hammer.

He crawled on. Now he reached the extremity of the wound. The spot where it had hurt, and where the mountain had roared, 'Ow!' How was the track going to negotiate this cruel V? Suppose . . . it didn't? The thought brought sweat.

The track didn't negotiate the V. A few boards did. Ben crept up to the boards. Blackness shrieked at him. From above and below and all sides. Some of the sweat dripped down into the blackness below. For the first time in his life, Ben pitied the stars.

He repeated his slogan. 'Wot yer gotter, yer gotter.' He got to the middle of the boards. Then, they swayed. He grabbed them to hold them up. Then, doubtful whether this was scientific, he grabbed himself, to hold himself up. The boards went on swaying.

He tried to move, but failed. He was holding himself too tightly. The situation grew more and more impossible. He decided to think of all the nice times he had had in the past. He found he hadn't had any. The situation now became quite impossible. If you can't hang on to your past while you're going into the future, what's the use? He gave up trying, and did whatever he was told to. Apparently he was told to start singing 'Three Sailors of Bristol City.'

Suddenly he stopped singing. He didn't know why. Again he was merely doing what he was told. Had the world he was about to leave had enough of the song?

All at once he discovered there was another reason why he had stopped singing. Voices were on the track behind him. Greene's and Faggis's.

27

The End of the Bridge

The voices grew nearer and nearer. Vague murmurings turned into coherent sound. A definite growl came from Faggis. An oath issued from the third officer. Thirty-five yards, thirty yards, twenty-five yards . . .

'Damn the darkness!'

That was Greene. Twenty yards.

'Black as hell!'

That was Faggis. Fifteen yards.

It is said that a chicken can run for a second or two after it has been decapitated. Similarly, Ben's mind went on working after all was lost. While the fifteen yards became fourteen and the fourteen thirteen, two solutions occurred to him. One was to roar like a lion and the other was to make a noise like a carpet. Neither would have helped him, but he was still earnestly considering their respective merits when Faggis suddenly paused and saved the necessity of a decision.

'Look here, Greene,' said Faggis. 'I wonder if we're a couple of fools?'

'Speak for your own half of the couple,' replied Greene. 'Come on!'

'Maybe it's your half'll be the fool if you do go on,' retorted Faggis. 'However, don't let me stop you.'

'Hell! What's the matter with you?'

'I'm trying to grow wise in my old age, Greene,' grunted Faggis. 'D'you suppose we may be on our second wild goose chase?'

There was a short silence, broken by the splutter of a match. Greene was lighting a cigarette. While Ben was praying that its feeble illumination would not reveal him, it suddenly went out.

'Hey! What's that for?' demanded Greene's indignant voice.

'For safety,' came Faggis's, in a lower key. 'How d'you know Sims isn't watching us?'

'What do you mean?' Greene's voice was still tinged with indignation, but it was noticeably quieter.

'What I say, Greene,' answered Faggis. 'He's up to any trick, that blackguard. May be waiting up at the end there to pounce upon us and pitch us over.'

'Like to see him try!'

'Well, I wouldn't! He's got the gun! And he's used it once since we last saw him, don't forget.'

'On that ugly blighter?'

'Yep!'

'That's where you're wrong. That was the fellow he expected to welcome us. It was the other darned blighter shot him.'

'Bah! You're guessing!'

'And, of course, *you* know!'

'No, I *don't* know! And that's why I'm wondering

whether we're a couple of fools to go on any farther till we *do*!'

'What's the alternative?' demanded Greene.

'Going back,' answered Faggis. 'Going back, and having a proper look round.'

Greene considered the suggestion. The men were clearly out of tune with each other, but neither could afford to ignore any proposal that might be good. Greene decided, however, that this proposal was not good.

'I tell you, there's no need to look round more than we've done already,' he said. 'It's obvious that Sims sent us to the beach to get rid of us. That's why we turned back, isn't it? It's obvious he wanted us out of the way so that he'd have time to clear off with the girl—'

'With *both* girls, you mean,' corrected Sims. 'And the scarecrow. The whole damned lot of 'em. How's he done it? And why's he done it? If he'd wanted to get rid of us, wouldn't he have got rid of them too?'

'P'r'aps he did.'

'Then where were they?'

'Never heard of a precipice?'

'Precipice your foot! He's got the scarecrow bound up and gagged, and you suggest he unties him and throws him over a precipice. And that girl—d'you think *she* wouldn't put up a fight—'

'I tell you, you don't know Sims—'

'And I tell you, you're too cocksure of your own little bit of knowledge, Greene! You talk about things being obvious, but nothing's obvious! Except that something darned queer happened while we were away. How do we know that Sims didn't have to sheer off for a while, and wait? Why, man,' Faggis went on, developing his theory, 'they may all be back at the cottage now, while we're plodding on like a couple of silly rabbits . . . See here, Greene! Maybe that's another of his little wheezes! Hey, yes! What about *this*? If he's got into any trouble—or been cut off—or if it suited his purpose for any other reason, how do we know *he's* not sneaking down to the beach, and making off again in the boat?'

'And what about *this*?' growled Greene, his indignation returning on the tide of his scepticism. 'Are you doing any good by raising your voice and shouting your ideas to the world? You told me to be quiet just now, and here you are shouting like a cup-tie crowd!'

'Oh, shut up—'

'I'm not going to shut up. You talk about fools, Faggis, but the difference between you and me is that sometimes I stop being one. The trouble is, you've got no *brain*. You can stick a man in the back, but you need someone to tell you when and how to do it. You get the wind up—'

'Wind up—'

'. . . The wind up, I said, and I stick to it! All these mad half-baked ideas of yours are the result of the fear that's working behind your drawl! I'll tell you where I'm smarter than you, Faggis. I know when I'm in the presence of a superior, and you don't. Sims is my superior, and I'm yours, and the sooner you realise it, the better it'll be. Well, *I'm* going on. What are *you* going to do? If you want to turn back, don't talk about it, but do it. I shan't weep any tears.'

There came the sound of a sharp breath. An exclamation followed it.

'Let go, you blasted fool!' cried Greene.

'Wind up, eh?' drawled Faggis, but with fury beneath the drawl. 'Carry on, Greene—but remember I can give *you* the wind up any moment I want to. Just like that! See?'

Another exclamation, low and sullen. A short silence. Then the third officer gulped:

'Yes, we *are* fools, Faggis. Panic and silly pride can drive you to murder, and my own folly drives you into a panic. Well, that little scene's over, so let's see whether we can now behave like adults again, and get a move on!'

He had scarcely finished speaking when another little scene, waiting only ten yards away, was preluded by a sudden cracking sound.

'What's that?' exclaimed Faggis sharply.

The sound was repeated, and now more loudly. A board seemed to be splitting somewhere, and the echoes in the V-shaped cleft ricochetted from rock to rock like thunder. The men swung round towards the point whence the noise appeared to come—ten yards ahead, where the track hit the deeply shadowed angle and twisted back on itself . . .

Crack! Split! Boom!

Then a pause. Then, a tiny crashing clatter, as the descending wood struck naked rock two thousand feet below.

'Well?' muttered Faggis.

But Greene was waiting no longer. He was hastening forward, and, as he hastened, there came another crack and another split, and more wood dropped swirling down into the void.

Greene did not know what was happening, but he had to know. Ever since he and Faggis had left the hut with the intention of returning to the beach he had been dogged by doubts and worried by ignorance. The return to the hut, despite its gruesome evidence of certain very definite happenings, did not remove the veil. They had left the hut again and had walked on into the veil. Greene had told Faggis that Sims was obviously double-crossing them, but this did not mean that he was certain of it in his own heart. It merely meant that with a man like Faggis—a man large-limbed and small-brained, and dangerous on account of both—definiteness was sometimes the only policy. You had to pretend to be sure, just to avoid following theories less probable or frankly impossible. Actually, Greene was certain of nothing beyond his own perplexity.

And now, on a track over which Sims might have travelled before them, a series of miniature explosions was occurring. The truth of these could be discovered, at least.

He reached the point from which the explosions came, with Faggis a couple of yards behind him. The track ended a short space before the extreme point of the cleft. It began again across a black chasm of space, some eight or nine feet distant, and spanning the chasm was a single, swaying board.

And even as they stared at the board, it vanished from their sight into the pool of velvet.

Then another sound fell upon their ears. It was probably the strangest sound that had ever been known by these primeval rocks. From the shadows across the chasm came a hysterical voice warbling:

> *'There were three sailors of Bristol City,*
> *There were three sailors of Bristol City,*
> *   And they were shipwrecked on the sea—*
> *   And they were shipwrecked on the sea-ee-ee!'*

28

Through the Night

Ben never knew how he got across that bridge. He never knew how he loosened the boards and sent them down into the depths. Perhaps they became loose under his frenzy. Perhaps he merely completed work commenced by Sims, who had traversed the fragile bridge before him and who may have been impressed with its possibilities. Perhaps anything. He was not in a condition to record or to remember. If you tell him that he stood on the ledge on the other side of the chasm singing 'Three Sailors of Bristol City,' like his own ghost, to Greene and Faggis on the opposite shore, he will blink amazedly and say, 'Go hon!'

The simple fact was, Ben was beyond knowing. There was just his body and the instinct of self-preservation. It is a collaboration that has saved many a drunken man's life, when sober he would have perished.

Sometimes, however, during the strange period that followed, even the instinct of self-preservation deserted him, and his body was entirely in the hands of God. Otherwise he could never have revealed himself by giving a concert on the ledge, but would have crawled away noiselessly in the hope of cheating the enemy's eyes. Did the enemy shout at him, or try to reach him, or throw things at him? Again, he did not know. For at least half an hour after the sailors of Bristol City ceased to be, his mind was an utter blank; and then it only emerged from the blank for queer, distorted, and temporary excursions in the regions of consciousness.

During the blank spaces he moved and sang. One song was particularly illuminating. It ran:

> 'Three blind mice
> Three blind mice,
> Three blind mice,
> And three blind mice.'

The song will never be officially recognised by historians, since rocks cannot write. At other times the songs were wordless, being merely weird sounds emanating from an uninstructed voice—a voice that, like the rest of his internal mechanism, seemed to have become disconnected and to rattle or spill about every time the callous body or dulled emotion got a jolt.

But it is by Ben's conscious, or semi-conscious, moments that we must mark his progress and judge how the angels were looking after him.

The first moment occurred, as has been implied, in half an hour. The record of time is ours, not Ben's, for time meant nothing to him. He came out of the blackness into a space of great height and light. There were no overshadowing rocks. There were hardly any shadows at all. At the top of the sky was the moon, illuminating Ben at the top of the world.

'That's funny,' said Ben.

And slipped back into the blackness again as he said it. Like a sleep-walker, he continued on his way.

The next moment was not quite so pleasant. He was lying on the ground. A large rock was near his feet, and his eyes, gazing downwards, were staring at the world through the wrong end of the telescope. He leapt backwards, bounced against a small fir-tree, fought it, won, and begged its pardon. The victory had to be paid for, as do all victories of physical force. The toll was exertion, a pain in the forehead (for the fir-tree had put up a bit of a fight), and darkness once more.

The third moment was of longer duration. It was also more significant. It was preceded by a series of confusing black lines, as though the blackness enveloping him were thinning out yet at the same time were becoming more definite. It resolved itself into these confusing black lines. The lines streaked across his path. He lifted his feet high to avoid them. Then they turned out to be shadows. The shadows of pines, cast by a moon no longer high.

He stared at the shadows, recognising them for what they were.

'Shadders,' he said.

Yes, he knew shadders. He clung on to the knowledge. He tried to step from it to something else that would keep him from swinging back to hovering nightmares.

'Trees,' he said.

Shadders and trees. But the nightmares hovered a little closer, seeking to envelop him again.

'Me!' he cried desperately. *'Me!'*

Shadders, trees and Ben. The concrete combination was growing. The little army of solid things! But so was the blackness! . . . It was his head—if only he could get rid of that. People kept on tugging at it. Sims, Faggis, and Greene. And sometimes they swept it with a broom, sweeping everything out of it . . .

'Shoe!' he muttered.

He was resisting. Shadders, trees, Ben, and a shoe. The first three seemed reasonable, but the shoe only confused him again. What was the shoe doing? Shoes didn't grow in forests! Or did they? Small shoes like this? Girls' shoes? Girls' shoes . . . girls' shoes . . .

Suddenly he stooped closer. The blackness stooped with him. He knelt down by the shoe. He picked it up. Something familiar about it stirred his dulled memory. He strove to reach the memory. He knew it was a peaceful memory—soft and warm and comforting. He began to cry. 'I know yer, I know yer,' he whimpered. 'I'm comin' ter yer—but give us a bit of 'elp!' He raised the shoe to his cheek. He thought he heard footsteps behind him. He shouted, and fell flat. He was caught again by the Demon of Darkness.

But the one thing the Demon could not do was to prevent his progress. He got up and walked on again, through land that left no trace and hours that left no mark. And when, for the last time, he came out of the darkness, he was sitting in a long, white road, with the shoe still clasped in his hands, and a face bending over him.

To Ben's surprise he found that it was not the face of Sims or Greene or Faggis, or of anybody he knew. The discovery was reassuring, and helped to keep him steady. As a matter of fact, it was rather a pleasant face. Old and lined and wrinkled, and not in the least forbidding.

'*Buenos dias*,' said the face.

''Allo,' replied Ben feebly.

That lasted for a long time. In silence, they tried to make each other out. Each seemed a puzzle to the other. Then the face tried again.

'*Buenos dias,*' it repeated.

'Yus, so yer sed afore,' muttered Ben; 'but it don't 'elp.' The next moment, however, he understood.

'Oh—dias—now I git yer,' he nodded. 'Well, yer can see I 'aven't dias, but it's bin a near thing!'

The old man shook his head. He was doing his best, but he wasn't one of the Intellectuals. He earned his living with a spade.

'*Inglés?*' he inquired.

'In wot?' blinked Ben.

'*Inglés.*'

'If it's a drink, yus,' said Ben.

The old man looked sad, and rubbed his forehead. Evidently it was not a drink. That wasn't where you put it.

'Look 'ere, let me 'ave a try,' suggested Ben, after a pause. ''Ave yer seen a man and a couple o' gals on a moke?'

The remark seemed to excite the old Spaniard, and also to hurt him a little.

'*Usted habla demasiado deprisa!*' he exclaimed, throwing out his arms.

''Ere, one at a time!' muttered Ben, quite unconscious of the fact that the Spaniard was asking him practically the same thing. 'Well, let's try somethink helse. Wot's the time? Ter-morrer, ain't it?'

'*No hablo inglés,*' sighed the Spaniard.

''Oo?' answered Ben.

'*Habla usted espanol?*'

'Oh! Spanol. No. 'Ave yer lorst one?'

The old man scratched his chin. His expression suggested

216

that it was interesting talking to monkeys, but one had one's work to do. Still, the old fellow tried once more, and pointed to the shoe which Ben was still clutching in his hand.

'*Zapatero?*' he asked, raising his eyebrows. '*Si? Zapatero?*'

'Wot *we* want,' replied Ben, 'is a dickshonero. Gawd, *wot's* Spanish fer a drink?'

He would have given a month's cheese to know. His mouth was parched, and his head was throbbing. Just a glass of something, to get a trickle down his throat, and a couple of hours on something less hard than a road, and he'd be all right. But this well-meaning old Spanish fossil couldn't help him to either.

'*Adios,*' said the Spaniard, with a regretful shrug, and pointed to the sky. '*Va á llover.*'

'Oi!' called Ben, as he moved away.

The old man paused. He was quite a decent old chap. Acting on a sudden inspiration, and wondering why he hadn't thought of it before, Ben remembered a valuable little piece of paper in his pocket.

''Ere, 'ave a look at thiseo,' he said, 'and put us on the rodeo.' He thrust his hand in his pocket. The paper was not there. He racked his brain desperately. 'Villapansies,' he blurted. The Spaniard shook his head. 'Villabonzo,' Ben tried again.

'*Ah, Villabanzos!*' exclaimed the Spaniard.

'Yus, Villabanzos,' nodded Ben, relieved. ''Ow do I git there?'

'*Villabanzos,*' repeated the old man. '*Por dónde se va a Villabanzos?*'

''Ow many more times?' demanded Ben.

'*Villabanzos! Aguarde un momento!*' He paused and screwed up his eyes, thinking hard. Then he opened his eyes wide and cried, '*Villabanzos! Si, si! Tome usted la segunda á la izquierda. Si!*'

'Yer know, you ain't 'elpin' me at all,' grumbled Ben.

'*Entonces pregunte usted otra vez,*' beamed the old man.

He flourished his arms as though he had done something clever, but Ben didn't agree.

'Well, wot abart this part, then?' he asked. 'Don Manuel.' Somehow or other he remembered that.

'Don Manuel,' muttered the old man dubiously. His face fell. 'Don Manuel.' He shook his head. '*No conozco á nadie en esta ciudad. Lo siento mucho.*' He struck his chest. '*Villanedo, si! Villanedo! Villabanzos?*' He shook his head again.

Then, with a gloomy '*Adios,*' which this time had a note of regretful finality about it, he raised his weather-beaten hand internationally, and walked away.

The interview had not been fruitful in one sense, but it had in another. It had done something to beat back the nightmare and to restore Ben's faith. If the old man had not helped him, neither had he hit him. After all, there were a few peaceful people in the world!

Ben rose to his feet. He immediately sat down again. 'I fergòt,' he said, and remained down for ten minutes. then, rising a second time, he found that he could just manage it, and very slowly he resumed his way.

Grey clouds scudded across the sky. It was early morning, and there was a moist nip in the air. The Spaniard had told him that it looked like rain, but Ben did not know that, and was unprepared for a sudden little shower that descended on him. The shower did not last, but it spoke of others to follow.

He walked for about an hour. His pace became slower

and slower. The poignant fears of the night were no longer upon him, and he had emerged from his frenzies and his black lapses; but he was fighting against a numb depression that was settling upon him, and also an intense heaviness of his legs. Likewise, his disconcertingly parched mouth. The little shoe was the only consolation he possessed, and he hung on to it as though it were an anchor.

Presently he passed another Spaniard. Naturally they were all Spaniards, but each one surprised him. This Spaniard did not respond to his 'Oi,' so he let him go. The next one he met, however, stopped obligingly. He was large and had a fierce black beard, but you couldn't be particular.

'We ain't goin' ter waste no time this time,' decided Ben. 'Am I right fer Villabanzos? Don Manuel. And I'm illeos.'

That got it all in! But the big Spaniard with the fierce beard stared at him so hard that Ben began to grow indignant.

'Wot's up?' he demanded.

He had meant to make the demand boldly, but his voice faltered. The big Spaniard went on staring at him.

'Well, I'm no funnier than you are!' muttered Ben.

He tried to move on. The big Spaniard wouldn't let him. He picked Ben up, and slung him across his shoulder. Then, slowly, he turned, and began to walk back in the direction from which he had come.

He walked gently and smoothly. The movement was curiously peaceful. It was more than peaceful; it was soporific. 'Gawd, ain't this comf'erble,' thought Ben. And slept.

29

In a Spanish Bedroomio

Ben went to sleep on a man's back. He woke up in a bedroom. It was the most peaceful awakening he had experienced for a long while, and he could not understand it.

His body felt refreshed and his mind felt calm. The quietude was comforting, not terrifying, and even the rain that pattered outside a small window across the room added to his sense of cosiness. Why wasn't life always like this? Then it would be a bit of all right!

Beside him, on a little table, was a small bottle. P'r'aps that was something to do with it! He often slept with his mouth open, and someone might have poured some Spanish medicine down into it. He recalled a recent dream in which he had fallen under a waterfall. Yes, that was when they'd done it! But why had they done it? He wasn't ill. He was only tired.

And now he wasn't even tired! He sat up suddenly. His back stood the test. He opened and closed his mouth. No cricks. He swallowed. All nice and smooth. That Spanish physic must be some stuff! He did not realise that, quite apart from the medicine, he had just emerged from a long, natural sleep, and that nature had been working on an unfit body that refused persistently to yield to its unfitness.

Well, so much for himself. Now for others. He hoped the others would prove as satisfactory.

At first there did not seem to be any others. He imagined himself to be alone in the room. Then, however, he became conscious of a bent figure sitting in a chair a little behind the head of his bed. Just a shadow in the corner of his left eye.

As his left eye went round, the bent figure rose and came towards him. It turned out to be an old woman of about three hundred and sixty. Ben stared at her in frank amazement. He didn't know people came so old.

The old woman paused, and stared back. If Ben had never seen anything like her before, she did not appear to have seen anything like Ben before. They were exchanging totally new experiences.

'*Eh?*' she muttered, at last.

'Sime ter you, mum,' answered Ben.

The answer seemed to excite her. Her eyes lit up, and she poured out a voluble question. He got a dim impression that she was inquiring about his cabeza. Not knowing what his cabeza was, or whether it should be mentioned if he had one, he continued to stare back, which excited her all the more.

'*Haga usted el favor de responder "si" ó "no!"*' she cackled, like an angry hen.

'I wish yer'd all stop sayin' that there 'oossted,' grumbled Ben. 'I'm fair sick of it.'

'*Cabeza, cabeza!*' she repeated. '*Dolor de cabeza!*'

She tapped her forehead as she spoke.

221

'If yer tryin' ter tell me yer barmy, mum,' said Ben, 'that ain't no news!'

She made a gesture of annoyance, and hobbled to the door. Opening it, she called out into the passage:

'*Eh! Alcoba! Eh!*'

Gaining no response, she grew more annoyed and stepped out into the passage, closing the door after her. '*Eh! Alcoba!*' she called again.

Her voice became fainter. She seemed to be descending stairs. Answering a sudden impulse, Ben jumped out of bed and ran to the window. No harm in taking one's bearings!

He looked out on to a moist street. It was uneven and cobbled, and the rain ran down large gutters. There were not many houses in the street, and what houses there were were low. One building towards the end of the road was a little bigger than the rest, and Ben concluded that it was supposed to be a church, but obviously the architect didn't know how churches went and had lost his plans half-way up. While Ben was regarding it with insular disapproval, a tall figure began to materialise round the church wall, but before he could see it clearly a sound in the passage sent him scurrying back to bed.

The door opened with a loud creak, and the old woman returned. Behind her was the black-bearded man who had carried Ben home. ''E must be Alcoba,' thought Ben.

'*Insensato, insensato!*' she muttered, pointing to him.

Alcoba waved her down, and advanced with a smile. He had very white teeth, and his smile showed them all.

'*Qué tal sigue usted?*' he inquired pleasantly.

'Oossted agine!' grumbled Ben. 'If yer wanter oossted, why don't yer?'

The black-bearded man tried another tack.

'*Cabeza?*' he asked. '*Dolor de cabeza?*'

'She's tried that one,' retorted Ben, 'and it don't work. I ain't got no cabeza!'

'*A mi ha dicho lo mismo,*' grunted the old woman.

'*No entiende ninguna palabra,*' answered the black-bearded man.

'Now, listen 'ere, Alcoba,' said Ben seriously. The black-bearded man raised his eyebrows. He had never been called 'Bedroom' before. 'Orl this oossted and cabeza bizziness ain't gettin' us nowhere! Why doncher listen ter me fer a bit, and see if I can git a word acrost ter yer. Fust, marth. That's ere.' He opened his mouth and pointed to it. ''Ave yer got hennythink ter put in it? I've got a 'ole in me stummick—that's 'ere—and I could eat orl the oossteds and cabezas yer've got in the lardeza.'

Alcoba stood silent before this outburst. It appeared to amaze him. The old woman, however, grew furious.

'*Quién hubiera imaginado nada tan disparatado?*' she cried.

Alcoba suddenly shook off the spell Ben's oration had cast upon him, and walked to the little table with the medicine bottle on it.

'Noneo of thateo!' exclaimed Ben vigorously. 'Wot I wants is a *proper* drink.' He made a loud noise, as of a man enjoying a proper drink. 'And, arter that, I'll ask yer ter put me on the road ter that plice I arst yer abart. Villabonzos. Get it? Don Manuel. Lummy, ain't there *nothink* we can do ter stop stoppin' like we're stoppin'? 'Ere. Beefinoza puddingoza beensinoza gorganzola, and if that don't mean nothink I give it hup!'

Apparently it meant nothing to the old woman, whose

only comment was '*Medico*,' but while her black-bearded companion clearly agreed with the comment, his expression suggested that the word '*Medico*' did not in his opinion entirely cover the position.

'*Si! Si!*' he nodded encouragingly. Then, turning to the old woman, he murmured something that ended with '*Carnero.*'

'Eh? 'Oo's that?' exclaimed Ben.

But they did not stop to explain, and left the room.

Carnero arrived five minutes later, and turned out to be mutton. This was a vast improvement on the interpretation Ben had put upon the word while waiting for it to materialise. With the mutton were potatoes and one or two other things less understandable, but Ben fell upon them all, while the old woman watched him disapprovingly. The black-bearded man, who had brought the tray, had gone again, for a reason which Ben was soon to learn.

'Spanish fer thankyer,' said Ben, when he had finished.

He felt better and better. He was ready to go on again. But when he began to get off the bed the old woman darted forward and pushed him back.

'Wot's that for?' he demanded.

'*No!*' she replied.

'Wot—yer could speak English orl the time?' exclaimed Ben indignantly.

He tried to leave the bed again, and again she shoved him back. She had more strength than one would have imagined, but it was not merely her strength that baffled Ben. It was her sex; also her age. Yer carn't knock an old woman abart—well, can yer?

''Ere, this is silly!' he protested.

She stood over him, glowering.

'Wot I wanter know,' he went on, 'is if yer on my side or if yer ain't? Yer've give me a rest and a meal, and I ain't fergettin' it, but yer ain't got no right ter keep me 'ere? I ain't done nothink ter yer. Now, look 'ere, mum, don't yer stop me no more, or p'r'aps I'll fergit me manners!'

He made a third effort. She almost jumped upon him, and shouted as she jumped. The man with the black beard came running in. Then all three began talking hard, and nobody had won when there sounded a sharp knocking on the door below.

'*Alguien llama!*' cried the old woman. '*Vaya á abrir!*'

'*Medico!*' exclaimed the man, and vanished.

A moment later he returned with an elderly gentleman. The elderly gentleman had grey hair, and he carried a small bag. A newspaper was sticking out of his pocket.

There was a consultation, conducted in low voices. Ben, obviously, was the subject of it. They continually looked towards him, and then coughed and pretended they had not. Every now and then a sentence floated meaninglessly across to the bed. '*Cuánto há que vino aqui?*' That was the elderly gentleman. '*Nada ma gustan sus modales.*' That was the old woman. '*Carnero.*' That was the black-bearded man, and for some reason he seemed rather ashamed. '*Carnero?*' repeated the elderly gentleman, admonishingly. '*Carnero!*' And his eyebrows went up and down several times.

Then the elderly gentleman turned directly to Ben, and studied him. Now he took the newspaper from his pocket, looked at it, and studied Ben again.

The old woman and the black-bearded man, watching

closely, seemed puzzled. The elderly gentleman turned towards them again, and held out the newspaper, pointing to one of the columns. They looked at the column, and then *their* eyebrows began working up and down.

''Ave I sed somethink funny,' wondered Ben, 'and 'as it got in a paper?'

But nobody was laughing. Faces were growing terribly serious, and even the black-bearded man, who had hitherto been the most friendly, began to scowl.

'*Zoologico?*' murmured the old woman.

'*Maniático?*' whispered the black-bearded man.

'*Asesino!*' muttered the elderly gentleman, his eyes on the newspaper. '*Asesino!*'

It dawned upon Ben that the remarks being made about him were not nice.

The trio drew a little nearer the door. The elderly gentleman seemed to be considering a course of action. Suddenly he put a question that evidently puzzled him.

'*Ah! Si!*' exclaimed the black-bearded man, and darted from the room.

He returned with three objects. The first was a shoe. The second was a knife. The third was a hammer. Ben recognised them all.

The elderly gentleman's face grew graver and graver. Hs also appeared a trifle less at ease than when he had first entered the room with his little bag. He was now very near the door.

'*Medico?*' he observed depreciatingly, tapping his chest. '*No! Oficial de policía!*'

'Wot's that?' cried Ben.

He bounded from the bed, but no more quickly than the trio bounded from the room. The key was turned in the lock. The next person to turn it, presumably, would be the *oficial de policía*.

When a door is locked, One turns instinctively to a window. Ben now adopted this obvious course, and as he did so he jumped back. Something came hurtling through the window and landed with a *plop* on the floor. It was a small, sodden shoe.

30

En Route for Villabanzos

A sodden shoe is not ordinarily classified among the world's most beautiful objects, but no object more beautiful to Ben could have entered through the window, saving the girl herself to whom the shoe belonged. His eyes were feasting on the unbelievable beauty when it was followed by a writhing snake. The snake was received with less enthusiasm than the shoe, and there was a nasty moment when the snake tried to sting him. Then it turned into a coil of rope; and, viewed in this light, it became immediately another thing of beauty.

The shoe said, 'I am below.' The rope said, 'Come to me!' Ben felt, with sudden bashfulness, like Juliet.

But his bashfulness did not prevent him from acting. He recalled that danger existed in the road beneath the window, where Medico and Alcoba would emerge at any moment, and possibly the old woman as well. If they found the girl staring up at their prisoner's window, they would probably arrest her for complicity! Complicity of what? He did not know. All he knew was that they thought he had done something dire, and that they were going to bring in the police.

He rushed to the window and stuck his head out. There, sure enough, was Molly Smith, staring up at him anxiously, while the rain descended on her upturned face. The sight of her produced a wave of violent emotion. She stood for Mother, and Home, and the English language! The emotion wasted a full second. Then the practical instinct reasserted itself, urged by the sound of an opening door below.

'Oi!' cried Ben, in a resonant whisper.

He darted back into the room again. The girl, interpreting the 'Oi' correctly, flew round a wall. When the door was opened, all was quiet and peaceful on the road.

Voices broke the quiet and the peace. There did not seem to be perfect unity among the voices. Creeping forward cautiously, Ben peered from the window, and with one eye watched the disputants. It was the old woman who was making the fuss.

Her point soon became obvious. The two men were going for the *oficial de policía*, and the old woman was not going to be left behind. The medico had said that Ben was an *asesino*, and she wasn't going to remain in a house alone with an *asesino*. Her previous boldness had apparently been due to the fact that she had merely regarded him as a *zoologico*. She won her point, the front door was secured, and the three gaolers left their prisoner in the keeping of mere walls.

With one eye—or, possibly, only half an eye—Ben watched the trio turn up the road and disappear beyond the apology for a church. Then he poked his head out of the window again, and risked another 'Oi!'

Molly responded immediately. He didn't know where

she had gone to, or where she now came from. She could move like lightning. After a quick glance up the road, she raised her face and whispered:

'Quick! Fasten the rope to something and slip down!'

'That's the idea, miss,' agreed Ben, and darted back to the bed.

He looped one end of the rope to the bed-post and then paid the other end out of the window. It ended six feet from the ground, and that was good enough. Even if it had not been, it would have been preferable to another six foot drop that might await him if he remained to interview the policeman! The very thought of the alternative shot him out of the window and down the elementary ladder.

'Be careful!' came Molly's voice up to him.

But it was she who needed to be careful. When Ben jumped the final six feet, he missed her by two inches.

'Well done! Well done!' gasped Molly. 'Do you think you can get the rope down?'

'No fear,' answered Ben, as he picked himself up. 'I don't want it!'

'It might be useful,' she urged.

'Yus, but not ter me,' he replied. 'As soon as I 'as a bit o' cord on me, miss, some'un comes along an' ties me hup in it.'

'How are you feeling?'

'Ready fer hennythink! But we've gotter 'urry—'

'Yes, I know! Follow me! I've marked our first funk hole!'

'Lummy, ain't Henglish loverly!' murmured Ben, as he obeyed.

They slid through the grey rain, taking a zig-zag course which the girl had evidently worked out in advance. Once they ducked down behind a derelict cart. Ben didn't know why, but he was trusting his leader, and banking on imitation. What she did, he did. When she ran, he ran. When she slowed up, he slowed up. When she swerved, he swerved, and once he swerved right into her, and they fell into a small ditch of coarse grass.

'Gawd, we 'ave bin in some funny plices tergether, ain't we, miss?' gasped Ben happily.

Nothing mattered to him just then. Not the ditch or the danger, or the rain. A vast loneliness had lifted from his spirit, and in its place was this queer miracle of companionship. Of course, she was a wrong 'un. But p'r'aps he could talk to her about that. After all, you had to be told, didn't you? 'Or dontcher?' he suddenly wondered. He could not recall who had told him.

Odd that such thoughts should have come to him in the ditch! It was hardly the place or the time for moral reflection . . .

'Keep still!'

He had been on the point of getting up, but the words held him down. They tickled into his ear, and he recognised the tickle. Well, he was quite comfortable. A knee was poking into his chest, but it was a very companionable knee, and a hand that seemed somehow bound round his leg was nice and warm.

Just the same, he didn't know why they had to keep still. Once again, he was trusting implicitly to her leadership.

From somewhere above them came the sound of boots scrunching in grass. Ah! These boots were the reason! Whose were they? The Spanish bobby's? He dug down harder into the ditch, while anatomy beneath him strove valiantly not to object.

The crunch came closer. There was a moist sound to it. You could almost see the little spurts of water as the boots came down. Left boot, right boot, left boot, right boot . . .

Mr Sims paused. He paused because he thought he had heard something. It seemed to come from just beyond that dripping bush over there. The wet ground dipped on the other side.

He altered his course, and moved towards the dripping bush. Then he paused again. He had been veering towards the right, but from the left came another distraction. Four figures, about a hundred yards off, making for the main street of the village.

One was an old woman. Another, a bearded man. Another, an elderly gentleman. The fourth, a sturdy *oficial de policìa*.

The procession interested him. He left the bush to drip upon its secret, and turned to the right. Thus, unconsciously, the Spanish law did Ben a service.

From behind the dripping bush two figures emerged. They, also, were dripping. As Sims went towards the village, they continued on their journey away from it.

'Do you know who that was?' whispered Molly.

'Lord Mayor?' guessed Ben.

'Sims,' she answered.

She felt Ben barging into her back again. His pace had suddenly doubled. But this time she kept her feet, and doubled the pace with him.

They reached their first funk hole. It was a small, dilapidated shed of black wood that seemed to be hiding itself in a little dip. It stood twenty yards off a road leading northwards from the village, and a path had once joined it to the road, but now the path was almost obliterated, while the shed itself was scarcely more recognisable than the path. Halt the roof of the shed remained, however, and could keep rain off if it drove from the east.

In this shed they rested, panting. Water ran down their clothes and made two little pools where they stood. But Ben was not thinking of the rain. He was thinking of Sims. Sims *here*? He couldn't figure it out, till all at once a startling idea struck him.

'Is *this* Villerbonzo, miss?' he asked suddenly.

'Villabanzos,' she corrected him, with a faint smile. 'You got the bit of paper, then?'

'Yus. But I lorst it agine. Is this Villerwotyersed?'

'No.'

'Oh, it ain't! Then wot's Sims doin' 'ere?' he inquired, perplexed.

'He's looking for me,' she told him.

'Lummy! Is 'e? And wot are *you* doin' 'ere?'

'Looking for *you*!'

'Lookin' fer—me?' She nodded. 'Wot for?'

'Aren't you worth looking for?' she asked.

It was the first he'd heard of it. The novelty of the theory confused him. He decided to try and work it out later, and meanwhile, after a solemn second or two, he inquired:

'Yus; but wot abart Miss 'Olbrooke, miss?'

'*She's* at Villabanzos,' answered Molly, 'and that's where you and I've got to get to, just as quick as we can!'

''Oo's with 'er?'

'Oh, my goodness! Who *isn't*? There's six of them—and a more bloodthirsty lot you never set eyes on!'

'Oh! And—that's where we're goin'?'

'Got to!'

'That's right.' Ben's voice was depressed.

233

'Well, haven't we?' she challenged the depression.

'Corse! Plices like that is made fer us! That Don Magnesia—is 'e in charge, like?'

'Don Manuel?'

'That's the bloke.'

'Yes, he's in charge. He's an innkeeper, but I'll bet he doesn't make his money selling lemonade! They've got Miss Holbrooke locked in a cellar—'

'That's nice fer us!'

'. . . And how we're going to get her out, God knows. But we're *going* to get her out, and, what's more, we can't waste any time about it! How are you feeling?'

''Orrible.'

A little frown crept into her face.

'Want to back out?' she asked.

'No,' he answered. 'That's why I feels 'orrible. 'Ave yer got a plan, like?'

'Yes, Sims will probably spend an hour or two more searching for me, and we've got to get her away before he returns.'

'I see. With 'im away, there's on'y six left. 'Ow fur is this Viller-wot-yer-call-it?'

'Seven or eight miles, I should think.'

'Oh! And 'ow do we git there? 'Op?'

'We'll get a lift somehow.'

''Oo's goin' ter hask fer it?'

'This is.' She thrust her hand into the neck of her dress and drew out a bundle of notes. Once before Ben had seen that bundle. In the coal bunker of the *Atalanta*. 'I've used a few of them already. Luckily, one of the six isn't above double-crossing his pals in return for a bribe. I'd never have got away if it hadn't been for him. I expect this bundle will be considerably thinner before we're through . . . Quick! Listen! What's that?'

A sound came from the road twenty yards away. A sound of trotting. She slipped quickly to the entrance to the shed and peered cautiously round the partition towards the highway.

'Look aht!' whispered Ben. 'S'pose it's Sims!'

'Yes, but it *isn't*!' she whispered back. 'It's an old man with a cart. I say, let's make a dive for it!'

She dived as she spoke. Ben dived out after her. A moment later the cart had stopped, and the driver was smiling amiably at Ben.

'Lummy, it's a pal o' mine!' exclaimed Ben, recognising the old man of whom he had first inquired the way. ''E ain't much good, but we can try 'im agine. Oi! Good arternoonio. Siggeo-wiggeo Villerbanzos?'

The old man shook his head, but all at once he stopped shaking it. Molly was holding up three-one-pound notes. If he could not understand the English language, he could at least understand English money.

'Villabanzos!' he exclaimed. '*Si, si*! Villabanzos!'

He made an elaborate gesture which clearly meant 'Jump in!' Three pounds rendered a journey to Villabanzos worth while, whatever other business may previously have been in view; and, obeying the invitation, Ben and Molly clambered into the back of the cart.

Then the old man made a noise with his mouth, rattled his whip in its socket, and spat. In response to the three operations, the bony horse broke into a gentle trot.

31

Exchange Is No Robbery

It was seven twisting miles from the dilapidated shed to Villabanzos. The miles did not merely twist. They also jolted. The horse and the road seemed to be in a sort of league against smoothness, and to be attempting to prove that advancement could be achieved without speed or luxury. The proof, doubtful at first, soon became conclusive.

But one can talk, even if one is not comfortable. Words can be gasped between bumps, and sentences inserted between twists. Thus, during the first half of the journey, Ben was able to give his companion an account of himself, and to listen to his companion's account during the last half.

The commencement of Molly Smith's story fitted into Ben's deductions. When she had entered the upstairs room in the little mountain hut, she had waited patiently for Sims to follow her and bring Miss Holbrooke back to consciousness. In due course he had appeared, and had begun to work on the patient in response to Molly's insistence; but he had not completed the work, and apparently he had never intended to. Having brought Miss Holbrooke back to partial consciousness, he had requested Molly to watch over her, and had suddenly inserted his injection needle into Molly's own arm.

'That's wot I thort,' muttered Ben, 'when yer didn't give me no signal. If yer'd bin orl right yer'd 'ave 'it the floor or somethink, wouldn't yer? Arter 'e'd left yer, I mean, and they was orl out o' the 'ouse?'

'Of course I would,' she replied. 'And I was a little fool! Though, honestly, I don't know how I could have stopped the brute, doing what he liked! He's a devil, if ever there was one! The next thing I remember is a sort of a bridge, and I can only remember that through a sort of nightmare. I expect it was the bridge *you* nearly toppled over.'

'Yus, that's right, miss,' nodded Ben. 'You was comin' out o' yer nightmare while I was goin' inter mine! Wot beats me is why Greene and Faggis, 'oo was arter me like I tole yer, didn't foller me acrost!'

'Well, I've got an idea about that,' said Molly. 'I remember seeing Sims trying to smash the bridge up after we'd got over. I suppose he wanted to make sure *he* wasn't followed. But he evidently thought there wasn't time, because he suddenly stopped, and we went on again. Do you think it's possible that, when you were making your last desperate wriggle to get across, you loosened the boards—you see, Sims had already started on them—and sent them down? Then Greene and Faggis couldn't have followed you, could they?'

Ben considered the theory. Then he nodded solemnly.

'It might 'ave bin like that, miss,' he agreed. 'I remember somethink did go dahn, but I thort it was me. But, look 'ere—that bridge was as narrer as a squeak. 'Ow did Sims git orl of you acrost?'

'I don't know. Probably there was just room for the cart—it was a very tiny one—hardly more than a barrow with a mule pulling it—and then one or two of the boards might have gone down before you got to it.'

'Mikin' it smaller, like? Yus, that's right. I hexpeck we're gittin' it. But wot 'appened arter that? You was comin' rahnd, wasn't yer—'

'Very slowly. I don't remember anything really clearly until we were going through a forest. It was there that I did a ridiculous thing, though it turned out all right, after all. I kicked off a shoe, in the hope that you'd find it.'

'Yus, and I did!'

'I know. Then—oh, goodness, I can't remember it all! I was so muzzy I could hardly think! We got somehow to Villabanzos, and—'

'*Pronto será de noche*,' interrupted the driver, calling over his shoulder.

'' Ooray!' answered Ben. 'That 'elps a lot!'

'*Si, si!*' cried the driver, and cracked his whip.

'Shurrup!' retorted Ben. 'Go hon, miss. 'E's barmy. Yer got ter Viller-wot's-its-nime—?'

'And Miss Holbrooke was taken to a cellar. Then there was a sort of consultation between Sims and those six men I told you about. One of them was Don Manuel, of course. He's simply enormous. They were deciding what to do with me, and after a lot of argument they stuck me in a room with a murderous fellow to guard me. *Then* what do you think I did?'

'Bit 'im?'

'No! *Vamped* him,'

'Go on!'

'It was—oh, beastly!'

'Wot—did 'e vamp yer back?'

'He tried to.'

'Sort of a twist, ain't it?'

'What do you mean?'

'Well, I ain't sure as I knows wot *you* means. This 'ere vamp. Is it ju-jittus?'

'You're right—it can be!' she exploded, and for a few moments she rocked without any assistance from the road or the horse. 'If we ever live through this, I'll come and listen to you for hours together!' Then she grew serious again. 'You vamp a person when you pretend you're fond of them. I pretended I was fond of the beast who was guarding me. And when, later on, I added a handful of notes, he helped me to escape.'

Ben was silent for a while. His mind was busy with a problem. Unable to solve it, he asked her assistance.

'This feller,' he said. ''Ow much did yer pertend?'

'You needn't think I let him kiss me!'

'That's orl right.'

Ben's vehemence impressed her.

'Would you have minded if I had?' she inquired.

''Corse,' he responded. 'Henglish gals don't wanter go kissin' no Spaniards.'

'The notes were instead of the kisses,' she smiled.

'Well, wot 'appened arter you got away?'

'This happened.'

'Wotcher mean?'

'I came back to find you.'

'Thank yer, miss. It mikes me feel—well, sort o' funny ter 'ear yer say that. But why didn't yer—why didn't yer—'

'Yes—why didn't I—what?' she queried. '*You* don't know. Nor did I. So, you see, *you* seemed the best thing.'

'But—Miss 'Olbrooke?'

'I didn't forget her. I wanted someone to help me.'

'Yer mean—me, like?'

'Well, of course. Do you know, I saw them take you into that cottage—you were carried in, weren't you?—and I'd have got to you long before if it hadn't been for Sims. When I spotted him, I had to be doubly careful. You see, I might have given you away, as well as myself!'

'Lummy!'

'Yes, lummy! He must have discovered my escape quite soon after I did my bunk. I didn't know how to get at you, or even what room you were in till I suddenly saw you at the window.'

'Oh! You saw me that time?'

'Yes. And I also saw Sims that time coming round the church! That was why I had to wait.'

'Good thing yer did, miss. That shoe o' your'n—I s'pose yer sent it hup ter let me know 'oo it was, like?'

'Yes.'

She poked out her sopping, stockinged feet, for sympathy.

'Yer a toff, miss,' murmured Ben. 'But if that shoe 'ad come in a minit sooner, it'd 'ave 'it the 'ole Spanish poper-lashun. 'Owjer git 'old o' the rope?'

'It was the same rope I got out of *my* room with,' she told him. 'The rope I was given by the fellow I bribed.'

'I'm blowed. You don't waste nothink! And now 'ere we are, goin' back ter Villerbandbox, with six blokes in front of us, and Sims be'ind us. Funny thing I'm orlways in a sandwich. Well—'ow are we goin' ter git aht o' *this* one?'

The question was so pertinent that speech ended for a while and thought took its place. The thought had not proved productive before Ben put another question:

'Wot 'appens if Sims comes along arter us afore we gits ter Villerbankox, and spots us?'

Thought was resumed. Their eyes were fixed on the road along which they had come. Yes, suppose Sims appeared now, at this moment, round that bend? What sort of a chance would they have?

Suddenly Ben's eyes nearly popped out of his head.

'What's the matter?' asked Molly anxiously.

'Got an idea,' answered Ben.

Relieved, she asked him to explain it, but for a few moments he couldn't. It was too big an idea. It was almost as big as the idea that had galvanised him in the little mountain hut when he had bound and gagged a dead man.

'Tell me, tell me!' exclaimed Molly. 'And do be careful, or your eyes will drop out.'

Ben gulped.

'Look 'ere, miss,' he said, lowering his voice unnecessarily, ''ow much did yer hoffer this old feller 'ere fer the ride? Three pahnd, weren't it?'

'Yes.'

'Well, 'ow much d'yer think 'e'd tike fer the cart?'

'The cart—'

'And the 'oss, yus, and fer somethink helse as well? 'Is clothes?'

She stared at him, as his idea began to enter dimly into her.

'More'n yer've got?' asked Ben.

'You mean—you'll take his place?'

'That's right. And drive hup ter Don Wot's-'is-nime, and pertend ter be Spanish?'

'But—even if you could *look* Spanish—'

'Hennybody could, in them togs!'

241

'. . . You can't *speak* Spanish!'

''Corse I carn't, miss,' replied Ben. 'I'm deaf an' dumb, see? It ain't much of a charnce, but can yer think of henny-think better?'

The old man under discussion turned his head and wagged it.

'Villabanzos,' he announced.

'Where?' asked Ben.

'Villabanzos,' repeated the old man confirmatively.

'Yes, it's only three houses and a pub,' whispered Molly, 'and the pub is *us!*'

'Well, I'm blowed!' murmured Ben.

So this was Villabanzos! This was the goal towards which his face had been set ever since he had left the little hut in the mountains! Three houses and a pub! The Mecca he had vaguely visualised was a place of palaces and turrets, and bull rings—a populous district in the underground of which resided one Don Manuel, of infamous reputation. Three houses and a pub might be easier to deal with, but, however you looked at it, it was a bit of a come down!

And where *was* the pub? He counted three small roofs among trees, but there was no sign of a Red Lion or a Bald-faced Stag. Even the three roofs were far apart and were almost lost among the deepening shadows.

'*Posada?*' inquired the driver.

Molly hesitated, then shook her head. Ben stared at her in astonishment.

'Yer know wot possyarder means?' he exclaimed.

'Yes—one of the words I picked up,' she answered. 'It means an inn. Don Manuel's inn. He wants to know if he's to take us there.'

'Oh. And 'ow fur is the passyarder, miss?'

'About half a mile, I think.'

'Well, let's try my idea now, and see wot 'e ses. Oi! Stopeo!'

The instruction was unnecessary, for the old man had already stopped. He was waiting for further instructions.

''Ow much can we give 'im?' whispered Ben.

Molly pulled the bundle of notes from her dress. The old driver's eyes gleamed as he saw them.

'Wot abart 'arf?' suggested Ben.

'You remember where they came from?' she replied, in a low voice.

'That's right. They're not our'n,' agreed Ben; 'but 'oo are we spendin' 'em hon? Miss 'Olbrooke, ain't it?' She nodded. 'Well, then, if there's ter be any payin' back to a deader's next-o'-skin, 'er father'll do it, won't 'e?'

The argument impressed her. It really was rather a good one. She handed Ben half the bundle. Ben climbed down to the road, and went to the front of the cart.

'One-o, two-o, three-o,' he said, taking three notes and handing them to the driver.

'*Gracias!*' beamed the driver. '*Muchîsimas gracias!*'

''E wants a lot o' grass,' commented Ben. 'Lummy, ain't Spanish silly? Now, look 'ere, Muchimus, would yer like some more gracias?'

He held up three more notes. The old man gazed at them, and raised his eyebrows.

'Oosted!' tried Ben.

'*Si, si!*' cried the old man, and began to turn his horse round.

'Oi!' shouted Ben, seizing the horse and putting it straight again. Then he glanced at Molly desperately. 'I must 'ave sed somethink! Wunner wot it was?'

243

'He thinks you're offering him the three pounds to take us back again,' suggested Molly.

'Then 'e must be a bigger fool'n 'e looks,' grumbled Ben. 'Wot do we wanter go back agine for? We're on'y jest 'ere, ain't we?' He turned to the driver once more. The driver was waiting in perplexity, anxious to please and to earn, but without the foggiest notion of how to do either.

'Now, look 'ere,' Ben began again. 'I'll mike it six. No, five.' He added two notes to the three he had held out. 'You can 'ave these. Oosted. No, not oosted. And we want *these*. Gracias.'

He pointed to the cart and the horse. Light dawned. The old man shook his head vigorously.

'Six, then,' said Ben, and added another note. 'Seven. Eight, Nine. 'Ere, a dozen!'

The old man stopped shaking his head. He became interested in the game. How much higher was it going! English people are not always understood, but English money is understood all the world over.

'Well, wot abart it?' demanded Ben, holding the twelve notes up.

The old man made no movement. He was just watching the pile grow. It grew to twenty. Ben began to get hot and indignant. It was a very old cart and a very old horse, and the notes were new.

At twenty-five the old man became agitated.

'*Aguarde un momento*!' he exclaimed, and held out one of the three notes he already possessed. '*Veinticinco pesetas? Si? Veinticinco pesetas?*'

'With knobs on!' replied Ben. Suddenly he remembered that he had forgotten the most important item. 'Oh, and I want yer clothes, too!'

It took some while to get this across. Comprehension did not dawn on the old man's amazed face for several minutes, and was succeeded by incredulity, amazement and indignation. But when the notes had climbed up to thirty-two, and he saw they could climb no higher, he jumped from the driver's seat, and began throwing off his garments in a sort of commercial frenzy.

No one will ever know what went on in the old Spaniard's mind during the two unique minutes that ensued. He did not know himself. Somehow or other he was acquiring eight hundred pesetas, and in order to earn the small fortune he had to relinquish a horse and a cart, both of which were on their last legs, and to exchange his outer clothing with a foreign lunatic. If there was something undignified in the transaction, he was not the first man in history to sacrifice his self-respect for finance. Eight hundred pesetas were sufficient to soothe his wounded pride!

The bargain completed, he vanished, confused but contented.

'And now what?' asked Molly, heroically fighting her desire to scream at Ben's appearance.

Ben, happily unable to see himself, turned his eyes towards the three almost concealed cottages. He noted that one of them was empty. No one in the world had better sight for empty houses than Ben.

'You pop in there and wait,' he said.

'You've decided to go on alone, then?'

''Corse! They mustn't see you, miss. Oi! Look nippy! Somethink's 'appenin'.'

Hoofs sounded on the road along which they had come. Molly dashed to the empty cottage, and had just reached it when a riderless horse raced by. Running after it was a tall, white-haired figure.

'Hell!' panted the figure, and then stopped sharply to stare at Ben and his cart. Ben stared back, galvanised.

'Hey, you!' cried the figure, hastening forward again. '*Lleveme al posada!*'

Thus Ben learned that Mr Sims could speak Spanish.

32

Ben's Passenger

There was no time to think. If there had been, the thinking would have been unproductive. Sims had climbed into the seat behind Ben as he spoke, and a totally new situation had developed with devastating suddenness. The only thing to do at the moment was to accept it.

Therefore Ben did not argue or protest. He clucked, attempting to do so with a Spanish accent. The horse pricked up its ears, listened for a repetition of the cluck, received it, and moved forward.

'*Habla usted inglés?*' asked Sims, after a moment's silence.

Just in the nick of time, Ben refrained from making any sign that he had heard. He remembered that he was deaf and dumb, and that his lips must be silent. His head, also, must remain invisible. Only its very lowest portion, which managed to escape from the large enveloping hat, could be seen by his passenger.

'Hey, there! *Habla usted inglés?*' repeated Sims. And then went on impatiently, '*Haga usted el favor de responder si ó no!*'

Vaguely Ben recalled that somebody else had said exactly the same thing to him once, but he didn't know what it was now any more than he had known before, and it wouldn't have made any difference if he had.

'Damn fool!' muttered Sims, and suddenly seized his arm and shook it.

'Let me see—can I feel?' wondered Ben.

The grip on his arm increased, and proved that he could. He half-turned in his seat and shook his head, pointing to his mouth and his ears—or to the places where they would have shown had they been visible.

'*Qué quiere decir eso?*' demanded Sims.

Ben went on pointing. Then Sims appeared to understand.

'Oh—deaf and dumb, eh?' he observed, and grew suddenly thoughtful.

He might have grown more thoughtful if Ben had not saved himself, again just in the nick of time, from nodding violently.

The horse loped on. It was not in any hurry to reach its destination. Nor was its driver.

'Well, if you can't hear me,' remarked Sims, after a pause, 'I don't suppose it's any good my telling you that I've lost my horse?' Apparently it wasn't. 'Or that I think Spain is a godforsaken country that ought to be blasted off the map.' The driver neither agreed nor disagreed. 'Or that, of all the things I have come across in Spain, you are about the ugliest—that is, what I can see of you!' The driver showed no resentment, but his heart thumped like a sledge-hammer beneath its picturesque covering.

The next instant his heart beat twice as fast and twice as loudly.

'Have you seen a girl anywhere about here?' roared Sims.

Somehow, Ben kept his seat, but the inside of a Spanish sombrero ran for the first time with British moisture.

They had been moving for three minutes. In another three, even at this slow pace, the inn of Don Manuel would be in sight. 'How do yer stop a 'orse?' thought Ben. Then he realised that no object would be served by stopping the horse. He had been caught by a tide, and he'd got to go with it. And, anyway, this had been his own idea, hadn't it—this visit to the inn in borrowed plumes? 'Yus, but not with Sims sittin' beside me,' he decided, in self-extenuation. He hadn't bargained for that.

'I wonder what you're thinking, my man?' said Sims. 'Queer how our secret thoughts are hidden from each other, eh? You look stodgy enough. But then I can't see very much of you. Shall I pull your hat up? Perhaps, if I did, I'd find some key to your thoughts! Secret thoughts, eh? Yes, I dare say you have them!'

'Gawd, why don't 'e stop?' thought Ben. His hat was now sticking all round him. His head felt like wet sand in an upturned pail; if the head had been shaken out, it would not have made a good castle. ''E orter stop. It's silly. 'E don't know I don't like it!'

'Perhaps you have a secret vice, Carlos, or whatever your name is,' Sims went on. 'Perhaps, despite your apparent lethargy, you are in love with another man's wife! Who knows? Sin lies behind the smoothest forehead—though I expect yours is lined, eh?—and romance stifles the hump-back. The thwarted instinct goes inwards, Carlos, and comes out again in the wrong place—twisted.' He laughed softly. 'And I know where to look for the place, and how to utilise the twist!'

'Now 'e's gettin' jest foolish,' decided Ben.

There was another short silence. Some way ahead, to the right of the lonely, tree-lined road, loomed a dull yellow building. Ben eyed it apprehensively. His passenger was eyeing it also.

'We shall soon part company, Carlos,' said Sims, with a little sigh; 'but I'd love to discover your secret before we part. You see, I'm quite sure you have one. I've an instinct for smelling them out. All I need is the tiniest lead. If only you had a voice one could hear, or a face one could see!'

'Lummy, 'e's at me fice agine!' thought Ben.

'But your hat conceals your face, and, as for your voice, you are deaf and dumb. So that's that, isn't it?'

Two men lounged out of the yellow building at the side of the road. One had a scar, and the other had a squint. '*Wouldn't* they!' thought Ben. He wasn't being let off anything.

'Yes, I really *am* sorry you are deaf and dumb,' said Sims, 'because if you weren't I could have asked you a question I'm terribly curious about.'

They were now almost up to the inn. A third man joined the other two, who had now grown considerably larger. But the third man was the largest of the lot. 'Why is it that, when people are agin yer, they're always big?' wondered Ben.

'Here we are,' said Sims, as Ben pulled the reins and the horse stopped.

He rose from his seat, and turned to dismount.

'Oh, by the way, that question,' he said, pausing. 'You won't hear it, of course, but I may as well ask it. Since you are deaf and dumb, Carlos, pray how did you know what I wanted when I first spoke to you, and how did you know where I wanted to go?'

'Well, I was goin' that way any'ow, wasn't I?' burst out Ben.

'Thank you, Ben,' smiled Sims. 'Thank you very much indeed.'

33

Flying Knives

Five men sat in a small, ill-lit room. One had a squint, another had a scar, and another was twice as large as any man had a right to be. The fourth was Sims, with his back to the slit of a window. The fifth was Ben, with his face to the slit. Only on Ben's face was there any light; Sims knew how to arrange his pieces.

Other people were in other rooms in Don Manuel's unsavoury establishment, but for the moment their business does not concern us. We are only concerned with the conference that was taking place around Ben's face.

The room itself was close and foul-smelling. 'And if *I* think a plice smells bad, it must smell bad!' decided Ben. He supposed it had something to do with Spanish onions.

'Now, Ben,' began Sims, 'we will get to business. You know, of course, that we mean business?'

'Cut aht the frills,' replied Ben. 'Wot is the bizziness?'

'You are going to tell me things, Ben,' said Sims; 'and the first thing is how you come to be alive after being shot?'

'Ah, yer'd like ter know that, wouldn't yer,' answered Ben.

'I'm going to know it. Are you related to Houdini?'

''Oo wot?'

'Or Maskelyne? If you ever get back to England, you'll be able to get a job at St George's Hall. If you ever get back. Well, speak up. We're waiting.'

'Yer can go hon waitin'.'

'Oh? So that's your humour?'

''Umer's right! Carn't yer see, I'm shakin' with larfter!'

'Then I'll have to make you shake with something else. Don Manuel, show our friend your little knife trick.'

The elephantine man grinned, and his hand suddenly shot out of a shadow. Something gleaming left it like a released arrow, flashed by Ben's head, and ended with a little ping in the wall behind him.

'Now will you answer me?' inquired Sims.

Why should he? They were obviously going to do for him anyway, and the sooner it was all over the better. So he grunted, 'No!' and, at a sign from Sims, Don Manuel's hand again shot out, and there came another flash of supple steel through the air. The blade passed this time within two inches of Ben's other cheek.

'One on the right, two on the left,' observed Sims, 'and the third, if it comes, in the middle.'

'It wasn't me wot yer shot,' muttered Ben.

'No?'

'Ain't I sed so?'

'Then who was it?'

'Little Red Ridin' 'Ood.'

'Think again.'

'Orl right. But wot's it matter now, any'ow? It was a

Spaniard wot come in dyin' like, and arter 'e begins ter hundo me 'e pops orf.'

'*Non comprendo*,' murmured Don Manuel.

'Pop off. *Morir. Expirar*,' explained Sims.

'*Si, si*,' nodded Don Manuel. 'Pop off! Ah!'

He laughed, and the other two Spaniards grinned, but with less intelligence. Although they gathered that something funny had happened, they hadn't the muddiest notion of what it was.

'You have still to tell me,' resumed Sims, whose eyes had never left Ben's, 'how the dead man came to be bound and gagged?'

'Are you a mug,' retorted Ben, 'or jest pertendin' ter be?'

'You bound him?'

''Corse! When yer dead yer dead, ain'tcher?'

'Then where were you?'

'Hunner the tible.'

'Really!'

'Yus, reely. And if yer'd come a step closer, yer'd 'ave got a sirocco in yer foot!'

Sims looked thoughtful. He was beginning to realise certain things that had not been apparent before. When Don Manuel began to address him, he motioned for silence. His mind was engaged on a new problem.

'I see,' he said, at last, in the soft voice Ben hated. 'There is, after all, a brain. One would not think it. But it is there. Yes, clearly, it is there. And what did the brain do, after I left? Did it wait under the table or emerge?'

''Oo?' jerked Ben.

'I'm asking you what happened next, Ben? You followed me?'

'No.'

'What did you do, then?'

'I took a trine ter Wigan.'

'I think that had better be your last humorous remark, Ben,' said Sims ominously.

'Well, yer asks sich silly queshuns,' retorted Ben. ''Corse I follered yer.'

'Why "of course"?'

'Well, I'm 'ere, ain't I?'

'You are undoubtedly here—and are likely to remain here. We will take it, then, that you followed me. How did you know where I was going to?'

'Eh?'

'How did you know I was here?'

That needed thinking about. Ben temporised.

''Oo sed I knoo yer was 'ere?'

'Well, then—*did* you know?'

'No. Yus. No.'

'Meaning?'

'Yus. Meanin' no.'

'You didn't know I was here?'

'Yus, I didn't.'

'Then how was it,' inquired Sims, 'that I found you barely half a mile away?'

''Omin' instink,' suggested Ben.

'I'm afraid that won't do,' replied Sims. 'You knew the name of this place before you arrived here.'

'Did I? Well, 'corse I did! When you pops in the cart, you tole me, didn't yer?'

'My precise remark,' observed Sims dryly, 'was "*Lleveme al posada*." Of course, you speak Spanish?'

'No, I don't speak Spanish,' exclaimed Ben, struggling to keep his head under this ruthless cross-examination. He knew what Sims was driving at, and he wasn't having any! 'If I could speak Spanish I'd tell yer somethink yer wouldn't fergit in a 'urry! Torkin' through yer 'at, you are. I took you 'ere 'cos there wasn't nowhere helse.'

'Then you'd never heard of Don Manuel or of Villabanzos before?'

'No, and I never wanter 'ear of 'em agine.'

'In that case, why did you inquire for them at the house you stopped at in the last village?' That was a nasty one. So Sims had been talking to them, had he? 'By the way,' added Sims, 'they're still looking for you in that village. You're wanted for murder.'

'Wot's that?' exclaimed Ben.

'Yes, you seem to have killed a couple of people somewhere near the coast. Did you kill Greene and Faggis as well, by any chance? What's happened to them?'

Ben was silent.

'What's happened to Greene and Faggis?' repeated Sims sharply.

'Lummy, 'ow do I know?' burst out Ben. 'I tell yer I don't know nothink! If yer goin' ter do me in, fer Gawd's sake do me in. I don't mind bein' dead, we orl gotter, ain't we—yus, and you too, the 'ole lot of yer, but this waitin' abart fair gits on me nerves. I ain't goin' ter hanswer no more questions, see? Orl right. Now tell 'im ter chuck 'is sirocco and mike a butterfly of me! 'Oo cares?'

Sims glanced at Don Manuel. Don Manuel bared his teeth at Ben, with deliberate intent to frighten. Ben closed his eyes.

'Well, I won't worry you about Greene and Faggis,' came Sims's voice through Ben's self-imposed darkness. 'Probably they are interesting the police, also, and may

256

already be under lock and key. But there is one question you have got to answer, Ben, and that without any more delay. How did you know the name of Don Manuel, and of Villabanzos?'

Ben closed his mouth, as well as his eyes.

'Did somebody tell you?'

Ben remained obdurate.

'Was it the girl who calls herself Molly Smith?'

'There,' thought Ben, 'I knoo that was wot 'e was arter!'

'And where is Molly Smith *now*?'

'Now I'm orl right,' thought Ben. 'If yer die pertecktin' a gal, 'Eaven's a cert.'

A few moments of silence followed. Then Sims's voice sounded again, softly but clearly.

'Let him have it, Don Manuel,' he said.

'Now it's comin'!' thought Ben.

It came an instant later. There was a sickening swish. A violent sensation pierced his forehead or his nose, or his neck. He couldn't decide which. All he knew for certain was that one had a huge hole in it. Then the voice of Don Manuel sighed:

'*Diablo!* I mees!'

'Gawd! 'As 'e?' gasped Ben, and opened his eyes to find out.

Yes, Don Manuel had missed, and since his aim as a rule was deadly, there was probably a reason for it. He and Sims, despite their differences in temperament, bulk and nationality, seemed to understand each other perfectly.

'Do you know, you're rather a nuisance, Ben,' said Sims, paying an unusual compliment. 'I said a few moments ago that you had the smatterings of a brain. You also appear to have smatterings of courage. Well, we'll have to try another method of making you talk. This method is invariably successful—but you're giving us a lot of trouble.'

He rose, and, at a sign, the man with the scar and the man with the. squint pulled Ben out of his chair and began to march him from the room. Ahead walked Don Manuel. Behind came Sims. The other men were on either side. 'Blimy, if we ain't like the Five o' Diamonds,' thought Ben.

He was conducted through a narrow passage to a stone stairway. The stairway wound downwards, ending in total darkness. Someone switched on a spotlight, and the procession, no longer like a playing card, proceeded in single file along a narrower passage. It halted at a door on the left. A key was turned. A large key, that groaned. Then Ben was pushed into a damp-smelling cellar.

The spotlight now played on a wooden trestle at the end of the cellar. Seated on the trestle was Miss Holbrooke.

She raised her eyes apathetically as Ben stared at her, and for a moment seemed too weary to show any special interest; but as her eyes met those of Ben, they flickered with a new though still vague emotion . . .

The door was closed behind Ben. For an instant Ben thought his guard had left him, but Sims's voice soon dispelled that illusion. With a hollow ring above the cold stone floor, it informed Ben why he had been brought here.

'From some reason which is quite beyond my comprehension, Ben,' said Sims; 'but which I shall be interested to explore when I have time to delve into the subtleties of psychology, I have been more patient with you than, I think, I have been with anybody else in the whole of my life. You interest me, Ben. When you are dead, I hope to have the pleasure of dissecting the inside of your face. I feel sure I shall find some unusual and intriguing things there. But my patience is now at an end. There will be no more questions and answers in this new method of forcing you to talk. When I have finished talking myself, you will tell me what I want to know, or—'

He paused. If he intended the pause to be used by Ben for horrible visions, the intention succeeded. Before he continued his discourse, Ben had had his eyes gouged out, his tongue slit, and his thumbs pulled off.

'You have shown a certain unintelligent bravery regarding your own skin,' continued Sims presently. 'The point you will have to decide is whether you care to show the same bravery regarding Miss Holbrooke's skin.'

'Wot's that?' cried Ben, and Miss Holbrooke suddenly took her eyes from his face and directed them towards Sims.

'Don Manuel missed you with his knives because I had so instructed him,' said Sims unemotionally. 'You will realise that, if I had killed you, I should have also killed my chance of obtaining the information I want. The same does not apply to Miss Holbrooke. Remain obstinate, and Don Manuel will not miss.'

Ben gulped. They'd got him now! He'd have to give away one girl, to save another! Of all the foul, black-hearted tricks . . .

'I am about to count five, Ben. Before I finish you will tell me who gave you the name of Don Manuel. If it was Molly Smith, as I suspect, you will also tell me how she obtained the information, and whether she obtained it before or after she left the ship. You may or may not understand the importance of that. It doesn't matter in the least what you understand. But you may be sure it *is* important, and that I am going to find out whether the information has been passed on to anybody besides yourself. And finally, Ben, you will tell me where Molly Smith is, because I am convinced that you know. Now, then, are you ready? Good. One . . . two . . .'

Don Manuel raised his knife. Miss Holbrooke stared at him unbelievingly. She was something like a rabbit, held down by the malevolence of a snake. Ben felt as though he were being held down, too, by the malevolence of incapacity. What did you do in a case like this . . . what did you do? . . .

'Three . . .'

Intelligence came to him suddenly. So suddenly, and so dazzlingly, that it almost hurt. Kill Miss Holbrooke? They wouldn't do that! Why, wasn't this a kidnapping scheme, and if they killed her wouldn't they be killing the golden goose? Alive, she meant thousands of pounds. Dead, she meant nothing! This was just bluff, bluff . . .

'Four . . .'

Then Ben's brain leapt a stage farther. Sims's compliment to it was being justified. Yes, it was bluff! But would Sims think Ben was clever enough to realise the bluff? Was not Ben, in fact, losing a fool's advantage by revealing the little cleverness within him—and could he not play a useful card now, at this poignant moment, if he pretended that Sims had beaten him? . . .

'*Five!*'

'Oi!' gasped Ben. 'Oi!'

Don Manuel's raised hand paused.

'Put that dahn—yer've done me!' shouted Ben. 'I didn't git it from 'er, I got it from Faggis, but I know where she is, 'cos I saw 'er afore I left that larst village, see, when she was runnin' away.'

'She's in that village, then?' inquired Sims sharply.

'No!' answered Ben. 'She was givin' some money to a chap ter drive 'er to a stashun. "I'm 'oofin' it," she ses, "and you better come too," that was ter me, see, but I couldn't, 'cos I was shut in the room, see, we was torkin' through a winder, see, and then she spots you and carn't wait, see, and orf she goes!'

Ben paused and stared at Sims to mark the effect. But Sims hardly seemed to hear him. His head was raised, and he appeared to be listening to something else.

'Quick!' he whispered suddenly. 'Outside! All of you!'

The door was opened swiftly, there was a rapid exit, and then it swung to again. Ben and Miss Holbrooke were alone.

34

Confidences in a Cellar

Fate, dipping into the extremes of affluence and poverty with a disregard totally unknown to its own puppets, had thrown Ben and Miss Holbrooke together and had interwoven their destinies, but it was in this cold-stoned Spanish cellar, towards the conclusion of their strange adventure, that they actually conversed for the first time. Miss Holbrooke had only seen Ben once before, and then only for a few passing seconds. She barely saw him now, on this second occasion. And though he had seen her more often, it had nearly always been during her periods of unconsciousness, so that he had almost come to regard her in his thoughts as a fellow-creature doomed to perpetual silence and inactivity.

When Sims's spotlight had played upon her, however, he had suddenly awakened to her vivid reality. She had looked pale and frail. The effects of the drugging were still on her. But her limbs now had movement, her face expression, and her eyes light. The reason for all this upheaval ceased to be a theory; it had become a living fact.

And though Sims's spotlight no longer played upon her, and she had become a vague shadow again, her reality remained. Silent and conscious of each other, they allowed a full minute to pass, while the hurried steps outside grew fainter and fainter, and the low, anxious voices ceased. They waited tensely for something to happen. The something that had caused Sims to order the hurried exit, and that appeared to have permitted this unpremeditated interview. For would Sims otherwise have left these two alone together, knowing how anxious they would be to talk? But the something they waited for did not happen—or, if it did no sign of it percolated down to this underground cellar . . . 'Cellar—I alius hends hup in a cellar,' thought Ben . . . No shouting; no cries; no explosion.

'What is it? I don't understand!'

Miss Holbrooke's voice came to him presently through the darkness.

''Oo does, miss?' replied Ben, and moved a little closer to the voice.

'Who are you?'

Ben tried to think how he could explain himself.

'Aren't you the stowaway?' she helped him.

'Yus, that's right, miss,' he murmured, and moved a little closer still. It seemed to be a bit warmer where she was, like.

'But what are you doing here?'

'Tryin' ter git away.'

'You're not—one of *them*, then?'

'Lummy, no!'

'Then—are they kidnapping you too?'

'Me? Gawd, I ain't worth 'arf a brace-button!'

Something indistinguishable happened a few feet off.

'Say, are you funny, or is it my head?' came Miss Holbrooke's voice again, after a little pause. 'I guess this dope's given my brains a holiday.'

'Doncher worry, miss,' answered Ben hopelessly. 'It'll orl come right.'

'What makes you say that? Don't they—?'

'Wot?'

'*Mean* it?'

'You bet, they mean it!'

'Then how can it come right?'

''Cos—well, wot's the use o' thinkin' it won't? Tike it from me, miss, yer never dead till yer dead, and then yer ain't. I bin killed 'undred an' two times, twenty of 'em terday, and I'm still 'ere.'

'Are you serious—have they really tried to kill you?' she asked.

'Well, they ain't tried boilin' me in fat yet,' replied Ben; 'but I hexpeck they got that dahn fer nine-thirty.'

'Oh, I *wish* you'd explain! This little mind of mine just won't function! Why should they try to kill you? Why? Why?'

'Oh, everybody does that,' he answered evasively. 'That ain't nothink.'

'You're not making it any clearer.'

'It ain't rightly clear ter me. Seems like people's told three things when they're born—git a job, git married, and 'ave a shot at Ben.'

'Ben?'

'That's me, miss.'

'Ben! I'll remember. And now tell me, please. We've got to stop all this guessing game and get down to facts. Try and help me, Ben—I'm feeling pretty punk. What special reason have they for trying to kill you?'

'Eh?'

'Please!'

'Well, seein' as 'ow I'm sorter friend o' your'n—ain't I?'

'I'm beginning to think so,' she murmured.

'Well, then.'

'I see. Yes, I'm getting wise. Are you my only friend?'

'No. You got another.'

'Who?'

'A gal.'

'But why—well, never mind that now. Where is she?'

Ben suddenly chuckled. Of course, it wasn't the time to chuckle, but you have to sometimes, when you get a bit of a chance.

'Ah, that's what they wanter know!' he answered. 'But I wouldn't tell 'em! Fust they tries ter kill me with knives. One each side o' me fice an' the third in the middle, they ses. And when the third come along . . . Gawd! I bin through a bit but I don't want that agine! And then they brings me 'ere, ter mike me think they'd do it on you if I didn't tell 'em.'

'But you *did* tell them!' exclaimed Miss Holbrooke, suddenly recollecting.

'Nah, miss. That was high-wash, that was. Yer see, fust I'm goin' ter. I couldn't 'ave you killed, could I? I was in a fair pickle, and me mind was like a pot o' jam with wasps in it. Tork abart buzzin'! But then I ses ter meself, when 'e gits ter four—lummy, ain't that countin' 'orrible?— I was bein' both of us, like, when it was goin' on, if yer know wot I mean—well, then I ses ter meself, "Go on, they wouldn't kill 'er, she ain't worth sixpence dead." And then I ses, when 'e gits ter five, "Why not tell 'em a lie an' put 'em orf the skent?"'

'Skent?'

'Yus, miss. That's the one word I knows 'ow ter spell. Skent. Wot yer puts on her 'ankerchiff.'

'Oh, Ben!'

'Wot?'

'Never mind. But how I'm growing to love England! England! Say, where are we now?'

'Spine, miss. Villerpanzy.'

'How did we get here?'

'One day, miss, when I got a couple o' years, I'll tell yer.'

'Yes, yes. Of course, there's no time now. We must do something. What do you suppose is happening upstairs?'

'Can't 'ear nothink, miss.'

'Go and listen. I would, but I feel so weak—'

Ben tiptoed back to the door. He heard someone breathing on the other side. Then he heard himself breathing on his side, and deduced, with relief, that he must be a sort of breathing ventriloquist. 'But I wish I'd on'y do it when I wanted ter,' he thought.

He turned to Miss Holbrooke, who was now sitting bolt upright on the trestle, trying to listen also.

'Nothing,' he reported.

'Of course, the door's locked?'

He went back again. He returned again.

'Yus,' he said.

'Then we can only wait,' she sighed.

'Yus,' agreed Ben; 'but it'll orl come aht right, I tell yer, like I sed. 'Cos why? 'Cos we got somethink ter wait for, see? That's why.'

'Something to wait for?' exclaimed Miss Holbrooke, with sudden hope. 'What?'

'I'll tell yer. Do yer remember that long speech wot was mide ter me afore Sims—that's the white-'aired bloke—afore 'e starts countin'? Well, 'e wanted ter know if Molly Smith—that's the gal 'oo's yer friend, like me—'e wanted ter know if she'd give me the nime o' this plice.'

'Yes, I remember.'

'Well, she 'ad.'

'How did she know it?'

'She 'eard 'im say it once. But 'e also wanted ter know if she'd tole hennybody helse.'

'Well?'

'She 'as!'

'Oh, *who*? My father?'

'I dunno, miss. And, rightly speakin', she 'asn't. Wot I mean is, she rote it on a bit o' piper, and if they've fahnd the piper, then they'll come along and find hus, see? 'Cos they'll see on it Don Manuel, Villerspangle—'

'Spangle? I thought you said—'

'Well, wotever it is. The end don't matter. You bet they'll find it, miss, and you bet they'll come along. Lummy!' he cried, all at once. 'P'r'aps they're *'ere*! P'r'aps it was them wot mide 'em orl 'op it jest nah!'

Miss Holbrooke's hand shot out and caught hold of his sleeve. The theory was almost too wonderful to be borne! A rescue party, upstairs . . . at this moment . . .

But only silence greeted their strained ears.

'And the girl—my other friend—where is she, really?' asked Miss Holbrooke.

'She's waitin' at the nearest cottage dahn the road,' answered Ben. 'A hempty one.'

As he spoke, the door of the cellar opened, and Sims's voice came across the cold stone floor to them.

'Thank you for a most interesting and enlightening conversation, Ben,' said Sims. 'I enjoyed every word of it.'

Then the door closed again, and the key groaned in the lock.

35

An Official Visit

When Sims had complimented Ben on his brain, he had realised there was no danger in the compliment and that it could lead the said brain into no greater display of subtlety than Sims's own brain was capable of. Once he had definitely placed Ben in the category of uneducated people who could nevertheless, when driven to extremity, do surprising things, he had increased his watchfulness; and he had subsequently read Ben like a book.

He was not surprised that Ben showed courage and kept his mouth closed despite the threat of Don Manuel's knives. He was not surprised, as he counted five in the cellar, that Ben might guess the bluff and still keep his mouth closed. He was not surprised that Ben should go one farther and tell a wild story concerning Molly Smith. But he knew the story was a lie, and that it marked the limit of Ben's brain. For, if the story were true, why should he have taken such pains previously to withhold it?

This evidence of Ben's limitations and psychology had given Sims confidence that his last trick, which he had had up his sleeve before entering the cellar, would succeed. He had, of course, heard nothing to cause the hurried exit, and the exit had merely provided an excuse for leaving Miss Holbrooke and Ben together without arousing their suspicions. Alone, they would naturally exchange confidences. Sharp ears outside the door would overhear those confidences. 'Yes, is it not time,' reflected Sims complacently, as he began to ascend the stone staircase after having possessed himself of the confidences, 'that I paid my own brain a little compliment?'

He wound up the stairs smiling, but all at once, just before he reached the top, the smile vanished. A breeze came towards him, as from an open front door, and voices. Sims realised, with a twinge of abrupt annoyance, that something *was* happening upstairs, after all!

Sims was a good linguist. Spanish was among seven languages he could speak fluently. He had no difficulty, therefore, in understanding what the voices were saying.

'It's no use protesting, Don Manuel,' said a sharp official voice, 'and I may remind you that to protest, in a case like this, is to raise suspicions.'

'Suspicions!' exclaimed Don Manuel piously. 'What should the police suspect me of?'

'The police might suspect you of many things,' answered the official voice, 'which makes it all the more important for you to avoid prevarication. There have been a couple of murders not so very far from here—'

'Virgen Santa! Have I then committed two murders?'

'Have you?'

'Oh, yes! Now hang me like a dog!'

'Perhaps I will one day, Don Manuel. We're still looking

for the fellow who killed a little boy in a wood eight months ago. But if you didn't commit these two latest murders—'

'*Dios!* Of course I did not!'

'Then help us to catch the one who did.'

'And who is that?'

'Well, we're not sure yet, but there are three suspects.'

'Then why worry about me? Must you have four?'

'Four have been concerned in one murder before now. Still, no one is accusing you of anything yet, Don Manuel, beyond your own attitude.'

'My attitude? Ho! And what should that be?'

'Helpful.'

'Well—is it not?'

'You seem anxious that I should not enter.'

'*Demonio!* Who likes the police?' muttered Don Manuel. 'Why do you want to enter?'

Sims, on the stairs, cursed him for a fool.

'To search for the people who are suspected,' answered the officer.

'Oh! And who are they?'

'Three foreigners. Two of them English, and the third— well, he may be.'

'But why do you think they are *here*?'

'One of them mentioned your name.'

'What is that?' cried Don Manuel.

'He was found exhausted in the road from the coast. He was taken to a house—the house of Pascual Cordova, who found him—and the only words he spoke that they could understand there were "Don Manuel, Villabanzos."'

'Which, of course, proved that he was a murderer?'

271

'No. But he had a knife on him, and also a hammer, and I am assured that he acted in a very strange manner. Now, as he had evidently come over the mountains, from the district in which, these murders took place—well, Pascual Cordova naturally suspected him, and so did the doctor who was called in. They very properly sent for me.'

'And then?'

'I arrived to find that the fellow had escaped.'

'So?'

'He had got out of the window of the bedroom in which he had been locked.'

'He jumped?'

'No. He climbed down a rope. And here *is* the rope? Do you know it, Don Manuel?'

There was a pause. Then Don Manuel's voice rang out indignantly.

'What is this? I helped him to escape, did I? That is a good one! Why, I have not left my inn all the afternoon!'

'Well, rope is very much alike. But, when I showed this rope to Garcia, he told me that you had been to his shop only two days ago, and had bought some very like it. You will note, the rope is new.'

'*Dios meo!* I am to be hanged now for buying rope! Well, well, I have always said the world is mad! But what of the other two? Did Pascuel Cordova find them, also? You doubtless pay him so much a dozen. I have always thought he was too rich for his brains!'

'No, Pascuel Cordova did not find the other two. In fact, all I know about the other two is that they passed through the village only a few moments after the first fellow escaped, and that they, also, showed an interest in Don Manuel, of Villabanzos.'

'I interest the whole world, it seems!' cried Don Manuel.

'That is why you interest me, also,' replied the officer, dryly.

'Well, and how did these two others show their interest in me?'

'By inquiring the way to you.'

'Virgen Santa!'

'They even had a piece of paper on which your name was written.'

'What!'

'"Don Manuel, Villabanzos."'

'Did you see the piece of paper?'

'No.'

'Well, then—'

'The villager they inquired of saw it, and gave us the information afterwards. He could not understand their language, but when he asked, "*Inglés*," they nodded. Then they disappeared.'

'Where to?'

'I presume, to the inn of one Don Manuel, Villabanzos. And I, also, am at the inn of Don Manuel, Villabanzos, with, as you will see, half a dozen men. So let us now end this conversation and get to business. Have you seen anything of these three foreigners?'

'Certainly not.'

'Do you know anything about them?'

'What should I know?'

'Very well. If you insist on prevarication! You have no objection if I search this place?'

'I have a strong objection.'

'Why?'

'I do not like my word doubted.'

'Yet you do not act in a way to invite confidence. Now, listen, Don Manuel. I speak for your good. If these men are not here, you will not suffer by my search—unless, of course, you are hiding anything else—'

'What else should I hide?' cried Don Manuel desperately.

'You are behaving like a fool!' retorted the officer, with contrasting calmness. '*Are* you hiding anything else?'

'No!'

'Then, if I do find any of the people I am after, it will not be with your knowledge that they have made your inn their sanctuary?'

'No! No! *Diablo*, no!'

'So I am nothing for you to worry about. These three foreigners were obviously making for this spot, and they appear to be desperate men who do not stop at murder. They may have slipped into one of your cellars, and they may be waiting till darkness to add *you* to their list. I expect you have money on the premises? If you woke up while they were taking it, your body would make a nice pin-cushion for their points. We search your inn, therefore, in your interests as well as in ours.'

The officer's ironical voice paused for an instant. Then it rang out sharply, and gave a command. Don Manuel fell back a step or two, as unwelcome visitors began to fill his doorway.

'Hey! Wait! Where is your authority?' he shouted

'Here!' replied the officer, displaying his revolver. 'And there are six other similar authorities behind me.' Suddenly his voice cracked out like a revolver itself. 'Out of our way! Sharp! Do you hear?'

Don Manuel fell back again, momentarily beaten.

'Yes, but where are you going?' he demanded helplessly.

'The cellars first,' answered the officer. 'From there, if necessary, we'll work upwards to the roof.'

Two men remained guarding the entrance to the inn. Four others followed the officer to the stone staircase that led down to the cellars. At the head of the stairs, the officer paused.

'One moment,' he said.

Don Manuel had also paused at a door on the entrance floor. The officer suddenly strode to it and, thrusting the innkeeper aside, threw the door open.

Five men immediately looked up. A sixth kept his eyes on a couple of dice on a drink-sodden table.

'Three,' he muttered disgustedly.

Then he, too, looked up.

The officer was equally interested in mathematics. 'Seven all,' he was thinking. 'But my seven have discipline and revolvers. That's equal to fourteen knives.'

He closed the door and returned to the stairs. He went down the stairs, with his four men behind him. No one obstructed him.

There were apparently four cellars, and the doors of three were open. He searched each, and found nothing. Then he turned to the fourth door. It was locked, and there was no key. He called to the innkeeper, who was hovering unhappily in the background.

'Where is the key to this door?' he demanded.

Don Manuel professed ignorance.

'Come! Let me have it!' the officer rapped out.

'How can I let you have what I have not got?' retorted Don Manuel, clinging to straws, and wondering why the key was no longer on the outside. The next instant a solution occurred to him. Perhaps it was on the inside!

The same thought occurred, evidently, to the officer who was peering through the keyhole. There was no key on the inside.

'Do you want to go to prison, Don Manuel?' asked the officer.

'Is it the law that one goes to prison for losing a key?' answered the innkeeper.

'One can go to prison for lying.'

'Very well. I am lying. Now take me to prison.'

'When did you lose the key?'

'It has been lost for over a month.'

'Why have you not had a new one made?'

'Because I have three other cellars, and they, as you have seen, are nearly empty. I do not need the fourth.'

'Have you another key that will fit?'

'If I had, why should I not already have used it?'

'Because you say you have no use for the room. And if you have no use for the room, why did you trouble to lock it in the first instance?'

'I did not lock it,' replied Don Manuel, his mind working furiously. 'It was a drunken man I had. One night he nearly turned the place topsy-turvy, and locking doors was a part of his humour. I kicked him out, and found afterwards that he had gone off with one of the keys. The key to that door. Now are you satisfied?'

On the point of replying, the officer changed his mind. He regarded the door for an instant, noting its massivity, and also the narrowness of the passage outside it. A difficult door to force, this. Then, with a shrug, he turned away from it.

'Well, well, it may be as you say,' he remarked; 'but if it is not, there will be a pack of trouble coming to you,

Don Manuel. Now, then. The rest of the house. And quickly! Do you think I can stay here all night?'

They left the passage, and ascended to the upper floors . . .

But Mr Sims, on the other side of the locked cellar door, did not take the muzzle of his revolver from Miss Holbrooke's throat till the search had been completed, the front door had been slammed, and the officer and his six men had left.

Then, swiftly and silently, he slipped to the door of the cellar and unlocked it.

'Congratulations on your wisdom, Ben,' he whispered sardonically. 'You knew that time, didn't you, that Miss Holbrooke's life really *was* in danger. A single squeak, and she would be lying dead at this moment.'

The door closed.

''E's Satan!' gulped Ben.

36

'The Last Resort'

This time Sims completed his ascent of the stone stairway, and he found Don Manuel waiting for him at the top with a large, self-satisfied smile.

'Well, he has gone!' the innkeeper exclaimed, rubbing his fat hands together. 'We have fooled him beautifully!'

'If so, whose fault is that?' replied Sims, in a chilling voice. 'Yours or mine?'

Don Manuel's smile began to diminish.

'Did I do nothing?' he demanded.

'You did quite a lot,' answered Sims. 'You made the officer thoroughly suspicious. And he has neither been fooled—nor gone!'

Don Manuel opened his mouth wide. Then he turned quickly towards the front door, but Sims called him back.

'Don't go there!' he barked sharply. 'Stay where you are! If we show we know he hasn't gone, that will be the end of it.'

'But—'

'Listen, Don Manuel! Let me do the talking. You

278

remember when we all left the cellar? I stayed behind, didn't I? The reason I stayed behind was because I knew someone in the cellar had played me a silly trick and I had to explode it with a better one. The someone *thought* I had gone, and gave the trick away. Have you followed that?'

'Yes, yes! You mean that idiot of a tramp—'

'Well, follow this, also. Someone in this inn has played a silly trick on the officer, and *he* is trying to explode it in just the same manner. He's outside at this moment, waiting for us to give *our* trick away—'

'Oh, and whose silly trick was it, then?' interrupted Don Manuel warmly.

'The trick itself was mine, and I now retract in calling it silly. It was the only trick to play, owing to your own lack of wit on the doorstep. The silliness was your attitude regarding it and your explanation of it. And your subsequent belief that you had fooled the officer with your damned ridiculous story. I could have riddled that sailor fellow's story in a second if I hadn't chosen to let him give himself away, and the officer could have riddled your story just as easily if he had wanted to. Bah! I knew the officer's game the moment he pretended to accept your explanation. He is a man of intelligence, and *you* hadn't the intelligence to perceive it.'

'I have the intelligence to perceive that you are worrying over nothing!' retorted Don Manuel.

'It is nothing, then, that he is waiting outside somewhere, with six men?'

'You jump to conclusions! Suppose he *isn't*? I am going to find out.'

'How?'

'There's a room at the top where I can get a peep.'

'Without being seen yourself from the road?'

'I may not have your monumental brains, Mr Sims,' said Don Manuel savagely; 'but I am not a congenital idiot!'

He turned and disappeared up a flight of stairs. Sims lit a cigarette. In a minute the innkeeper returned, with a sullen expression.

'You were right,' he admitted at once. 'I saw one of them. Dogs!'

'Where?'

'In the wood down the road. Like a shadow moving.'

'And you still think I am worrying over nothing?'

'Yes! For what can they do? They wait. So do we. What do we suffer? When they grow tired, they will go away.'

'Or come back?'

'Not they!'

'You're confident! Well, suppose you are right, we are still in our difficulty.'

'How?'

'If they do not move for an hour, nor can *we*.'

'We don't want to move.'

'Wrong again, Don Manuel. We do want to move. We have *got* to move! The officer and his six men are merely our—local difficulty. Another difficulty—we might almost call it an international one—may come along at any second.'

Don Manuel cast up his eyes, and shook his head.

'I do not understand you,' he muttered, 'and please do not reply, "You wouldn't!"'

Sims smiled. 'Sometimes I refrain from the obvious,' he observed.

'Well, your "international difficulty" is not so obvious!'

'Then I will explain it. The officer outside is after the murderer of the two men near the coast. But others are after the kidnappers of Miss Holbrooke in the cellar below.'

'But they do not know where she is!'

'I have just learned that they *may* know! Your name and address, Don Manuel, were left behind on the ship from which we took Miss Holbrooke.'

'*Diablo!*'

'Which means that we must get Miss Holbrooke away from here at once. I should say, at a guess, that your inn is about the unhealthiest spot at this moment in the whole of Spain. Two more people know of it as well,' he added.

'Are there any who do *not*?' cried Don Manuel. 'What two more are these?'

'You have a short memory. The officer spoke of two more Englishmen he was after—'

'Yes, yes! Of course! The other suspects!' Don Manuel paused, then sought Sims keenly with his beady eyes. 'The two fellows you double-crossed, eh, Mr Sims?'

'For our mutual benefit, Don Manuel,' replied Sims, unruffled. 'They would reduce your share as well as mine if they were with us.'

'But they have not come here!'

'No. And why have they not? And what will be their humour if they do come here? And—where are they at this moment?'

This question, shot at the innkeeper, rebounded and struck the questioner. He paused abruptly, and thought, frowning, for several seconds. Then he said:

'Yes, this is clearly the unhealthiest spot in Spain! The local police—Miss Holbrooke's friends—Greene and Faggis—the girl—'

'I forgot her!' interposed Don Manuel, growing more and more uneasy. 'Where the devil is *she*?'

'Not half a mile away.'

'What!'

'That is another thing I discovered from our lunatic in the cellar.'

'Half a mile—do you know the spot?'

'I can walk straight to it.'

'And what are you going to do about it?'

'I am *going* to walk straight to it.'

'Now who is the fool?' cried Don Manuel, with exasperated triumph. 'You will walk straight to it, and the officer will walk straight after you!'

'I sincerely hope so,' replied Sims.

'You hope—? I give it up!'

'It will be a blow to me if he does not walk after me. Believe me, I shall leave most suspiciously. And, while he is following me with all his men, *you* will be leaving this unhealthy spot—for ever, I should advise you—and taking Miss Holbrooke with you.'

Don Manuel looked at Sims hard. Then he looked towards the door behind which his six other ruffians had returned to their dice throwing. Then he looked at Sims again.

'And where do I take Miss Holbrooke?' he murmured.

'I think you and I never repeat the name of the place,' answered Sims, and now he also threw a glance towards the door, 'saving by the definition, "The Last Resort."'

'So—it has come to that now!'

'It was always intended to come to that, Don Manuel—though not,' he added, as the innkeeper's eyebrows shot up, 'in this particular fashion. But if circumstances had not forced us to act now, we should undoubtedly have flitted to our last resort—*the place only you and I know of!* Begin with many, Don Manuel, but work down to a few. To those, in fact, who *must* remain, and to no others. It saves risk. It saves double-crossing. It increases the final share. Eh?'

'I thought I was a devil,' muttered Don Manuel, 'but, *Deos,* by your side I am almost respectable!' He closed his eyes, considered, and opened them again. 'Well, devil or not, you are right. There is no hope here.' He held up four fingers. 'Four separate points of danger outside'—he added the thumb—'and a leakage within! Someone helped that girl to escape, be sure of it.' He closed his eyes once more, and now spoke with them closed. 'Then there is, as you called him, the lunatic in the cellar. What do I do with him?'

'I should like to have dealt with him myself,' sighed Sims; 'but, as I shall not be returning, you will have to deal with him yourself.'

'Deal with him?'

'Deal with him. In the most definite sense. In fact, kill him, Don Manuel. And when I say "kill him," I mean that, also, in the most definite sense. If you propose to do it with a knife, see that you stick your knife into him fifty times. Forty-nine will not be enough. If you drown him, hold him under the water with a ton weight. Yourself, for instance. If you shoot him—no, he cannot be shot. I have tried that myself. I fancy the only certain way of really killing our lunatic is to cut him up into five pieces and to have one piece deposited in each Continent.'

Don Manuel grinned.

'Leave him to me,' he said.

'Unfortunately, I have got to. But are you as confident that you can deal with Miss Holbrooke? That you can get her away from here without anybody knowing? Alive, of course.'

'I shall think of something.'

'Lacking your sublime faith, I shall think for you. When I leave, you will proceed to the cellar, and you will kill Ben. By the way, that is his name. Let everybody see you kill him. Then, get your men to put him in a sack, and say that the body must be taken away, to save suspicion when it is found. Volunteer to take it yourself. Send your men back to their dice. And then—'

He paused. Don Manuel frowned impatiently.

'Well, and then?'

'Then pour Ben's body out of the sack, and put Miss Holbrooke's in. When you go forth to do your good deed, the lunatic's body will be in the locked cellar, and Miss Holbrooke will be in the sack on your back.'

'She will make no objection, of course?' queried Don Manuel, after a pause.

'She has travelled innumerable miles without making any objection. Here is something to stop her complaints. And here is the cellar key.'

Sims handed two objects to Don Manuel. The innkeeper took them thoughtfully.

'Yes, it is a good plan,' he confessed. 'But suppose someone sees me with the sack?'

'It is dark, and there will be no moon till after midnight.'

'And I go to "The Last Resort"?'

'Yes.'

'And you meet me there?'

'Naturally.'

'You think I will not double-cross you?'

'You are helpless without me. Alone, you would burst like a pin-cushion.'

'And what will *you* do—meanwhile?'

'I shall round up as many dangerous elements as I can, and see that our officer outside gets a good bag.'

'What if this good bag should include *you*?' suggested Don Manuel.

'In that case,' replied Sims, 'you will be well advised to get rid of Miss Holbrooke, as you will have got rid of Ben, and to take a very fast boat to the North Pole. But I shall not be included in the officer's bag. The bag will include, I imagine, Molly Smith—she will not escape a second time—and whoever happens to be at this inn when the officer returns to it. Every one in it at present, in fact, except our two selves, Don Manuel; and we shall not be in it. Now, is everything clear?'

'It is as clear,' nodded the innkeeper, 'as an empty hive.'

A minute later, Mr Sims walked out of the inn to draw the police away, while Don Manuel, followed by his six ruffians, went down to kill Ben.

37

The Events on the Road

Before dealing with the events in the cellar, let us follow the events on the road, for the events on the road eventually led back to the cellar, to merge in a culmination not dreamt of in the philosophy of any of the participants.

The road was dark and dripping as Sims stepped out upon it, and the average traveller would have faced it with a sour expression; but Sims's expression was the reverse of sour, and he even turned his head and called cheerily to the closing door.

'That fool of an officer, Don Manuel, would give a lot to see what has just walked out of your locked cellar!' he chuckled. 'But he'd give more if he could see the *next* place I'm going to walk into!'

The fool of an officer, concealed under a spreading branch, heard the remark, as he was intended to. But he was not quite such a fool of an officer as Sims's description assumed. When Sims swung by the clump of trees behind which he and his men were hidden, he thought rapidly for an instant, and then, picking out four of the men to accompany him, he signed the other two to stay. Both Sims and the inn were to remain under supervision.

Sims knew he was being followed, and was merely wrong in the matter of mathematics. He had reckoned on seven followers, and there were only five.

In contented ignorance he proceeded along the way, humming softly to himself. He heard many sounds. The rain made a steady, insistent patter on the road, and his boots scrunched at each long stride with the rhythm of a metronome. Every now and then a little stream of wind, stealing silently into the night and ending in a sudden flurry of discovery, shook the tree branches on either side of the road, and produced a violent dripping. Occasionally a little rustle, distinguishable only to the acutest ears, marked the fear or restlessness of some small creature. Sims's own humming added its music to the orchestra.

But if he heard the footsteps of others as well as his own, if he heard an occasional soft slither through the road-bordering trees, or a suppressed exclamatory whisper that marked some minor tragedy among the trees—a little unseen pool, a hole that caught a boot, a branch that swept a face—he gave no sign.

'My ears are deaf,' he reflected. 'I know nothing. But I wish the damned fools would make less noise!'

The noise he complained of at that particular moment was the echo of his own footsteps.

Presently he recognised it as an echo. He recognised also the explanation of the echo's clearness. The trees on either side of the road were now closely packed, forming tall walls of foliage through which he passed. He was walking through an outdoor passage, and sound could only escape above; on each side the walls of trees threw it back.

He increased his pace. There were two good reasons for this. The first was that he feared the thickness of the trees would force his pursuers out into the road, and then the farce of his pretended ignorance would be more difficult to keep up. They might even overtake him! That would be catastrophic!

The second reason was that he was thoroughly soaked, and he wanted to get the business over.

With an instinct that had helped him many times in the past, and was akin to the instinct of a blind man who knows when he is near a wall, Sims smelt the last lap of his journey. He knew as certainly as though he had been told that, only a little farther on, the empty cottage waited for him. It would be tucked away somewhere on the right—yes, the wall of trees seemed already to be thinning a little—and he vaguely recalled a roof or two while he had been chasing the confounded horse Don Manuel had lent him, when he had come upon Ben so strangely caparisoned. Yes, it would be about here. Undoubtedly, undoubtedly it would be about here. An accurate recollection of time and distance checked the deduction. In another half-minute . . .

Yes, in another half-minute—*what*?

It swept over Sims that he really did not know. He had embarked on this adventure partly through necessity, but partly, also, through self-confidence. 'I can deal with any situation,' was Sims's motto, and his life had justified the motto. But he had to admit that it did help him to know what the situation was!

'Let me get my mind quite clear,' thought Sims, during the final half-minute. 'Clear not only on myself, but on everybody else who may affect myself. At this moment,

Don Manuel has killed Ben and is conveying Miss Holbrooke to "The Last Resort." Six fools are waiting at the inn for his return, and for my return. We shall not return. But the fool of an officer behind me must return, with his six fools, and then they can all have a merry time. Miss Holbrooke's friends may also turn up at the inn and join in the merriment. Well, well, that's all to plan. But meanwhile what am I going to find at this empty cottage?'

As the question flashed through his mind, the cottage roof grew darkly out of the thinning trees. Farther along the road, considerably farther, was a tiny glimmer of light from another cottage, but no light came from beneath this nearest roof. A little track sprawled from the road to the building, with a drunkard's generous disregard for straightness. Had it indeed been trodden out by inebriates? Sims paused for an instant, but his mind was not concerned with the birth of the track. It was concerned with the question of what the track was going to lead him to.

'Assuming Molly Smith is still there,' he thought, 'I must lead the officer to Molly Smith, and vanish during her capture. Molly Smith must be captured, just as Ben had to be killed. A thought! Should Molly Smith be killed? By an unfortunate incident in the process of capture? Well, perhaps. We'll see. It would retard the ultimate pursuit. Luckily for her, Molly Smith cannot speak Spanish. If she could, she would certainly have to be killed.'

He was walking along the crooked track now.

'But Molly Smith can make gestures,' his mind ran on. 'She can use her eyes, and she can point. If I could remain on the spot, I could easily convince the fool of an officer that she is dangerous and that I am not. But I cannot remain on the spot. I have got to vanish. That will be suspicious, and will make Molly's gestures all the more eloquent!' A point grew clear to him, and slackened his pace. 'No, Molly Smith must not see me! Or, if she does, then an accident of some sort should certainly occur to Molly Smith. As it has happened to Ben.' He smiled suddenly in the darkness. He could smile on the scaffold itself. 'And as it shall happen before long to Don Manuel!'

But suppose Molly Smith were *not* there? The dark roof was now very close.

'Yes, suppose she has left?' thought Sims. 'Or is now leaving. Well, if she is now leaving—if she has heard us—she will be caught. The fool of an officer will, I assume, have sense enough to leave a man or two in the road. But if she has left, then the cottage will be empty. How shall I act?'

Another twenty yards to the entrance. The grasses rose tall and long, and licked one's boots.

'I shall be surprised. I shall be amazed. I shall be grief-stricken. I shall become a greater soliloquist than Hamlet, and shall pour out my soul to the world. "Villanedo!" I shall cry. "They've taken her, after all, to Villanedo! They'll kill Pascuel Cordova and his old woman—" Yes, that will set them running. Myself, too, eh? Leading the chase! But I double back in the confusion and the darkness . . .'

His hand groped quietly towards his revolver pocket. The cottage door rose before him. It was open. Beyond, the black gap of uncertainty!

On the threshold of the black gap Sims paused, and perhaps he did wonder as he stood there, with eyes strained for what lay ahead and ears strained for what lay behind, whether he had been entirely wise, and whether his innate self-confidence were going to be justified. But it was too late now, however, to draw back. Probably, at that moment, his pursuers were silently spreading out and surrounding the cottage, and to turn tail at this juncture would be to court disaster. He must enter the cottage, discover whatever waited to be discovered, and twist the discovery to his own advantage.

He passed through the black gap. He passed into sudden silence. The rain no longer pattered down upon him, and though he still heard it, it was now merely an off-stage accompaniment to a scene that had changed. Things stirred outside. Here, inside, all was static. Coldness without movement seemed to have settled in the empty cottage; it did not come to meet one, as a current, but one walked into it, and shivered in its motionless embrace.

Then, abruptly, the silence was broken. Something creaked, and a door began to open somewhere at the back. A slit of faint yellow appeared and widened to an inch or two. Assumedly, then, had the approach to the cottage been made from the rear, a tiny light would have glimmered . . .

Sims steeled himself, smiling as he did so. He always kept his smile by him. It was good company, and could wither a difficulty with its cool contempt. A creaking door and a slit of light, produced by the timidity of a girl, were certainly not sufficient to drive it away.

But a moment later Sims realised that the creak and the light had not been produced by a girl, and as he realised it he sped with amazing rapidity to the staircase. He identified the staircase by a second slit of light cast by the first slit upon the bottom stair, and by the time the door was wide he was half-way up the staircase and safely round the bend. Then a man's voice spoke from the doorway; disagreeable, contemptuous, familiar.

'Nerves again, Faggis,' said the voice. 'There's nothing out here!'

'I'll swear I heard something,' retorted Faggis's voice. 'And so did she!'

She? Sims, on the stairs, noted the allusion with satisfaction. All three of them? Excellent! With the police locking them all up for a night or two, and the tramp out of the way, the road to 'The Last Resort' would be immeasurably simplified, and there would only be Don Manuel left to deal with . . .

'Well, come out and look for yourself, if you want to,' answered Greene. 'Maybe you can hatch something!'

'Oh, you're probably right!' growled Faggis. 'Sailors are supposed to have good sight, so if you don't see anything, I don't expect there is anything. Anyhow, what we've got to fix our minds on is—what's happening at that blasted inn!'

'I've told you—nothing's happening there!' This time it was Molly's voice.

'So you say,' sneered Faggis, while the door of the room half-closed again. Sims, on the stairs, descended a little, and strained his ear closer. 'But if nothing's going on at the inn, what were *you* doing here?'

'Yes, and why did you duck round the wall when we spotted you from the road?'

'You don't think I love you, do you?' demanded Molly.

'No one loves anybody in this sort of game,' remarked the third officer; 'but they have to pull together. Were you in this double-cross from the start?'

'Don't talk rot!'

'Rot? You knew the address of this Don Manuel!'

'That was just a lucky accident.'

'And you were obviously making for his place, when you dropped in here?'

'No, I was coming away.'

'And you warn *us* to keep away—'

'Of course! I want to save my skin, if you don't want to save yours. Heavens, haven't I *told* you? They've killed the tramp, there are twenty men with knives, and Sims has told them what to *do* with their knives if any of us turn up.'

'Blast him!'

'I'm with you there! But what's the use of talking? If you want to get the knives stuck into you, go on to the inn. If you don't want to, turn back.'

In a corner of the little hall-way was a pile of straw. Sims, from the stairs, suddenly eyed it.

'And what'll *you* do?' inquired Faggis. 'Turn back with us?'

'No.'

'Why not?'

'Ever heard of hating?'

'Yes, and of loving,' said Greene, with a sudden little laugh.

'What's that mean?' came the sharp response.

'Why, that if I've got to find my way out of this god-forsaken country,' observed Greene, 'I mayn't object to a spot of consolation along the road.'

'Well, you won't get it!'

'Won't I? You never know! Anyway, the road's too darned wet and dark to tempt *me* out on it again tonight. And there's another thing. That one-eyed village back there isn't any too healthy. So I'm *staying*, my dear—'

'And so am I,' drawled Faggis. 'You won't forget, Greene, that she's *my* working partner and not yours, will you?'

Sims descended a few more steps. He still eyed the straw

in the corner of the hall. Above it was an opening in the wall where once had been a window. Beyond the opening was a clump of moist bushes.

The voices in the room droned on, but Sims hardly listened to them. He had heard all he needed.

They were staying inside. And the fool of an officer and his men were staying outside. Curse Spanish caution! Yet, after all, if the men rushed the cottage, could Sims effect his own escape without first creating some sort of diversion?

He had taken his bearings. He could smell the plan of a house. He knew where windows were before he saw them, and also where they weren't . . .

Suddenly the girl's voice rose angrily. Sims was now at the bottom of the stairs.

'I'm not a prude, heaven knows!' Molly cried. 'But, Faggis, tell that little worm what happens when people try to kiss me? *You* know!'

'No, he needn't tell me,' replied Greene. 'I'd rather like to find out for myself.'

'Sure,' said Faggis. 'But you forget, Greene, *two* things may happen to you.'

'Eh?'

'Hers first, and mine after.'

The straw was no longer immediately under the opening where once there had been a window. Sims was under the opening. The straw had been shoved a foot or two nearer the middle of the hall.

There was quite a pile of it, and some of it had been heaped near the rickety wooden balustrade.

'Do you remember that moment, Greene,' asked Faggis, 'when I held you over the precipice?'

Evidently Greene did remember the moment. But, until pain was actually there, Greene had more pluck than Faggis.

'Quite a Squire of Dames, eh?' he snapped sarcastically. 'Well, then, how about tossing?'

Immediately afterwards Greene felt the pain. A resolute little hand smacked his cheek, and the sound of the smack penetrated into the hall. At the same moment, a sound from the hall penetrated into the room.

'What's that?' exclaimed Faggis, raising his head.

'Little feline!' cried Greene.

'Shut up! Listen!' hissed Faggis.

'The devil! Can't you live two minutes without hearing something?' rasped Greene, thoroughly out of temper.

But then he noticed the girl was listening also. He could have got his kiss now with ease. What had suddenly put her off her guard?

Greene twisted his head round towards the half-open door. He discovered that he, too, was listening. Something was crackling in the hall. There was a queer, stealthy, insistent swishing sound . . .

After ears, noses! Now they no longer listened. They sniffed.

'Burning!' gasped Faggis. 'Something's burning!'

And after noses, eyes! Through the aperture of the door came a little puff of smoke.

In a trice, they were all in the hall-way.

An incredible thing had happened. They were alone in the house, and the sole illumination, a candle, was still melted to the window-sill of the room they had just left. Yet the house was on fire! Flames licked up from a heap of straw, and had already caught the rotting balustrade.

They stared beyond the burning straw. It was empty. The

windowless aperture yawned peacefully through the smoke, telling no story.

'Hell!' cried Greene suddenly. 'If we're not quick, we'll be caught!'

'How in thunder did it happen?' exclaimed Faggis, still hardly crediting it.

'*Wouldn't* you be the person to stand and ask?' shouted Greene.

As he shouted, he dived past the flames and disappeared into the darkness. A moment later he tried to cry out, but found himself incapable.

Faggis stared towards the spot into which he had disappeared. Blackness woke fitfully in this new and unaccustomed light. Rain dripped through it. Now flashing and illuminated. Now dim. Now heard only. Now flashing again.

Abruptly, Faggis woke up. He followed Greene. But he was bigger and stronger than Greene, and his shout of utter consternation escaped. As arms closed round him he fought like a demon against demons; only the other demons had all the advantage, since they had been aware of him and he had not been aware of them. Also, there were more of them. To Faggis, in his startled frenzy, there seemed a thousand. He struck out wildly. All the hideousness of the past days seemed to have loosened itself at this moment. It was downing him. He struck, and struck again. Each blow seemed weaker than the last. Smash! Ah—one of the demons felt *that* one! The joy of it momentarily sweetened his frenzy and renewed his waning strength. He struck again. Another demon went down. He laughed insanely, and, all at once, recalled that he had feet. One was free. He kicked violently. Another demon went down. Three! How many were there? There could not *really* be a thousand! If he went on like this, there must presently be an end!

Then there came another crack. A different kind of a crack. Something that was not quite cricket spat at Faggis. The demons vanished. Everything vanished. Faggis fell to the ground like a log . . .

In a clump of dripping bushes just outside the aperture where once there had been a window, Sims stooped, waiting. Fool, Greene! Fool! He had been too easy. But Faggis—by heaven, Faggis was putting up a fight! Sims could hear it. He could also sense its progress.

The shadows menacing his clump of bushes grew fewer. Three . . . Two. Confound that last shadow! Didn't it realise it was needed elsewhere? Go away! Go away! You don't know there's an old man hiding in a bush, you don't! Go away . . .

The shadow disappeared. Sims smiled. Ah, that good companion, his smile! How it steadied him! He smiled all the way to the road. He smiled as he dived across the road, and slid into a track that, he knew, would lead to another road—the last road of the adventure! The road to The Last Resort!

'When you are not a fool yourself,' he reflected, 'it is not so bad, after all, to have been born into a world of fools!'

Another, who was not a fool, slipped after him out of the aperture where once there had been a window. She, also, ran unseen up the tangled garden path to the road. But she did not cross the road and enter the track that Sims had entered. She swerved swiftly to the left, and, as a shot cracked in the chaos behind her, raced madly through the dripping darkness towards Don Manuel's inn.

38

The Battle in the Cellar

Don Manuel, accompanied by his six ruffians, went down to the cellar to kill Ben, and Ben heard him coming. And something told Ben, even before Don Manuel told him through the door, that this time he meant it.

In the darkness of the cellar, sitting so close to Miss Holbrooke that his hand unconsciously touched her skirt, Ben tried to work it out. A dangerous weariness had suddenly settled on him, and, although he did not know this, the future of himself and of his companion depended entirely upon whether this weariness, which seemed to have entered from nowhere, was going to increase or evaporate during the next few moments. Out of our varying moods spring our actions, and it is by our actions that we are judged by superficial critics. This action brings, joy, this tragedy, this a smile, this a tear; this, life, and this, death. Who takes the trouble to inquire into the mood itself, and to seek the source from which that came? Only the psychologist, who refuses to give up guessing, or the humanitarian, who refuses to give up hoping; and both the psychologist and the humanitarian meet in the darkness and confusion of an unfathomable design.

Though unfathomable, the design exists. Cosmos depends upon it for her equally unfathomable need. And we, too, depend on our lesser designs, even if we are nothing more significant than a weary tramp in a cellar, wondering what to do next.

'Yer can jest let it come, like yer was in the gas, and git it over that way,' reflected Ben. 'Or yer can jump up like and 'it abart. But wot's the *use* of 'ittin' abart? If I 'adn't kep' on 'ittin' abart, I wouldn't be 'ere now, would I? I'd be lyin' com'ferble somewhere, and nobody'd ever come arter me agine. Jest lyin' nice an' com'ferble . . . Or does yer float? Well, that'd be orl right. I'd like ter float.'

He was really very tired. He was so tired that he hardly had the energy to listen to the approaching steps outside.

'Arter orl, wot does it come to?' he demanded of himself. ''Ere we are, and there we go. So wot does it come ter?'

He felt he hadn't quite answered the question. The feeling annoyed him. His limp hand, hanging at his side, became conscious of the skirt it was touching. The skirt, in some queer, silent way, seemed to be begging him not to float. At least, not just yet. And he *did* want to float!

'Yer know, *I* b'leeve it's a sort of a sea,' he reflected, 'On'y yer don't 'ave no rudder.'

The skirt insisted.

'Yus, it's orl right, if the gal's your'n!' his thoughts protested, with startling frankness. 'Gawd, if I 'ad a *gal*— but I don't *git* nothink! Yer jest goes on an' on an' on, and arter that yer goes on goin' on an' on an' on. It ain't fair! Stright, it ain't! I wanter *stop* somewhere, and if it's floatin'—well, I'll 'ave that!'

The steps paused outside.

'Lummy, it fair kills yer, livin' like this,' thought Ben.

There came a sound at the door.

'Funny thing!' thought Ben. 'I don't seem ter be feelin' nothink.'

A key turned.

'Gawd, me 'ead's hempty,' thought Ben. 'Do they clear yer aht fust, like, so's ter mike yer lighter?'

A voice came through the door before it opened.

'*Asesinar*,' said the voice. '*Keeell!*'

'Wot I wants, afore I pops orf,' decided Ben, 'is jest a good old blub. Wunner if they'd wait fer it?'

The door moved. So did the skirt that touched Ben's numb fingers. Miss Holbrooke had been thinking her own numb thoughts, but the opening door sent a sudden shiver through her, and the shiver reached Ben through a little piece of expensive cloth.

And then, suddenly, Ben ceased to think about floating. He could stand his own shivering, but he couldn't stand anybody else's, and this communicated shiver corkscrewed straight into his heart.

Lummy, he *didn't* care if he died, straight he didn't! But this girl beside him—that was different! *She* hadn't got to look forward to attics and cobwebs and cold stone seats! She had silk and satin to live for, and gold chairs, and p'r'aps that nice young feller who'd been hanging round her on the ship. Then there was another thing. Even if she did want to die, she hadn't had Ben's practice, and you mustn't spring horrors on a girl like her without proper warning!

Here Ben's logic was at fault. Immediate physical danger threatened only him. In the instant that followed, however, he forgot that, and his worn-out brain visioned Miss

Holbrooke lying dead with nine knives in her, and Don Manuel playing quoits over her body. Her pretty face dead white. Her legs crumpled up under her. The skirt he now touched—covered with blood.

The vision was in his harrowed mind. The reality was beside his tortured body. The two were about to merge and to become one. Unless . . .

Unless what?

'Unless ME!' thought Ben.

A chemical explosion sends a bullet winging through space. An emotional explosion discharged Ben. Don Manuel at first frankly disbelieved the sight that sped towards him through the air, because in a properly constituted planet such things did not happen. Men crossed a floor on the ground. But here was Ben crossing it three feet above the ground, and making noises as he came. Not one noise; several noises. One like the offspring of a lion and a pea hen. One like a soda waterfall. One like a whistle with a sore throat. One like a sore throat with a whistle. These, and other noises equally unusual, all joined together in a sort of human whizz, and landed with their origin on Don Manuel's elephantine chest.

Possibly all tramps make this sound when travelling through air at nine hundred and nineteen miles per second, but no previous tramp had ever provided evidence.

For a quivering instant, the small human bullet and its large human target stuck together. Don Manuel's chest was too flabby to bounce off. But it reeled back, and, as it did so, a swinging arm caught Don Manuel's cheek; an arm that, feeling like lead, delivered it.

The blow on the cheek stung the astounded innkeeper to momentary action. He raised a huge paw to strike back, uttering an incoherent oath as he did so, and it was this movement, working upon a mind strangely guided in its anguish, that determined the conclusion of the world's shortest and sharpest battle. For in the raised paw was the cellar key—the key to security and salvation—and Ben's bleared eyes beheld and recognised it.

If Ben's momentum had been spent, he would have dropped off the innkeeper's chest like a dead fly from a wall, but fortunately he had not yet ceased to press into his opponent's flesh. Risking everything, he seized Don Manuel's nose with one hand, and dived at the key with the other. The first capture made the second easy. The key dropped into his hand, as he himself dropped on to the floor.

One thing remained. It was to complete Don Manuel's tip. The only way to do this, if you could not reach the head and shove it back, was to seize the legs and pull them forward, and to kick with all your violence whatever portion of bulk started descending upon you. Ben accomplished these matters, thereby causing Don Manuel to continue his sway backwards into the passage; and when the innkeeper felt his legs going as well as his body, his head went too. A moment of stark terror urged him to assist his own exit. He really believed, in this unique moment, that he had suddenly been confronted with something occult; and, before the belief had passed, the cellar door was banged to, and the key was turned on the inside.

Then Don Manuel, gasping and dazed, found himself grappling with another miracle.

'*Ay Dios mio!*' he cried, and rounded on his men. 'Where were *you*?'

But they merely blinked back his own bewilderment. Virgen Santa! When things like this happen . . .

From the other side of the door rose a violent sobbing. Ben was having his blub.

He felt two arms round him. His strength was gone. He was being drawn back somewhere. His head rested peacefully against something warm.

'Ain't key this 'ow was!' he wept.

Was that what he meant? It didn't sound right. He tried again.

'Isn't 'oo arterwards?'

'Sh! Just lie quiet,' came the whispered instruction.

She was right. He couldn't say what he meant. The words wouldn't come in their right order and the alphabet was all mixed up. And, in addition, he didn't know himself what he meant, so how could he tell anybody else? Much best just to enjoy yourself and cry . . .

In the distance were sounds of banging. Close to, however, all was quiet, saving for the beating of a heart. He listened to the beating. It wasn't his heart. He knew *his* heart. That just went an ordinary plonk, plonk, plonk, plonk. But this was somebody else's. You couldn't describe the sound of this heart. He listened, permitted, to the precious music. The permission was as wonderful as the music. A sudden idea came to him.

'Did '*e* win,' he wondered, 'and am I floatin'?'

He hoped Don Manuel had won, so that he could go on floating for ever. But the banging grew louder, and the sweet sea became a little agitated. He raised his head suddenly. The banging was now louder still.

'Wot is it?' he gulped.

'They're trying to break the door down,' answered Miss Holbrooke.

'They carn't,' he muttered, groping for consolation.

'Still, if they *do*,' she whispered, 'you must stay quiet this time. You've been—wonderful!'

''Oo 'as?'

'I don't know what to say about you.'

'Go on!'

'But, remember, there's nothing more you can do. They won't kill *me*, and if you go on trying to protect me, they may kill you.'

Ben thought about it. The door was still standing, but it could hardly stand for ever. Then he said:

'There's one thing I ain't tole yer yet, miss. I've come dahn from William the Conquerer! So I *gotter* proteck yer, see?'

He staggered to his feet as he spoke, and, despite her protestations, began shoving the trestle towards the door. Realising his determination, and also the wisdom of it, she helped him. While the smashing and the swearing went on outside, and the hinges creaked, they found a few other oddments in dark corners, and added them to the fragile barricade.

'It ain't much,' observed Ben; 'but everythink's something.'

'Listen!' whispered Miss Holbrooke, all at once. 'They've stopped!'

Yes; silence had suddenly fallen outside the door. What was happening? Had they given up?

A few moments later this hope was dashed to the ground. Footsteps returned, with an accompanying sound of clanking metal.

'They mean it this time, miss!' muttered Ben solemnly.

'I'm afraid so,' she replied. 'And—if they break through— don't forget what I've said!'

The noise recommenced. The banging had a new ring now. It clanged. It vibrated. It split.

An ominous line showed in the door. It was a little crack, and gradually it increased in length and breadth. Light glowed through it, marking its growth. Soon, other points and lines of light appeared, and while they augmented, the hinges shook and creaked.

Now one of the cracks was an inch wide, and through the width came a coiling finger. Ben had a piece of a packing case in his hand. He brought it down on the finger. There was a howl, and the finger disappeared.

'Shall we call it a drawer?' bawled Ben.

Bang! Smash! The crack was now so wide that bits of faces could be seen through it. But, worse than this, the lower hinge was definitely giving way. Another minute, at most, and the door would be down and the enemy would pour in.

Bang! Smash! Lummy, that was a narsty one! Bang! Smash! Bang . . . Ben felt a hand on his sleeve.

'Remember!' came the whisper.

'Not if they touch you, I won't!' retorted Ben, gripping his bit of wood. 'Think I'm agoin' ter let them lay a 'and on yer? If they . . . Oi! Look aht! Look aht!'

The door groaned and yielded. The weakened hinges gave way, and there was a crash of wood. Then Don Manuel's huge form appeared in the aperture, his face shining with perspiration, and his eyes evil with revengeful fury. He raised an arm. Something gleamed in it. Ben fell on his stomach, and the gleaming thing flew above him, embedding itself in a beam.

He knew he was done for now. It was just a question of guessing where the next blade would enter him. Head?

Neck? That'd be narsty. Middle of the back? Place where mother spanked you? "Allo, mother!' he thought, struggling against nausea. 'With yer in 'arf a tick!'

The next blade was a long time coming! Funny, that! And what was this new noise in the passage? A new sort of shouting. A new sort of rushing. A new sort of banging . . .

'Bet it's a trick!' decided Ben. 'I ain't movin'.'

But what was happening? All sorts of things were drumming in his ears. Cries and scuffles and—lummy, wasn't that a shot? P'r'aps he'd *better* move? He tried and found he couldn't. It takes it out of you, all this dying!

'Yer know, I'm beginnin' ter think I wasn't *made* ter die proper,' he reflected, as the new sounds grew louder. 'I b'leeve they'll 'ave ter tike me up in a go-cart, like they did Elijijah!'

39

The Fruits of Actions

Voices poured all about him. He felt like a lawn being sprayed by a vocal fountain. Some of the voices were recognisable, some were not. Some had a right to be there, some, by all the rules of logic, hadn't.

Time went mad. People and places played hide-and-seek in it. A large man, but not as large as Don Manuel, was hugging Miss Holbrooke. That was yesterday, wasn't it? A young man with a vaguely familiar face was running about like an excited little dog. That was tomorrow. Now *he* was hugging Miss Holbrooke. That'd be about half-past three. A comic opera soldier was sitting on Don Manuel's head, and another comic opera soldier was sitting on his feet. That'd be Tuesday and Friday. An officer was yelling orders. That'd be next week.

But, equally confusing, was a series of illogicalities in which he himself figured. Now he was on the floor. Now he wasn't on the floor. Now he was in the middle of a crowd of questioning faces. Now the large man was hysterically shoving notes in his pocket. Now he was all by himself again. Now he was leaning against a wall. Now he was tripping over a stone stair. Now he was in a hall that seemed to have had an accident. Now there wasn't any hall, but just rain and darkness.

And why was all this happening? Why hadn't he remained on the floor, or in the middle of the crowd of faces? Was it because one particular face wasn't there? Because, since people were kissing and hugging each other, and comic opera soldiers were sitting on comic opera brigands' chests, the centre of Ben's necessity had changed and he was free to follow other hazy impulses?

Certainly, no one was now worrying about him. The only person who might have done so was herself in a state of collapse. So why not totter up, and slip out, and search for one who surely ought to be present to make that chaotic party complete?

Darkness and rain! Was she out in it somewhere? He must find out! He turned to the left, that led to where he had last seen her. She was to wait in the empty cottage until he could come to her . . . and now he was coming to her . . .

Was he? Or—was *she* coming to *him*?

He stopped suddenly, and strained his eyes. Out of the moist blackness resolved a figure.

''Allo, Molly,' he said rapidly.

Now the figure stopped and stared at him.

'Ben!' she gasped.

They advanced towards each other, and almost fell into each other. For several seconds neither spoke. Then, with sudden intelligence, Ben told the longed-for news in half a dozen words.

'They've come,' he announced, 'and it's orl right.'

For an instant the amazing news made the girl rigid. Then, suddenly, reaction set in, and she began to sob. As suddenly, she stopped.

'Little fool I am!' she muttered angrily.

'Then so'm I,' replied Ben. 'I've blubbed buckets!'

'Stop talking like that, or you'll set me off again!' she gulped, and took his hand. A little warm tear fell upon the hand in the middle of the cold rain. 'If everything's all right, what are *you* out here for?'

'Don't be silly,' retorted Ben.

'Do you mean—you were coming for me?'

''Corse! Wotcher tike me for?'

'A pal, if ever there was one! I say, you're a good sort! But you must go back now.'

'Yus. We're both goin' back.'

'I'm not!'

'Wot's that?'

'I said—I'm not.'

'Go on! Why?'

She raised her head quickly. Rapid steps sounded on the road. She dived for the trees.

Wondering, he dived after her. The rapid steps drew nearer the spot on which they had stood. They passed the spot, and faded towards the inn.

'Do you know what that was?' whispered Molly.

''Oo?' asked Ben.

'Some Spanish policemen. You'd better follow them.'

'Not if you ain't goin' ter.'

'But I can't.'

'Why not?'

309

'My job here is done now—and—have you forgotten?—
I'm wanted for another job at home!'

A poster grew into Ben's mind with startling incongruity
on this lonely Spanish road:

'OLD MAN MURDERED
AT HAMMERSMITH'

The poster had formed her first background! Was it to
form her last?

He rebelled at the idea. The murder had been Faggis's!
Not hers! She herself was merely a misguided little pickpocket—and, lummy, look at what she'd done since!

'Doncher worry, miss,' he said seriously. 'Arter orl yer
done in this 'ere job, they won't think nothin' o' that
other!'

'Yes, they will,' she responded definitely. 'Law's law, and
I'll always be on the wrong side of it.'

'Not if yer git on the right side!' he urged.

'I was *born* on the wrong side,' she answered.

'Then wot abart me pullin' yer hover, like?'

She looked at him long and earnestly. The rain descended
on their upturned faces, but they were unconscious of it.
Then, abruptly, she shook her head.

'Listen, Ben,' she said, and her voice was very solemn.
'You're a pal, if ever there was one. I shan't forget you.
But, though we're both down-and-outs, we're made of
different stuff, and the stuff we're made of doesn't mix.
Do you get what I mean?'

'No,' replied Ben doggedly.

'What do you do when you're hungry and haven't got
a penny?' she challenged.

310

''Old a 'orse,' answered Ben.

'Well, I pick a pocket. Some difference! So, you see you're better without me. Good-bye.'

Better without her? He considered the proposition. Without her, he would go back to the inn, and join in the rejoicings, and receive his meed of praise and profit. He would return to England, doubtless, not as a stowaway but as the legal passenger of a steamship or a railway company. Mr Holbrooke would shower cheese upon him. He might even get his picture in a paper. Lummy, that'd tickle his mother, wherever she was—up or down!

Yes—but all that was without Molly Smith . . . And now she was suddenly slipping away from him! He stopped thinking, and slipped after her.

'Oi!' he panted.

She turned at his voice, and he caught her up.

'Didn't you hear me tell you to go back?' she cried tremulously.

'Yer know, miss, you ain't got me right,' he answered. 'I'm a fair blinkin' sticker, I am, and I'm agoin' ter see you 'ome!'

They walked through the night; away from an inn where ugly scenes had led to strange reunions; away from an empty cottage where two disillusioned rascals awaited the uncomfortable processes of the law; away from a little village where, for many a day to come, the odd habits of the *Inglés* would be discussed, and also the strange return of a native in a comic foreign suit; away from a long precipitous mountain track, and a broken foot-bridge above a yawning precipice, and a lonely hut where two prone bodies had been found under a neatly spread table-cloth;

and away from an ocean liner that had slid out of the Thames one day with queer folk aboard, and was now throbbing across distant seas.

And, while they walked, Sims waited in an isolated, uncharted spot for a man who never came . . .

'Funny thing, life, ain't it?' said Ben.

THE END

Also available

The House Opposite
J. Jefferson Farjeon

The return of Ben, the prince of tramps with his rich Cockney humour and naïve philosophies—in a story of criminal goings-on told from both sides of a London street.

Strange things are happening in the untenanted houses of Jowle Street. There are unaccountable creakings and weird knockings on the door of No.29, where the homeless ex-sailor Ben has taken up residence. But even stranger things are happening in the house opposite, from where a beautiful woman in an evening gown brings Ben a mysterious message—and an errand that puts him in more danger than he bargained for.

'A mixture of humour and excitement, which Mr Farjeon knows so well how to handle.' DAILY MIRROR

'An undiluted joy . . . Ben is the plum of the book; his personality impresses itself upon the imagination.' LIVERPOOL POST